When All the Girls Stopped Singing

When All the Girls Stopped Singing

A Novel

Susan Burgess-Lent

Current Words Publishing | Los Angeles

When All the Girls Stopped Singing

Dianne Pearce, editor
David Yurkovich, cover and design

International Standard Book Numbers:
978-1-957224-65-7 (paperback)
978-1-957224-67-1 (ePub)

Published by Current Words Publishing, LLC, Los Angeles, CA.
Find us at: currentwords.com

To Dave, for your beautiful loyalty

"There will come to you news of one you didn't provide for,
for whom you never fixed a date for meeting. The days will
reveal to you what you didn't know before."
Tarafah ibn al 'Abd

I belong to no race nor time.
I am the eternal feminine with its string of beads.
Zora Neale Hurston

When All the Girls Stopped Singing

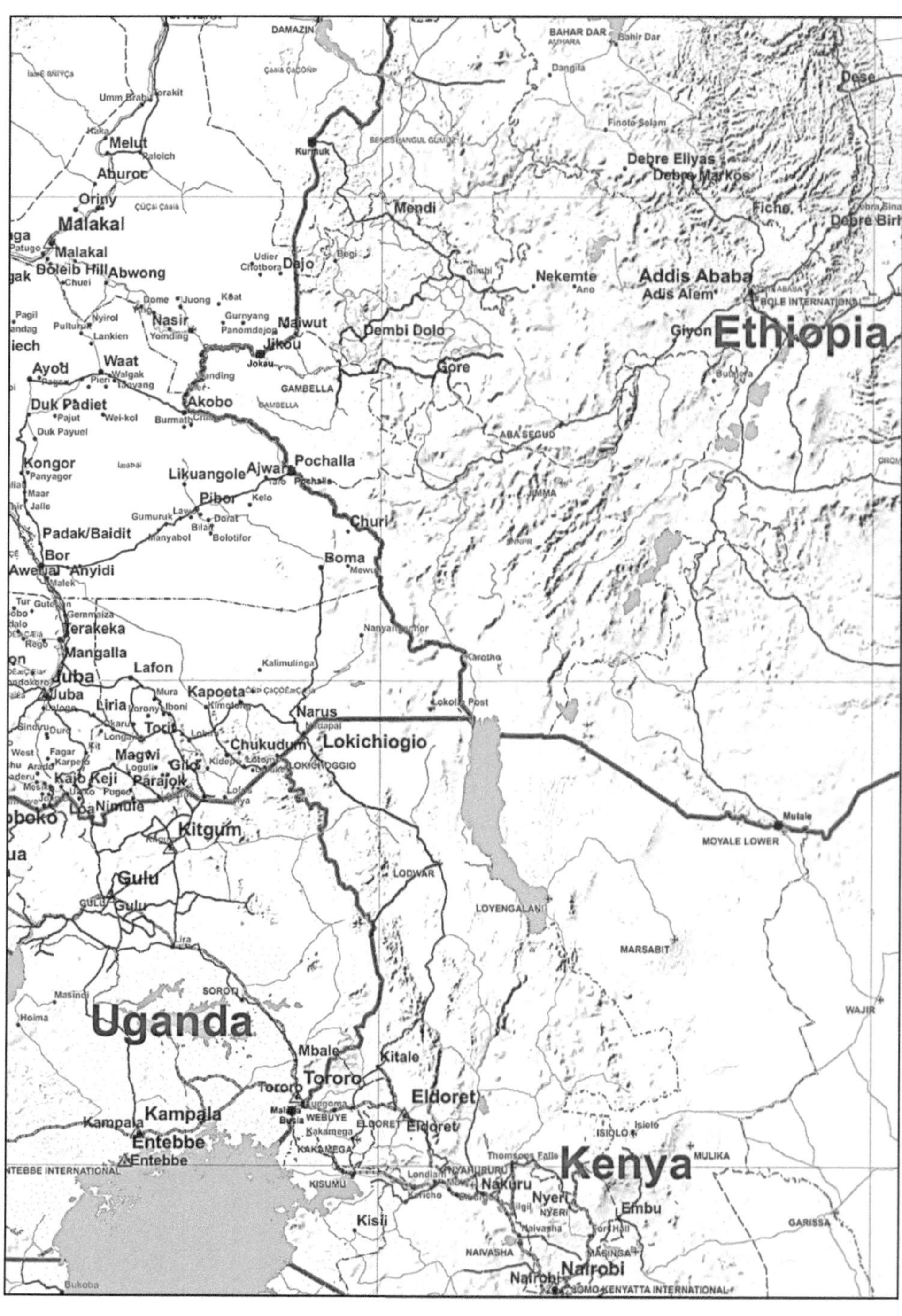

Ethiopia
Uganda
Kenya
Malakal
Melut
Aburoc
Oriny
Doleib Hill
Abwong
Nasir
Jikou
Jokau
Waat
Ayod
Duk Padiet
Duk Payuel
Akobo
Kongor
Panyagor
Likuangole
Ajwara
Pochalla
Pibor
Churi
Boma
Padak/Baidit
Bor
Aweil
Anyidi
Terakeka
Mangalla
Lafon
Juba
Liria
Torit
Kapoeta
Narus
Chukudum
Lokichiogio
Magwi
Glu
Kajo Keji
Parajok
Nimule
Kitgum
Gulu
Gulu
Lira
Lodwar
Mutale
MOYALE LOWER
LOYENGALANI
MARSABIT
WAJIR
Masindi
Hoima
Mbale
Kitale
Tororo
Tororo
Eldoret
Eldoret
Kampala
Kampala
Entebbe
Entebbe
WEBUYE
Kakamega
KAKAMEGA
KISUMU
Kisii
Kericho
Nakuru
NYERI
Nyeri
Embu
GARISSA
NAIVASHA
Nairobi
Nairobi
JOMO KENYATTA INTERNATIONAL
Bukoba
Kumuk
Mendi
Dajo
Dembi Dolo
Gore
Nekemte
Addis Ababa
Adis Alem
BOLE INTERNATIONAL
Giyon
Debre Eliyas
Debre Markos
Ficho
Debre Birhan
Dese
BAHAR DAR
Bahir Dar
Dangila
Finote Selam
DAMAZIN
GAMBELLA
GAMBELLA
JIMMA
SNNPR
ABA SEGUD
Maiwut
Kong
MULIKA
Isiolo
ISIOLO
Thomsons Falls
NYAHURURU
Londiani
Karotha
Lokichoggio
Lokicha Post
Nanyangachor
Kalimulinga
Mewun

CHAPTER ONE

Washington, DC

As is her duty, Zora Monro shows up at the party celebrating ten years of her organization's survival. A three-foot high white banner emblazoned with *Human Rights Defenders* adorns a wall of the trendy Washington club. Months of diminishing donations mandated a slim offering of fruit and cheese platters. Nobody had thought twice about requiring a cash bar. Local supporters and a gaggle of interns crowd the tables and red banquettes. Zora wears a black halter dress, confident that her thirty-nine-year-old body is decently fit. She waves at one of her favorite interns, the one who has affably indicated she understands about not yet ruling the world. In the amber light of the bar, she eases onto a stool.

Her working days as spokeswoman for HRD require rabble rousing against mass murderers. She slogs through daily reports of large-scale psychotic behavior, in particular the Sudan regime's unfettered practice of slaughtering civilians. The haughty impunity of senior officials, their sneering guile about "counterinsurgency" warfare, used to fuel her resolve to nail the bastards. She no longer knows what perverse anomaly in her character sustains this obsession.

Tom Tishman approaches smiling, his suit jacket off, his burgundy tie loosened over a blue, French-cuffed shirt. "Let me buy you a drink," he offers. "Whiskey, rocks, right?

She nods, wondering uncomfortably how her boss knows her cocktail preference. He chats easily with the young blonde bartender, trading opinions about the previous night's loss by the city's star-deficient NBA franchise. Watching him, she remembers thinking, at the beginning, that charisma had found a new embodiment. Tom drew people into causes that, in the best of times, were sobering and, in the worst, utterly wrenching. His passion infected anyone in proximity. She'd felt, at the beginning, he was a great and visionary man.

He turns his attention to her, his tropical-sea blue eyes roving over her face. "I'd like you to speak tonight," he says, smiling with his mouth but not his eyes. "Short notice, but I'd like to get out in front of a new initiative." He can disarm her. He is too handsome with his tousled black hair, respectably salted with grey, and his carefully trimmed three-day beard. An ex-Marine, Iraq War vet, his military bearing argues he will suffer no fool. She sips her drink, suspicious of his purpose.

He continues his even gaze. "I've been invited to a meeting of Sudanese rebel groups and government mediators in Addis. I think we're close to a breakthrough in the peace negotiations. I want to keep in close touch so you can shoot out press releases."

His use of "we" is a troubling new wrinkle. In theory, HRD never compromised its voice by engaging in political nice-making. His last trip to the refugee camps on the Chad border—the Sudanese government would never allow him into the country—that trip, in her opinion, had ushered him into the company of disaster tourists: folks who dropped in for a quick look-see, proclaiming outrage at the suffering of the destitute masses, offering reckless assurances of help. There'd been several of those visits.

Unlike him, she has never been an eyewitness to the devastation. She's been stranded stateside reading reams of disturbing reports and reviewing ghastly photos that haunt her days and invade her dreams. As a spokeswoman, she feels bitterly without credentials. Trips to assess events on the ground are reserved for Tom. The exclusion chafes her like a tight collar.

She inhales deeply. "You think the rebel leaders are aware of what's happening to their purported constituents? They don't go to the camps. They shuttle between luxury hotels, trading accusations of duplicity."

A flash of annoyance tightens his lips. The alcohol already has softened her tact. She presses on. "We accuse the regime of violating international humanitarian law. They ignore every ceasefire and peace agreement they've ever signed. They wait for the wavelet of international finger-wagging to pass and then get on with their scorched-earth campaigns."

He sips his cocktail. She hadn't meant to tread down this path, haranguing him. It's the price they both pay for refusing to deal with an ugly week-old incident.

He'd come on to her. No. He'd *groped* her. *In the damn copy room, no less.* He'd seemed as stupefied as she when he cupped her breasts, like a child eager to learn the heft and feel of a coveted toy. When she dislodged his hands, they'd backed away from each other in shocked silence. In that furtive moment, the rapport between them took a fatal bullet. Her personal hero, the champion of people's rights, proved himself just another guy who tragically surrendered to a dick-first impulse.

She'd not spoken of the incident to anyone, not even him, as if the burden belonged to her. This in spite of everything she knew and believed about what a woman violated should do. His once appealing scent, his musky cologne, now afflicts her. Resting his arm on the bar, he speaks in a measured tone. "There are appropriate channels and methods. And we will work them. Now go speak."

She slides off the stool and steps onto a small dais near the bar. Scanning the room with a solemn expression, she begins: "Friends and supporters. Human Rights Defenders has advocated since the beginning to end the genocide in Sudan." She pauses, surveying the audience of mostly white faces. "I've believed that if we continued to broadcast the grisly facts, that teeth might grow in the mouth of U.S. Sudan policy. That we would mobilize and deploy resources to end the annihilation of a people. Now HRD's CEO Tom Tishman is taking a role in renewed peace talks among the rebel groups. The regime is sending a mediator." She pauses, catches Tom's eye, looks deliberately away. "We hope that working channels such as these advances our mission."

"The truth: we're dealing with the *Third Reich* of Africa. We go about reshuffling the deck of *reasons to act*. But the ace that will ratchet up global response is not on the table. For too long, the word *genocide*—or its sanitized euphemism *ethnic cleansing*—has provoked little more than brief moral panic." Her colleague Mookie, standing at the margin of the crowd, flashes a quick thumbs up.

"Your presence here tonight signals your willingness to take action that ends *this* genocide." She glances at faces in the crowd. "Am I right?" The crowd applauds with scattered whoops of approval.

"Renew your financial support of HRD's work. Send a clear message to Sudan's displaced women and children that they have not been abandoned. Thanks for coming tonight!" A small wave of applause follows her off the dais.

Tom is moving to take her place there, his expression wounded. "I never thought of you as a saboteur," he chides in a harsh whisper.

She leans near his ear. "Appearing to collaborate with the rebels is a piss-poor strategy that hardly dignifies our mission. And you're a jackass for suggesting it is."

"I won't put up with reckless bullshit from you." He brushes past her, waving at the crowd, smiling.

She retreats quickly to the bar, sits with her fist over her mouth, speculating about the impact of her remarks. A few painful minutes pass before she realizes that he's gaslighting. She may not have spit-polished her argument—wait, yes, she had. Even a month ago he would have taken her meaning and *agreed* with her, even driven the conversation toward new strategies. The copy room incident is a symptom. Something fundamental has gone sideways.

Her phone vibrates. She bobbles it, puts it to her ear.

"I've taken your momma to GW Hospital ER," come the pinched words. It's her Aunt Bert. "She is…." the call drops. Stunned, Zora stares at the phone, unable to grasp that her 'always fine' mother has ended up in an emergency room. Gathering her purse, she dashes outside to hail a cab.

Her phone call to Bert shunts to voice mail. When the taxi arrives at the emergency entrance, Zora fumbles with her purse, pushing a ten into the driver's hand. Rushing down a long hall, through double doors, she finds Bert at the nurses' station. Her face is drained to pallor.

"Oh thank God you're here!" Bert wails, tears spilling down her cheeks. She grasps Zora in a desperate hug. "Baby girl," she whispers, "your momma's gone."

CHAPTER TWO

Near Fangak, Sudan

I remember the season when my life was sliced to pieces. It was before I knew that other people kept time in months and years. I learned that when I was thirteen years old. I carry pictures in my head. They are heavy like water in a jerry can. As hard as I try, I cannot set them down.

The horsemen come at night. Riding thunder. Their guns throw sparks. Tukuls burst into flames. Blinding orange. Friends fall to the ground. Screaming. So much screaming. Grandfather drags me into a hole. His hands cover my eyes. I smell the fear in his sweat. Insects slither over my leg. We huddle for thousands of heartbeats. The stink of burned flesh hangs in the air.

I blink away the pictures in my mind. The sun is a fire on my back as I lift a bundle of dry grass. Grandfather is waiting. Walking with the bundle balanced on my head, I pass two children huddled in a scrap of shade. They wait with empty eyes for their mother. I know she is dead. Across the clearing, the granary is a black hole. On the dusty path, a young boy weeps over the bloody body of his father. I blot out their names, make them strangers. I cannot hold all their pain. I skirt the scorched ground where a tukul once stood. At first light, three burned bodies were found here.

Thirst tightens my throat. I trudge on. I know how long I can walk before my legs grow weak. Seasons ago, when I was driven with other women across strange land, I learned how to be small, without needs.

"Abuk!" grandfather calls. "Mind your work." His voice calms me. His patient eyes never lose their love. But today they are dark with sadness. Everything is ruined. We must make shelter from the sun.

I put the bundled grass beside grandfather. I watch him form and weave bunches into a small bamboo frame. He turns to look at me, nods toward the water gourd. After I drink, I accept the light touch of his hand on my cheek. Then I return to gather more grass.

Not so long ago, my skin glowed. My new woman's shape made young men glance twice and then follow with their eyes. Now my shoulders sag like an old woman's. I have stopped singing the tales of brave men and cattle wealth. There is no longer reason to sing.

With a short knife, I cut the dry stems, dropping them into a pile. I keep a slow rhythm to my work. I tell my mind to be empty. When my face drips with sweat, I lift two more bundles and return to grandfather. Again, he offers me the water gourd. I gulp from it until he raises his hand. "Child," he says quietly, "rest for a while." I sit obediently at his side in the shade of the canopy he has partly finished.

"I have something important to tell you." He peers at me, his face weary. "We will leave this place." He waits for my reaction, but I stay silent. He rests his hand on my shoulder. "We must go north where no bombs fall. Where no raiders attack us."

I nod. "When?"

"Soon."

A sudden breeze lifts fine grit that coats our skin. My dry lips form a tiny smile. "I know the way," I say. "I remember."

CHAPTER THREE

Zora pushes through a shroud of grief to get dressed for the service. She calls Bert who picks up after one ring. "Just gonna call you," Bert says. "I've followed your momma's handwritten instructions. No church service and she'll be laid to rest beside Joe at Oak Hill Cemetery and her grave is to be marked with a white marble headstone inscribed only with her name and dates and some lilies are being delivered to the grave site."

Zora sighs. "No frills, huh?" In the long silence, she senses they both are wrestling with raw impulses to wail. "Tell me B," she finally manages. "Did momma … say anything to you before she died?"

For a moment Bert is silent but Zora can hear her ragged breathing. "She said only one word and I wasn't sure but it sounded like 'pan-ee.'"

"Pan-ee?'"

"She was basically helpless when I found her."

Zora flinches at the image. "One of her mysteries to solve then."

"Yeah, but let's get through today." Bert urges. "You ready to go? You want me to pick you up?

"No, but thanks." She wants no company, no attempts at salving the screaming pain of a loss she finds unbelievable. And no obligation, yet, to comfort Bert.

"See you there, baby girl."

In the turmoil of days since the hospital, Zora replayed weeks of encounters with her momma, realizing she'd failed to grasp the significance of her momma's increasingly taciturn behavior. She'd made twice weekly visits to do laundry or cleaning or drop off groceries or take-out meals. She did her best to let her momma be, an accommodation learned over a lifetime of trying to extract meaning and motive from her intractable secretiveness. She had not rescued her from stubborn decline. If that is a daughter's duty, then a tanker-sized load of guilt would be waiting just beyond the numbing grief.

Under a cloudless sky, Zora steps among the headstones to the newly dug grave, shoving her hands into her jacket pockets to steady herself. Her right fingers wedge against a slip of paper. Without seeing, she knows it's a message from momma. Over the years, her momma's notes, secreted in books, in pockets, in folded towels and lunch bags, could have filled a few shoeboxes. She'd kept only one box stuffed with zany crayoned clues for treasure hunts that had occupied many a childhood afternoon. Momma had had a knack for anticipating when her notes would be discovered.

Withdrawing a twice-folded pink paper, she reads the looping cursive:

> *My shining star,*
> *Look in my files in the pantry. All is revealed there.*
> *I've always loved you. Always.*
> *Momma*

Astonished, she jams the note in her pocket. A wizened man in a black suit sets a large floral spray near the casket. The cloying scent of lilies wafts through the cool air. Mookie, her favorite colleague from work, approaches in a tailored black dress that restricts her usual deliberate stride. Bert slides beside her in a wide-brimmed navy-blue hat that nearly obscures her delicate face. Then comes a group of momma's women friends, wrinkled and shrunken beyond her last memory of them, caught in "the time when your friends go dyin' on ya," as momma, with head-shaking disbelief, had referred to her seventh decade.

Father Corvus, pastor of the church Ella attended sporadically, beckons them to circle the casket. Zora hears little of his readings, instead watching frowsy poplars scatter yellow leaves in a freshening breeze. Her tears pool behind a dam of confusion that permits no release.

The ranks of her kin had grown sparse. Her mother's parents had passed within a year of each other when Zora was a toddler. Her mother's only brother is ten years into a thirty-year sentence in San Quentin prison on a murder charge. Her father's parents, the Monrowskis of Chicago, are resolute strangers. Evidently, they never forgave their blue-eyed genius of presumptively pure Polish lineage for marrying a black woman. Of her many paternal uncles and aunts, only Bert had stayed close.

She hears the "Amens," the murmured words meant to comfort, and yields to gentle embraces. Bert whispers that she will stay if needed, but Zora shakes her off, agreeing to come soon to the wake at momma's house. She watches the mourners drift off to waiting vehicles.

A small backhoe shovels dark clay until her mother's resting place is nothing more than a brown scar on the verdant, granite-studded slope. As she kneels to arrange the lilies, the knot in her chest heaves apart. "Momma!" she wails. "Why you make me wait till you're gone to tell me … wherever it is you decided to tell me?" She looks away, overtaken with anger that seems to sucker-punch her grief. "Now you're gonna send me on another one of your treasure hunts?" Nearby, a flock of sparrow flashes skyward, a winged sigh. "Is that it?" She rises, backing away on unsteady legs, and walks slowly through a maze of headstones.

"Zora!"

She startles at the voice. Jackson stands beside her car, his face composed like a concerned politician, even here in a field of people that he could not impress. She'd been one of the naïve women who'd mistaken his lustrous smile, his intimate attention, for personal interest. That was months ago at a Congressional reception. Congressman Jackson Sykes had pursued her with breathtaking professionalism: extravagant bouquets, but never to the office, and late-night cocktails and hot athletic fucks in the Jefferson Hotel. What was not possible between them soon whispered at the boundary of her heart's hearing, finally spilling out in a deafening harangue: he was a *politician*. His wife was no fool. Over glasses of expensive Chardonnay in her kitchen, as he'd ramped up another seduction, she'd ended it. He'd been gracious, undismayed in a way that had wounded, as if the *game* had been all that mattered.

He smiles as she nears. "I thought you might need a ride."

She couldn't engage. Not today. "I appreciate the thought, Jackson, but I drove myself."

"Girl," he gently chides, "grief is not a thing you wrestle on your own." He opens the passenger door of her car and signals his driver, waiting in a town car nearby, to follow

"Jackson, what do you want?"

"This is just a ride home after sayin' goodbye to your momma." He holds out his hand for her keys. "A gesture of respect."

As he drives, she gazes out the side window, silent. They cross over the Beltway where traffic inches past a messy accident. Georgia Avenue, lined with small family shops, seems to be going about normal business on a day when her normal had ceased to be.

She realizes, with stunned certainty, how carefully her mother had planned her departure. She knew she was dying when she'd written the note. She'd correctly guessed the grey tailored jacket her daughter would wear to her funeral. Evidently her illness had not diminished her capacity to scheme. The note said she'd left files in the pantry. Wait. Jesus! *"Pan-ee."* It had been her last attempt to point the way.

"Strange days in Sudan," Jackson says. "I have some information to share. When you're ready."

She nods. His detailed knowledge of the ongoing crisis interests her. For him, the genocide is a flashy piece in an ever-evolving global chess game. The meaning of horrific events, of the obligations they impose, seem not to overwork his conscience. Sometimes she envies him that.

The car turns onto Sixteenth Street, the road she's dubbed 'God's Strip Mall.' Anyone of faith could find an edifice of worship somewhere along these miracle miles. She wonders if, in a month of Sundays, she could hear one whisper of comfort in all their soaring sacred spaces. Provisional relief, perhaps the best she can hope for, awaits discovery in the pantry of her mother's kitchen.

CHAPTER FOUR

Marley's *Redemption Song* wafts from the open door of her momma's house. The front parlor is crowded. Zora catches the end of the retelling of a hilarious-in-retrospect gaffe by Joe's best man. Several friends rise to greet and hug her. "Maybe you should be recording those scandalous allegations," she teases, prompting laughter.

She moves on to the kitchen. Bert kisses her cheek. "Got your favorite cheesecake here." She nods and takes a fingerful, provoking B's faux disapproving glance. Her aunt had been momma's staunchest ally for nearly forty years. When she'd lost her young husband in the Vietnam War, she'd retreated brokenhearted on a widow's allowance to her parent's home in Chicago to ponder her options. Her longing to attenuate her grief and to ascend beyond the meager expectations of the Monrowski household had coincided exquisitely with momma's need for help with the new baby. She'd moved to Washington to assist in Zora's upbringing.

Unlike her beefy siblings, Bert is thin as a post with an angular, delicate face and washed-blue eyes. Like Zora, she seems not to fit neatly into the family scheme of physical characteristics. Recently Bert and momma had had a dustup that neither would discuss.

Bert has prepared too much food but skimped on the booze. She never wanted to encourage drinking after Joe got sober. Despite a warming blaze in the fireplace, the room where everyone is gathered feels chilly in the way of a place deprived of its soul. Nobody has the heart, it seems, to stay long.

After earnest condolences are repeated and the company departs, Zora carries the plates and left-over food to the kitchen. She knows better than to offer help to the dominatrix of party cleanups. Briefly she skirmishes with nervous curiosity about the pantry, then wanders to the shrine of family photos in the hallway. The centerpiece is gold-framed black-and-white portrait of momma's dusky round face nestled against her father's pale narrow one. They'd just been married. She knows from the stories—and sees in the photograph—that her parents had been helplessly in love. No doubt they'd needed that heady, irrational fuel to weather the social disdain for their unmatched skin colors. According to Bert, the font of family history, momma had been Joe's muse, the inspiration for every splendid melody that flowed from his piano. He and momma performed rapturous musical tête-à-têtes in D.C. clubs. She always appeared in low-cut shimmering gowns, polishing every lyric with her startling smoky voice. Zora had heard the tapes. Nobody sang *My One and Only Love* like momma in her prime.

Back then, her parents had been scaling the rock face of fame. Promoters came calling. The gigs started paying well. They toured. The rub was that momma wanted acclaim almost as much as she wanted Joe's children. Two miscarriages inflicted near-fatal heartbreak before she gave up performing. Bitterly claiming that the punishing schedule "messed up my ovaries," she'd forfeited full flowering as a chanteuse for the quotidian thrills of motherhood.

Zora touches her father's cheek. She never knew him beyond the legend. Shortly after his passing, Ella had announced jubilantly that she was expecting a baby. Joe's family made no secret of its disaffection. Momma evidently hadn't needed them, not then.

Beside this photo is another black-and-white: her mother in a sleeveless flowered dress, one arm cradling baby Zora, the other clenching a diaper to a clothesline. Wild curly hair frames her cheeks. Her generous mouth is wide open in song. She is a women unleashed.

Suddenly Zora is impatient for Bert to leave. She wants solitude for the hunt.

"*Kochanie*," Bert calls from the kitchen. The endearment in Polish became, years ago, a nickname. "I'm done here." She comes into the hall, pulling on a jacket. "Ahhh, the wall of legends." Scanning the photos, she clutches a hand to her mouth, sighing slowly, as if she will cry. "You want me to stay here with you?"

Zora shakes her head. "I'm leaving soon." She kisses Bert's cheek. "Thanks for ... all of it."

Bert nods with a sad smile. "Don't stay long." She steps to the door and then turns. "Your momma's not here anymore." She lets herself out.

The hushed house grows dim as the late afternoon sun retreats. Zora knows her momma is, in fact, still here. She goes to the kitchen and stands before the pantry door. The small windowless room beside the stove had always attracted the jetsam of the household. No unmotivated person would venture in there. A perfect concealment.

She opens the door. In one corner, a vacuum cleaner, a garden rake and hoe tangled in a hose and, oddly, a fishing pole, belonging perhaps to one of momma's men friends. A set of sagging shelves holds two cartons labeled "Sunday dishes," a plastic tub full of baking pans and a bin labeled "Fix-it stuff." Knowing that her mother took evil delight in misdirection, she opens each box to confirm its contents. She inspects and moves aside several boxes of Christmas decorations that block a cupboard. The bottom door of the cupboard is secured with a hasp from which hangs an open padlock. Whether this is a thoughtful gesture or a bit of forgetfulness, she cannot guess, but she's relieved there will be no search for a key. She removes the lock and pulls the handle. The door breaks loose like a tooth from a jaw, its hinges attached only to the door. She holds it like a booby prize, chuckling softly, then sets it out of the way. Inside the dark, narrow space are two wooden boxes hand-labeled *1* and *2*. She pulls out the top box. Taped to its lid is a folded pink note exactly like the one she'd found in her pocket. With swift pain, like a paper cut to the lip, she wishes for her mother to shamble into the kitchen in a housedress, put on a kettle for tea and sit for a chat that would sweep away her anxiety. She opens the note and reads:

> *Dearest Daughter,*
> *In Africa, it is a mother's job to tell her daughter what she must do.*
> *It is a grandmother's duty to tell her why. This box holds your grandmother.*
> *Listen to her first.*
> *Love you always and forever,*
>   *Momma*

In Africa? Since when is her mother pulling down aphorisms from Africa? Suddenly, the weight of the house, its cargo of secrets, settles around her, squeezing light and air from the small room. She cannot stay any longer.

After moving the boxes to the front door, she stands gazing into the parlor. Back in the day, musicians had gathered there, sharing tunes, laughing and gossiping, feasting on "Soulish cuisine," the name they'd given to the unlikely fusion of Ella's soul food and Bert's Polish country cooking. They'd been a big, boisterous family. None of that was left now. She carries the boxes to her green Honda, stacks them on the passenger seat, and drives home in the drizzling dusk.

Cool air washes her face as she pushes open the door to her dark apartment near DuPont Circle. She stacks the boxes in the foyer, breathing in the scent of roses sent by the HRD staff. She drops her purse on the floor and sheds her jacket. Street light filtering through the shutters paints orange stripes on the oak floor in the living room. Everything stands ordered, clean but somehow shabby. Exhausted, she drops into the sofa. Her gaze wanders over the chipped edge of the coffee table, the faded upholstery of the easy chair, the traffic-worn Persian rug. At thirty-nine, she lives like a thrifty student, surrounded by the aging debris of her short, chaotic marriage, now ten years distant.

She has no children, no innocents to blame for the meagerness of assets. Rather, she devotes her days to mapping lunatic brutality, expecting to find solid, righteous ground. On all fronts that matter, satisfaction eludes her. It may be that momma is offering a posthumous re-direct.

Rising, she switches on the light in the dining room and carries the boxes to the table. As she takes the lid off box 1, a vague scent, like the incense burned during Mass, rises from the notebooks inside. Worn at the edges, tied in a bundle with sisal, the notebooks look like objects from an archeological dig. She wants their meaning surrendered without weeks of analysis. "But where is the adventure in that?" momma would have said. Had she forgotten about loving adventure?

Removing the sisal tie, she reads the handwritten labels on the two thick notebooks: "Dinka Culture" and "Sudan Wars." Incredibly, her mother had been trudging over much the same territory as she. Fully aware, or so she imagined, of her daughter's work, she'd never once hinted at the depth of her connection. Zora tries to imagine a reason for such stubborn withholding but cannot.

Opening the notebook "Dinka Culture," she finds a raft of loose pages detailing a prickly on-line debate that "Jieng," not Dinka, is the proper tribal name. Then a list of the many clans, with their territories sketched out on a map. Bor, Rek, Tonj, Njok, Agar Gok. To an outsider, the list reads like a log of outposts on a Star Trek expedition. Other maps show the distribution of oil tracts; their owners, multinational corporations, are noted with red labels.

She finds a page describing the outsized Dinka vocabulary for their cherished cattle: hundreds of words to describe color and shape and movement. There's a small Dinka-English dictionary. A note paper-clipped to the cover proclaims: "The only source!" with an address of missionaries in Rome. Even with a pronunciation guide, she cannot decipher the sounds that would derive from the unusual alliances of vowels and diacritical marks.

There are passages about the Dinka belief in Nhailic, the creator of the first humans, Garang and Abuk. After the Europeans came to their lands, many Dinka signed on to Christianity. Having surrendered to this God, the clans probably were in no mood to do it for another. When confronted with the next hegemony of Islam, they took up arms. That conflict has been dismantling their lives for more than two generations.

There are also entries about the tribe's musical traditions. Of course, Zora knew her momma would have loved the fact that singing was the domain of women. Favorite Dinka songs celebrated a wealth of cattle and good harvests and bravery in battle. Aid organizations, Zora knew, had been campaigning for a conversion to songs about peacemaking. Embattled as the women were, she thought it would be a miracle if any of them still sang about anything at all.

Alone on a page Zora finds a single double-underlined note: "Both men and women are fond of beaded necklaces." *Momma never left specious clues.* Somewhere would be a prompt or an artifact to illuminate its meaning.

Zora stands stiffly and stretches. Her momma had taken her mission of discovery much farther than she. It had been too easy to think of the war-affected as victims, never fully appreciating that formidable traditions had taught them nuanced ways to inhabit their piece of the planet. Her vantage point had revealed only the many and cruel ways the tribe was staring down its ruin.

She drifts to the kitchen, pulls a beer from the fridge. The revelations feel like elements of an empathy-building exercise. *Why had Momma felt it necessary to make this notebook? Why had she never spoken of her obsession with these people?*

The second notebook, "Sudan Wars," holds much less appeal for Zora. She already knows too much about the killing and dying. But she sits again to read what her mother has assembled: a comprehensive chronology of the war beginning with the coup that installed a brigadier as president of Sudan. There are clippings of commentary about arrests of opposition leaders and the shuttering of newspaper offices. There are red-starred entries, scores of them, about attacks on villages. In a separate section are the texts of a dozen United Nations Security Council Resolutions on the conflict. Always, the international body had been "seized of the matter," to tragically little effect.

Her mother studied events with an unblinking eye. In lengthy passages, she railed against the "savagery of evil men," and stated that "God has abandoned my people." Her connection is ardent, personal. *Were they "her" people because of their blackness? What other tie would bind her to them?* Weary of reading, Zora rests her head on the open notebook, and dozes fitfully.

The loud clatter of the 5:25am garbage truck startles her awake. Bleary, irritable, she wants no more of "grandmother's" offerings. Her momma may have been a stickler about precisely following clues, but Zora knows she wouldn't have wished it to feel like punishment.

Though she needs sleep badly, Zora can't restrain her curiosity about box 2. She pulls off the lid. On top of more notebooks, in a plastic sleeve, is a black and white photo. The image, faded with age, is of a gaunt, dark woman. A ragged cloth covers her hips. Her untenanted gaze speaks of desecration. Her thin arms cradle a naked infant. A thrill of dangerous discovery courses through Zora but her boggy brain refuses to allow its passage into conscious thought. Slipping the photo into her purse, she shuts the lights and retreats beneath the comforter on her bed.

Just after noon, when most of the HRD staff is at lunch, Zora slips into her office. At her desk, she aimlessly rearranges a few files, signs on to her email, reconsiders, signs out. Opening her purse, she takes out the photograph. Touching the long oval face of the woman, she wonders how the skin would feel, as if that knowledge could grant meaning or connection. The sorrow in her face makes Zora look away.

The phone warbles. She stabs the speaker button.

"Zora, it's Jackson. How you doin'?"

She's surprised to hear from him after their chilly post-funeral parting. "I'm okay."

"I was expecting to leave a message. You didn't take time off." Jackson's tone grants her the comfort of concern.

"I needed to get out of the house." Zora lightens her tone. "You called because?"

"I got something you'll find…*provocative*."

"I'm listening."

"CIA sent a private jet to pick up Sudan's security chief for meetings in Washington."

Zora sits up in her chair. "U.S. intelligence is hosting Osama bin Laden's old buddy?"

"Yeah."

"And…?"

"Not much I can tell you over the phone."

He always plays her this way. With his Congressional privileges, Jackson can pick through all sorts of sensitive intelligence. His power game is to offer a teasing headline, intimating he'll give more, then require a rendezvous.

"Meet me for dinner?"

Being right about a man is so tedious. Zora sighs. "Let me call you."

"Don't jive me," he says with a hint of warning.

"*Me?* Never. Later."

"Hey, ZoMo." RayJ leans into her office. His fetish for nicknames inspired the contraction of her first and last names. She had long ago shortened the unlikely Polish surname Monrowski to Monro and had never adopted her former spouse's name. No one but she had been happy with either choice. He stands in the door with a troubled expression. "Sorry about you losin' your moms."

She murmurs "Thanks." The usual awkward exchanges about death do not rise up between them.

"You wanna hear some news, or should I leave you alone?"

"I'm here. Shoot."

"Got video from the Sudanese anti-torture group. Five political detainees. Stripped, hands bound, multiple wounds, dead on the ground. We know their names and their faces are visible. Weird part is," he hesitates, "they got…erections." Zora scowls. RayJ takes a step into the office. "I ran it by an ER doc I know. He said that can happen when there's spinal trauma at time of death."

Zora shakes her head in sorrow, "Imagine how your people would feel if that was you—and the video goes viral on YouTube."

He rests his hand on the doorjamb, his eyes appraising her. He is taller than her six feet, a shade darker than her acorn-brown, lean, and, she imagines, buff. At their first meeting, his laughing chestnut eyes worked some sweet hoodoo on her. Tragically, he's at least ten years younger than she.

"I'll tell Mookie you're lookin' for her." RayJ puts the DVD on the corner of her desk, backs away, and slips out of the office. She dislikes being triaged, *especially by his handsome self.* Whenever her distress seems beyond his pay grade, he hands her off to the only other person-of-color in the office: Mookie, a full-bodied woman with shoulder-length weaves, who commands attention merely by showing up. Though both she and Mookie are on the verge of forty, Mookie treats her like a kid sister, always wheedling to develop in her the gravitas she's decided is required of a black woman professional. Being of mixed-blood, Zora's never found dependable quarters anywhere in the tenement of racial identity. She is not aggrieved about the accident of her birth. She likes her brownness. On the other hand, Zora knows that gravitas requires learning; she's respectful of Mookie-isms that guide her along.

Zora views a small collection of photos on her computer sent by a journalist who'd managed to slip into the killing grounds. A woman sits on a flat rock, an azure *tobe* wreathing her ebony face. The tiny hand of an infant rises above the dirty swaddling cloth. Five young children in torn, filthy clothes cluster around her, clinging to the vestige of her protection. *The children might be hers, or she might be the only mother left, and they have become hers, and she has no idea how she will care for them where there is no food, no shelter.* A stooped man trudges through a dust storm clutching a small body in a thick blanket. His white *keffiyeh* and the driving sand obscure his face. *He is preparing to bury his hope in the shifting landscape of desert warlords.* A young girl peers with dark vacant eyes, *as if all possibility of feeling has been sawed away, like a shattered limb. On the tender threshold of womanhood, she may have been raped. Probably more than once. The shame will define what is left of her life.* Zora thinks of them as neighbors consumed by a malevolent disaster. With a small shudder, she imagines her bond with them might become more personal.

Mookie strides into her office and perches on the corner of the desk that been permanently cleared for her seating. "What are you up to?"

"Just I got into these photos," Zora points at her computer. "At home I was looking through some of my momma's papers. Check this out." She hands Mookie the black and white photo from box 2.

Adjusting her owlish new red-frame glasses, Mookie peers at it. "Looks like she could be your kin."

Zora shakes her head, unwilling to agree. "I found it with a bunch of notebooks Momma kept about Sudan. I had no idea."

Mookie arches her eyebrows. "Damn, a whole secret life."

"I wanna know *why* the secret." She takes the photo from Mookie and slides it into her purse.

Tom pokes his head into her office. "Hey, Zora! No extra points for early return." He rolls his eyes as if to erase the tactlessness of his greeting. "Glad to see you. When you have a moment, could we talk in my office?"

"Sure. Be there in a couple of minutes."

When he leaves, Mookie shuts the door. "I think Tom boy's gone off his feed."

Zora nods. "Whatchu think's goin' on?"

"Well, if he was a woman, it'd be complicated. But he's either got a new shortie, or an old enemy's got him by the balls."

Zora looks out the window, considering how Tom liked swimming in predator-infested politics. If he were being compromised in some way, the organization would suffer.

"He's squirrelly with me," Mookie complains. "See what you can pry outta him."

"Probably not much."

"We all know he likes you best," Mookie teases, heading for the door, waving her fingers. "But *I* got your back."

The prospect of talking with Tom annoys Zora. She feels too raw. But he's traveling soon. Deferring resolution of the tension between them would be a mistake. On her way to his office, she ducks into the ladies' room. Resting her hands on the sink, she draws a couple of deep breaths to calm herself. Reflected in the mirror is a troubled face. She's a woman old enough to be fully in control of her life, but a wave of chaos seems to be rising from a source and direction she cannot see.

Tom welcomes her into his office with a sweeping gesture and closes the door. Floor-to-ceiling windows overlooking the square below flood the room with sunlight. She sits at one end of a brown leather sofa opposite his desk. The space has the ambiance of a war room, complete with the stink of cigar smoke. Large maps of Sudan, Yemen, and Sri Lanka paper one wall, each spotted with pushpins of various colors. His collection of photos on the wall behind his desk includes one of him shaking hands with President George W. Bush.

"My condolences for the loss of your mother," he says as he sits at the opposite end of the sofa.

"Thank you."

Tom drapes his arm across the sofa back, aiming, she imagines, to appear relaxed in spite of his strained expression. "We have to get a few things straight between us," he begins, looking past her to the map wall.

Not knowing whether he is referring to the argument at the club or the grope in the copy room, she waits.

"I'm concerned," he says quietly, "that you might not be able to put out the right messages about my mission."

Naturally he would lead with his needs, even put her on the defensive. "Why don't you tell me more about your mission?" she suggests.

"I told you: I'm facilitating negotiations among the rebel groups."

Despite his terse tone, Zora forges ahead. "Isn't our credo to remain politically neutral?"

"I'm not at liberty to discuss the details."

"Tom, it's *me*," she says calmly. "You gave me the impression that something new was in the wind. I'm here to remind you that we've been down a lot of roads with these guys—always at arm's length in keeping with our mandate."

He seems to formulate his words carefully. "The government wants to finish a peace deal."

"The military regime?"

He scowls as if she were a clueless newbie.

She arches her eyebrows. "You're connected with the Khartoum government? I thought they hated you."

Tom rises and moves to sit behind his desk. "You've got to involve all the players if you want a deal that works."

She shakes her head. "You really think the regime is going to change its stripes? How do you excuse over thirteen hundred bombing raids on civilian targets in the past twelve years? You know they won't stop, not for any signed piece of paper." Zora watches him distance himself, shuffling papers at his desk. "The regime is professional at turning good men into their bitches." She rises and steps to his desk, plants her hands on a stack of documents and leans toward him. "Tom, I repeat: it's *me*. What have you gotten yourself into?"

He regards her with an expression both sad and defiant. "I've gotten myself into what I think will be a definitive solution." He pushes back in his chair. "If you cannot back me up, then I'll have Mookie take over with the media on this one."

The threat should sting but, to her surprise, does not. "Okay, how about letting me go to Sudan and listen to the displaced civilians' negotiating position?" The idea emerges fully formed, without the tiring exercise of weighing pros and cons. "Haven't they been left out of the equation?"

He huffs dismissively. "So now it's about *you* and *your* mission?"

"No, it's about sticking with our watchdog role. It's about mobilizing support for human beings trapped in a genocide."

He runs his hand through his unruly hair, a signal Zora knows to mean he will end the conversation. "Zora, take some time off and get yourself back on point."

"I'm not off point," she answers, calm. "I hope somebody you trust has got your back."

He tents his arms on his desk, joining his hands into a fist. "See you when I get back."

"I'm not finished." She succeeds in trapping his gaze. "What you did to me in the copy room. That requires an apology."

Embarrassment flashes in his eyes and is extinguished. "You got it."

Something more heartfelt, like the actual words, "I'm sorry," would have done a lot to restore the respect she'd imagined existed between them. But then Tom appears to be no longer himself. "I want it *never* to happen again," Zora says, "or I will happily nail your ass to the wall."

He nods. As she leaves his office, she hears him pick up a call, speaking jovially in Arabic. She knows he'd been an avid student for months.

CHAPTER FIVE

Gathering her purse and jacket, Zora hurries down the back stairs and out the shipping dock. She crosses to a small shop to buy a pint of chocolate ice cream and walks home along busy Connecticut Avenue. At the door of her apartment, the restraints in her life meet her like a needy pet. She cannot remember when last she lost herself in the pleasures of hobbies. Like her momma, she does not sing anymore, not even in the shower. She does not know what made her stop.

Shucking her blouse for an oversized work shirt, she slips the photo she's carried all day from purse to breast pocket. Keeping it close feels necessary, through its meaning remains hidden. Clearing away the "grandmother papers," she takes the lid off box 2. On top are two large notebooks: "Marriages and Births," and "Notes on Family History." She opens the ice cream, certain she'll work down to the waxy bottom of the pint before this inquiry is finished.

Among several copies of birth certificates is what appears to be an original on yellowed paper dated 1832, preserved in a plastic envelope. Her mother must have lifted it from some registrar's office, suggesting special meaning, at least to her. The infant's name, Yagoub Kiir, is penned in formal script Above *Father* Adam Kiir and *Mother* Sawni, no surname. *Place of Birth*—Pahokee, Florida. The discovery shifts her into a dark eddy of memory.

When she was nine, her mother had taken her on a driving vacation to Miami. Along the way, they'd stopped in a small Florida town. The main street was empty in the swampy heat. Her momma had bribed her with a chocolate ice cream cone and the promise of three fabulous, fun days on beautiful Miami Beach. Zora was to wait on the bench in front of the town hall while her momma went to "check on some records."

As the sun-basted clock in the square chimed noon, her momma churned out the squeaky door of the building. Grabbing Zora's arm, she rushed her across the street as though fleeing a noxious gas. "Momma, what did you find?" Zora blurted.

"Nothing you need to know, child."

"But ain't they—?"

"Child, use proper English."

"*Aren't* they my family, too?"

Her momma had squeezed her eyes shut as if stricken by pain. "My early kin in these parts got all messed up." She'd caught herself and artfully recovered. "You're *my* special girl. You're gonna be a shining star in this world." They'd marched to the car through the heavy air, never again to speak of the incident.

Zora examines a sheet of parchment containing a diagram of the Baines clan, her mother's people, going back to the nineteenth century. A Post-it attached at the top instructs: "See front index of Family History Notebook." She duly opens it and begins at the root of the tree, Mabior Kiir. Notebook entry: *The only indication of his place of birth is a reference to Fangak, Sudan.* She wondered how her momma found birth records going back, she counts them, *six* generations.

Mabior's wife appears to be unknown. His son, Adam Kiir, married Mina (no surname). They appear to be first of the clan born in America, undoubtedly as slaves. Any black America might find such roots, but only with extraordinary dedication could one hope to untangle the web of names and places. Evidently her momma had been possessed of such doggedness. Still, many entries had been punctuated with a red question mark.

Adam and Mina produced three children. Ezra drowned during the transit to Cuba; Peter fate unknown, and Amina, sold as a slave to the Baines family plantation in north Georgia. She bore two children by the master, George Baines: a daughter Alma and a son, Ezekiel.

The clan's early begetting had been fraught with sorrowful outcomes; any one of them could have provoked her momma's comment about being "all messed up." But her tone had been harsh, as if she *blamed* them for the untidy customs of slavery.

Her momma's great, great-granddad Ezekiel kept the Baines name after he was emancipated. His boy Josiah, survived to become Ella's great grandfather. His son Caleb migrated north and married Bernice Jones. Zora's maternal grandparents and settled in southeast Washington DC and had died before she was born. That left momma and her brother, my uncle Miles, who would not have a chance at begetting unless his prison sentence for murder was commuted. Her momma had devoted herself to his release until she ran out of hope and money to file appeals.

On the family chart beside *Ella Amina Baines*, in a box outlined in red, is *Joseph Albert Monrowski. Zora Julia's* box is connected to theirs, not with a sure, solid line, but with a row of dots. Ella kept the Baines name, but Zora was given the Monrowski surname that she'd shortened to Monro at the first legal opportunity.

The phone startles her. "*Kochanie*," Bert greets her. "What are you up to?"

Zora hesitates. Yesterday the hunt felt personal. Now it seems bigger and weirder than she wants to handle alone. "Did Momma ever talk to you about family genealogy?"

"No." Bert allows a wounded note in her voice. "No, she didn't." There's a long pause. "So that's why you stayed after the wake? She let you know she'd left some records?"

"Jeezuz, your intuition creeps me out. Yeah, a classic "note-in-the-pocket" communiqué. Two boxes—stashed in the pantry."

"And you were ... *debating* whether to share?"

"Bert, I'm sharing now."

"I'll be over directly."

Zora paces around the table. *Why in a family tree of solid-lined connections do I get the dotted line? Am I not momma's daughter?* As the story went, the only semi-interested party, Joe's family, had not hidden their discomfort from her momma when she'd trundled her new infant to Chicago for inspection. Bert's account of The First Sighting, with a scandalous imitation of Grandma's mournful "*Czarny dziecina*" (black baby) wail had been a stellar, if distressing, bit of family lore. Evidently, no one had seen her momma during her pregnancy.

The rapping of the knocker announces her aunt's arrival. Bert enters bearing a golden-crusted pie, her signature offering for nearly any mood, occasion, or objective. Zora plants a light kiss on her wind-pinked cheek and leads her into the kitchen. "You're actually putting effort into destroying my girlish figure."

"Guilty pleasures keep us strong," Bert answers, pulling plates from the cupboard. "I see you're not eating meals. No plates in the sink." She slices the pie and presents a serving to Zora. "You're upset."

Zora avoids her gaze, takes a bite of pie. "Incredible! As always."

Bert wrinkles her nose. "Oh, come on, talk."

Zora spears a chunk of apple. "I'm hip deep in the sorry history of the Baines clan." She wolfs two more forkfuls then leads Bert to the paper-strewn table.

"Quite a haul," Bert observes, sitting at the head of the table.

Zora hands her the family tree diagram. As she examines the diagram, her jaw goes slack.

"That's pretty much my feeling. I was just getting to the thick of Momma's 'Notes on Family History.' Want me to read to you?"

Bert nods, her expression suddenly forlorn.

"The entries start in 1970, before I came on the scene. Momma wrote: 'Back in 1834—exact dates are just not to be had! —African traders captured a Sudanese man named Mabior Kiir. A kindly, eccentric gentleman translated this information from Arabic records squirreled away in the basement of the Emory University Library. No telling how they got there. Kiir was noted as a 'fine Nubian buck.' Evidently his captors decided he would serve well as a camel driver on their trans-Sahara trade expeditions. I imagine the toll of such a crossing was extraordinary, but he managed to attract a buyer running slaves out of West Africa. He was sold and put on the slave ship Urraca bound for Cuba.'"

"Incredible," Bert whispers. "Do you have any idea how hard it was to find such records back then?" She heaves a sigh. "There were so many vessels and routes, and do you know that over the course of four centuries more than ten million slaves were taken from Africa? And not just to America, but to the Caribbean, and Brazil, and Great Britain, and the Netherlands. And to find bills of sale and owner financial records, and sort through the miserable mess of slave birth records and marriage records—"

"For sure. Let me go on." Zora props up the notebook. "'During the crossing, forty-six of 490 slaves died. It's a miracle that Kiir survived in the belly of so vile a vessel.'"

"Absolutely!" Bert exclaims. "The most horrible brutality inflicted on men and women, and so many children! And these voyages took three *months*!"

"How do you know this?"

"It is a special interest. An obsession for a while."

"You never mentioned it to me."

Bert shrugs. "Nor did I mention my intensive studies of celestial navigation and ancient papermaking techniques."

"Now you're showin' off."

Bert shakes her head. "It's not possible to know everything about someone."

Zora stares at the page, waiting for a wave of nameless anxiety to subside, then she continues reading her momma's narrative. "'Kiir jumped ship as it reached Cuba. He made it to south Florida, perhaps swimming!? and found refuge among the Seminole Indians. It was common for the tribe to shelter runaway slaves, probably because they also experienced the brutality of the white man's oppression. Kiir evidently married a Seminole woman and their only surviving American-born child was Adam. He would be my great-great-great-grandfather.'"

Bert cups her chin with her hand, tapping her fingers hard against her cheek. "Amazing! Ella traced her roots to a slave from Sudan."

The doorbell sounds. Annoyed, Zora rises to answer it.

"You never called," Jackson says gently through the crack of open door. He's wearing a splendidly tailored gray suit with a butter-hued silk tie. His dark eyes suggest a seductive agenda.

"Jackson, I'm sorry. I meant to, but –"

"I heard about your dust-up at work."

"Really?" She wonders *who's turned mole. And why?*

"I thought," he continues, "you might like some help unwinding."

"It's … not a good time." Zora opens the door enough for him to see Bert coyly waving her fingers.

"Oh." He clears his throat. "If you want the contact I mentioned, call me."

"I will." She can't recall him mentioning a contact.

With his self-assured smile, he turns and steps unhurriedly down the stairs. Zora shuts the door. Bert is grinning like a schoolgirl swollen with a juicy rumor. "The Congressman?"

"He's *married*," Zora tells her.

"But given to a bit of Congressional junketing, it seems."

"He's a *source*."

Bert's prim expression dissolves into sputtering laughter.

"B, please just stop it." Zora hands her the photo of the woman and infant. "Take a look."

Bert peers over her bifocals, then examines it closely through the lenses. "Oh my, oh my."

Zora drops empty box 2 on the chair cushion. A thin file, invisible against the bottom of the brown box, flutters for attention. She peers at it for a moment, then picks it up and opens it. Inside are copies of several letters. The first is an exchange between her momma in Washington and a priest named Father Tomaso in Sudan. Her momma requested the priest's assistance in identifying surviving relatives of the Kiir clan. He told her the clans know their people well, but many had been scattered by the drought and raids. Zora reads silently, handing Bert each letter as she finishes. Two more letters exchange views on the dire fate of "her" clan in the Fangak area. Then, her momma had asked him to look for "unattached" children. Zora's hands begin to tremble.

"What have you found?" Bert takes the letter, working her teeth hard against her lower lip as she reads.

Zora's voice is a husky whisper reading the final bit. "A key is taped inside this folder labeled *Safe - front closet*." She shoots Bert a puzzled glance. "I didn't know momma had a safe."

Lifting the key from the tape, Bert nods. "When you were in grade school, she had it installed after some robberies in the neighborhood. I'd forgotten, and you know I haven't lived here for more than, what, ten…twelve years."

Bert's departure from Ella's home had been amicable, Bert claiming, after a job transfer, that the commute to the College Park National Archives facility would be the death of her, and that she needed an apartment there. She and Ella'd had some heated words about selling the DC house, but Ella had stayed on alone in the big place, lavish with memories.

"All these fuckin' secrets," Zora complains. "Why lock up stuff where I would miss it?" She tilts back her head, stares at the ceiling. "Maybe she hoped I'd sell the house and never know the whole story." She drops the folder on the table. "Damn her."

Bert's face drains of solicitude. "Your momma, God rest her soul, loved you more than life itself. She most certainly *was* silent about the truth while she was with us. But she left the facts for *you*." She jabs a finger at Zora. "I'm damn sure she expected you'd go where they pointed."

Zora shakes her head, waiting for courage to surface.

"*Kochanie!* If you want to know what this all means, we have to go open the safe." Bert pulls on her coat, puts the key in her pocket and strides to the door. With her back to Zora, she waits silently. After a long moment, turning, she asks, "Are you able to command your legs?"

Zora slowly slips into a jacket and follows Bert to the car.

The yellow row house with white trim is nestled between two unkempt brethren on 11th Street in Southeast DC. Ella had stayed on through waves of neighborhood criminal enterprises and changing resident skin tones, dismayed but never cowed. Zora and Bert climb the brick steps spattered with a crimson watercolor of tree litter. Ella always had kept the entry swept. In the shadows of the porch, Zora fumbles with the house key.

"Fear is not your friend," Bert says quietly. Taking the key from Zora, she unlocks the big white door, pushes it open, and switches on the foyer light. The rooms beyond are frozen in shadow. The house feels foreign, melancholy.

"Are you ready?" Bert asks quietly.

"I've shown up."

Bert opens the hall closet. The collected coats and jackets, impeccably arranged by color like bands of a rainbow, defy disturbance. Griping the hangers, they carry armfuls of coats to a table in the parlor.

When the closet is empty, they find a faint outline on the back wall. Bert bends a wire hanger to pop open a panel. Inside is a red metal safe the size of a shoebox. On the upper corner of its door is a round button with an image of a woman's finger pressed against red lips. An intricate gold design surrounds the lock.

Zora feels herself sliding out of normal time into a strange undertow she knows will rearrange everything. She inserts the key in the lock and turns it. The door releases with a sigh to reveal a carved wooden box nestled atop two neon-green envelopes.

"Ella was all about presentation," Bert murmurs.

Zora does not hear. She removes the box. Sitting on the stairs, she opens the lid to find scrolled papers secured by a beaded necklace. The "grandmother" notebook's reference to necklaces means this is *not* a random souvenir. For a moment, she studies the intricate string of crimson and lemon-yellow beads, a seemingly random design interspersed with dark tubular bits of bone or wood. She knows it is an heirloom that once belonged to a relative.

Gently sliding the necklace from the scroll, Zora unrolls the papers. The first, a note from Father Tomaso, promises "Your long-awaited request will soon be fulfilled." The second, a telegram, lists an address in New York City and the date July 5, 1982, "... to receive arrival." The final paper, a document meticulously handwritten and bearing a violet-inked seal, releases an infant girl to Ella Baines.

Zora struggles to breathe. "The photo…is my mother!" She pulls away from Bert. "Why would she hand me over to a missionary? What kind of shit is that?"

Bert waits a respectful moment. "That *shit* is usually an act of desperation."

"It's rank exploitation!" she retorts. "A priest pressured a poor pregnant woman to get Momma what she wanted—a trophy from Africa."

Bert blinks as if she's been slapped. "You were *not* a trophy."

"How do you know?"

"Ella never used people. Don't be disrespectful."

"Who are you to tell me?" Dropping the papers on the floor, Zora stands and glares at her. "For Christ sake, we aren't even remotely related."

"You're wrong!" Bert protests, her face roiling with hurt. "We've *always* been family. *Love* made us family."

Zora works her mouth as if she will spit. "So, love justifies the lie about who I am?" She steps back from her aunt, glaring. "What's more important than where you come from?"

Bert purses her lips, defiant. "I suppose what you make of yourself."

Zora hisses at this tidy, correct response to so raw a question. "Damn you both!" she yells and flees into the dark parlor.

In her old refuge, the ledge of an alcove window behind a wide, high-backed chair, she sits with her arms locked around her knees. Wanting to shout or cry, she kicks open the lace curtain. A full moon spills hard white light on the house across the street, illuminating its facade like a shrine. An ancient eccentric named Mr. Jones had lived there, each summer finessing a patch of vegetables in his tiny front yard. Once, when she'd gone to cadge a fresh tomato, he'd seemed unusually preoccupied, as if he'd just gotten some painful news which, she later learned, he had: the death of an old Navy buddy. Leaning on his rake, he declaimed: "We come into this here world alone and all by our lonesome self; that's how we leave it." He often made odd pronouncements, but this one had gotten under her skin. In her girl's mind, she'd fretted about the loneliness of the "leaving," an event far beyond her imagining. But she also decided he was mistaken about the "coming into this here world" part. With breezy confidence, she'd reminded him that birth requires a momma and a baby——hardly a "lonesome self." He'd regarded her sadly, saying one day she, like every other black folk, would learn what it meant to feel like a motherless child. In his thick old man's voice, he'd said that day would remake her soul. Remembering this Zora decides "that day" has arrived.

The image of her sad, hapless real mother haunts her thoughts. If she's still alive—and that seems unlikely—she would have an explanation for what she did. Perhaps a brutal one. *Does this daughter have the courage to know why her mother gave her away? Or should she let time sweep that question into oblivion?*

The whistle of the teakettle, a signal of familiar comfort, summons her to the kitchen. In the dim glow of the range light, Bert arranges a tray with a teapot and two china cups, the fancy hand-painted ones from her grandmother. As she sits at the table, Bert offers a tentative smile and settles the tray between them. Zora shifts in her chair, rests her hand on the old papers assembled neatly on the table. "The news didn't strike me dead," she says quietly. Pouring tea, Bert nods.

Zora fiddles with the lid of the sugar bowl. "Any idea why momma kept up the charade?"

Bert considers the question, her eyes gentle with a memory of her sister-in-law. "I think the longer Ella waited to tell you, the more dangerous it seemed. I bet she thought you'd leave her, go search for your birth mother, and never come back. She never managed to tame her terror of losing you."

Zora had not imagined her intrepid mother helpless with fear. Maybe her constant singing had not been as much performance as a way to keep joy ahead of the fear. "It's a lot to take in, B."

Bert touches her cheek. "Ella was a complicated woman. She worked hard to find you. And it seems you *are* related."

"By a few drops of blood. Maybe." Zora shakes her head. "But why'd she keep digging *after* she got me?"

Bert shrugs. "I suppose family ties became an obsession. Maybe she was hoping to find more blood relatives on this side of the ocean to, I don't know, to keep you company."

A large vehicle, siren bleating, roars down the street. They wait for the noise to fade.

"I got you for company," Zora says. Bert snorts, relief animating her face. Zora stirs a spoonful of sugar in her tea. "This news oughta get me off the hook for not being a musical prodigy."

"Well, I suppose."

They drink their tea in silence, surrounded by the artifacts of their long-ago life as a tight triad of women. Zora pulls the necklace from her pocket, working it gently through her fingers like a rosary. "I'm going to Sudan to find my mother."

"Of course you are." Bert meets her eyes, "And God help us both." She reaches into a sweater pocket and slides a fat green envelope across the table. "Your momma left cash in the safe. Twenty-five thousand."

CHAPTER SIX

As the taxi rumbles down the potholed street, Zora glances at her notes. One of Jackson's staff had sent a profile of Executive Travel. The owner, Mr. Senoja, had been background-checked in preparation for Jackson's Congressional fact-finding trip to Sudan a few months earlier. Over an unavoidable dinner the night before, Jackson had raved about Senoja's knowledge of Sudan, his finesse with security matters. He'd told her to shrug off the State Department's advisory against travel to Sudan, and referred to his former guide as a "real brother," as if that were sufficient professional recommendation.

The taxi is taking Zora to meet the man himself. The northeast Washington neighborhood, crouched in the shadow of the Capitol, offers a mélange of spiffy row houses fronted by clipped shrubbery, and old homes with peeling paint and weedy yards. The brick houses with their cramped stoops remind her of Chicago's Polish enclave where Momma had taken her for her one and only visit in the '80s. Grandma Monrowski had forbidden her to mingle with neighbor kids on the street, an ill-concealed attempt to shield herself from the shame she felt over Zora's color. Zora had contented herself with a metal swing in the fenced backyard surrounded by beds of coddled roses and dahlias. All around her the old brick houses had seemed to exhale disappointment or fear, but in her innocence, she'd ignored the contagion.

The taxi pulls up to a two-story beige house, its graveled yard enclosed by a waist-high, black, wrought iron fence. A small bronze sign beside the door reads "Executive Travel Ltd." Zora slides from the taxi just as man bolts from a door two houses away. A glass vase with red flowers arcs through the air and explodes like a bomb on the concrete behind him.

"Ya fuckin' son of a bitch," screams a woman. She stands in the door, hands on hips, a flowered wrapper barely covering her ample brown breasts. "Ya oughta be a jail bitch, ya scumbag." The young blonde man, dressed in jeans and a brown suede jacket, stands at the curb, his face a mask of indignant anger. As the woman continues her screeching harangue, a large dark-skinned man in a suit steps out the door of Executive Travel. He grins at Zora, cants his head at the disturbance, and rolls his eyes. "Ms. Monro, so glad you are here. Please wait. This will take but a moment." He strides over to the young man and stands close, his words inaudible to her in the rumble of a passing truck. The young man hustles into his car and drives off.

The woman at the door straightens, yells "*Mr.* Senoja, don't ya be gettin' up in my bidness."

Senoja turns to the woman. "Naomi," he commands, "I will stay out of your business if you keep your business off the street. Now go inside." Her posture softens. A pout rises on her face. Dogs in a nearby yard begin barking then yelping as if being beaten. Mr. Senoja steps to the foot of her stoop. "Go in," he encourages. "We do not want the police here again."

She shakes her head, wiping her hand across her forehead.

"I will check on you later," he offers, "help you clean up the mess."

With a compliant sigh, the woman withdraws and shuts the door. Senoja ambles back to Zora, satisfaction on his face. "Messy affair," he explains, cupping his hand to her elbow. "Please come."

"You handled that smoothly."

"I like to think is it my style rather than my size that defuses people." He opens a steel security gate, then a large oak door. She follows him into a reception room. An intricately woven Persian rug graces the oak floor; a striking painting of a desert landscape dominates a burnt-orange wall. Bob Marley's "No Woman, No Cry" provides a musical undercurrent. Mr. Senoja leads her down a short hallway to a large office. "Ms. Monro," he says as he motions her in, "you are even more beautiful than the talented Congressman could describe."

His chivalrous manner disarms her. Despite his considerable bulk, he moves with athletic grace. The gray silk of his double-breasted suit whispers as he arranges a chair for her. His bald head glistens like polished mahogany. Just above his right ear a curious dent mars the smooth curve of his skull. His face beads with sweat. "I have never been able to adapt to the weather here," he says. His voice would be gruff if not for a clipped Afro-Brit accent.

"Humid for late September."

He points at her as if she's intuited his thought. "Then we shall have iced beverages, yes?" He sits behind his desk, touches an intercom, and speaks briefly in Arabic. "Now, tell me," he turns his full attention to her, "why would a stunning professional American woman wish to journey to Sudan?"

"Did you also flatter the Congressman when you asked him this question?"

He offers a honeyed chuckle. "You are much more beautiful than the Congressman. And there are many agendas."

She smiles, indulging his bantering tone. "This trip is not about my work. It's a personal matter, a search for family."

"Ah ...." He folds his hands on the desk. "As you know," he says, apology in his tone, "Sudan is a war zone. Are you certain this would be a good time to go?"

She shrugs. "The war has been raging for more than a generation. Will there be a better time?"

"That would be difficult for me to say."

"Mr. Senoja." A dark-haired woman enters, her head bowed, carrying a tray with two large, iced drinks. She sets it soundlessly on the desk and leaves.

"This is *karkedeh*," he announces. "Hibiscus tea. A popular drink in Sudan." Handing a glass to her, he raises his own. "Some believe that if Sudan does not kill you, then you are invincible." He catches her eye. "I have completed many journeys there."

She tastes the tea, deciding it's an acquired taste. "Then either you are living on borrowed time or very good at what you do."

He laughs. "Some might say they are the same. The job is a dangerous game."

She cannot decide if "game" is a slip or a boast. She glances at the photos arrayed on the burgundy wall behind him. "Tell me about yourself."

He bows his head deferentially. "I was born in Uganda. My parents moved our family to London when I was ten years of age. I was schooled there, but never took well to the discipline of the headmasters." He allows a self-effacing grin. "I attended university and completed military service. Then I came to America to start a new life. My business has been good. I serve many high-profile clients. Their satisfaction has been most gratifying to me." He lifts the top of a crystal jar near his phone and plucks out a Dot candy. "I love the red ones," he confesses, tipping the container toward her. "Please, help yourself."

She takes a couple of green ones. "And where is your family now?"

"My father has passed. My mother returned to live near Kampala; my sister is in London." He slides a document across the desk. "The details of my professional history."

She takes time to read it. A few Congressional junkets, two trips with celebrity ambassadors for UN agencies, even an expedition with a scientific group studying changes in wildlife migration patterns. "You have lots of experience."

He nods. "And now if we may discuss practical matters." He opens a blue folder and hands it to her. "My services are comprehensive. I arrange air transportation, visas, and travel documents. I secure lodging, as you may specify. My associates in Sudan provide ground transportation. I speak Arabic fluently. I will be armed for your security."

"You carry a gun?"

"Once we are on the ground in Sudan, yes. At all times. A Glock 9mm."

"I'm never comfortable around guns."

He regards her calmly. "My dear Ms. Monro, I have never had to shoot anyone in the course of a journey, but it is an efficient deterrent in certain situations we may encounter." He rises and moves to a large map of Sudan on the wall beside his desk. "Now tell me the places you wish to visit."

She sits back in the chair, oddly pleased by his seamless showmanship. "The people I am looking for were in the Fangak area— but that was years ago."

He purses his lips. "A volatile area. Many people have fled to Khartoum."

"Still, Fangak is a start. Is the area accessible?"

"Yes, but that village may be seriously compromised." He draws a circle with his finger on the map. "Militia have raiders in that area."

She considers how crazy it is to travel in a war zone with an armed stranger as a guide. But the Congressman and other clients had returned undamaged—as far as she could determine.

"Do you know the name of the clan you are seeking?"

"'Kiir' is all I have to go on right now."

"A common name."

She'd wanted to appear less clueless. "I'll see what more I can find."

He nods and turns a page in his folder. "It is customary," he continues, "for women to dress discreetly."

She arches her eyebrows.

"Nothing severe. Long skirts or loose trousers are suitable." He sits again at the desk. "Sudan is a very hot place." His eyes hint of sexual calculation.

It soothes her ego to be regarded in this way, but this is not the sort of vibe she wants. "Mr. Senoja." She leans toward him. "I have never traveled with a man I didn't know. I wouldn't want—"

"Ms. Monro, let me assure you that I maintain a strictly professional relationship over the course of a journey." He reaches in the jar and holds up a Dot. "This is my one vice." He pops it into his mouth and smiles.

She decides he has had good practice tamping down potential deal breakers.

"I must now cite two necessary restrictions—for your safety. A camera will only bring unwanted attention. I therefore recommend you do not bring one."

She nods. *Of course, I will ignore this recommendation. Who would go on a journey of such consequence without one?*

"Is that something you do when you're nervous?" he asks.

"What?"

"Twist the hairs near your collar?"

Frowning, she rests her hand in her lap.

"Ms. Monro, it is my job to notice what people do. I mean no offense."

"None taken," she says, sensing he has leveraged a subtle advantage.

"Second, I must insist that you strictly follow my direction if a threat should arise."

"Such as?"

"If we are confronted by armed men." He crosses his arms over his broad chest. "Sometimes, it is not clear what they are seeking. I must be in control of whatever negotiations are required."

"Fair enough since you speak the language. But I do *not* want to find myself at your side in a gun battle. I expect you to do everything in your power to avoid one."

"It will be so, I assure you." He clasps his hands together.

"That's a stunning ring," she observes.

"Yes, it is." He holds his fist clenched between them. A raised scar at the base of his middle finger runs like a small black snake across the top of his hand. "It was a generous gift from a satisfied client. Now, Ms. Monro, have you determined when you wish to depart? I can make all preparations within two weeks."

To calm a niggling anxiety—is it the decision to go or the man before her?—she rises and steps over to the wall to look at a group of photographs. Senoja smiling from the driver's window of a Land Rover. Jackson grinning from the back window. Two tall, impassive, black men in fatigues flanking them. Other photos reveal similar scenes with other government officials she recognizes. "Two weeks?" She turns, catches him averting his gaze from her legs. She sits again. "Tell me, how much will this cost?"

"It depends on the quality of comforts you require." He takes a pad from the desk drawer.

She knows the country is a wasteland, that fetching clean water can require a multi-kilometer trek on dirt tracks, that everything she might carry is, for most of the natives, beyond imagining. "Bare bones will work for me."

He jots a note on the form then reads: "Round trip airfares from Washington to Khartoum for two, brief accommodations there, a chartered plane, supplies for the field, food, a vehicle for the overland journey, fuel, driver, and, of course, my services as a guide, guard, and translator." He studied the list. "Shall we budget for two weeks?"

"That's barely enough time to recover from jet lag."

He chuckles. "Then I will give you a base weekly fee, and you can decide on the number of weeks." Pressing his lips together, he checks off items. "I am eliminating the standard Congressional fee. They tend to require many creature comforts." He winks.

"Our tax dollars at work." She helps herself to a couple of Dots as he taps at the calculator. "Do I hear the sound of my nest egg shattering?"

He looks up from his calculations. "It is a trip of great importance, yes?"

"That remains to be seen. Perhaps I won't find anyone."

He regards her solemnly. "It is the nature of Sudanese to know the whereabouts of their clansmen. We will surely find *someone* who is your kin—or knows their whereabouts."

The idea of the journey suddenly terrifies her. She could cocoon in her job, zipper her mouth, and stay cozy with a paycheck. *Why in God's name endure the unpredictable dangers of a war zone? What could I possibly learn from an obliquely related person, if I find one, and with whom I share no language, culture, or life experience?*

"Alright," he says. "The base cost of air travel: $8,000. The weekly cost of all other items and services: $5,000. Two weeks total $18,000, three weeks $23,000 and so on."

She thumps her chest as if she's taken a bullet.

He smiles indulgently. "I really do take care of *everything*."

So, there it is: a risky, expensive expedition. Thanks to Momma, the money is there, but her resolve inexplicably is faltering. "I appreciate all the information," she tells him, rising as she gathers the documents he has prepared. "I'll call you within two days with my decision."

"As you wish." He comes around the desk. "It has been a great pleasure to meet you." He bows slightly. His firm handshake telegraphs a signal she cannot decode.

"Does everybody call you *Mr.* Senoja?"

"No," he says softly, meeting her eyes. "My friends call me Senoja. I would like to think we could become friends."

After she leaves, he moves to the window and slightly parts the dark wood blind on the window facing the street. He watches her slip into her car. "Mmm, mmm," he murmurs. "I love this job."

CHAPTER SEVEN

RayJ strides into Zora's living room. "Sorry I'm late. Sudanese army's been bombing Bentiu." He drops into the easy chair, chuckling as Zora chants "la, la, la" with her hands over her ears. "A network is beggin' for footage," he says loudly. "Take a miracle to find any."

"You just *had* to mess with my willful ignorance." Zora pushes aside the fat black duffel she's been packing. "I fell out of good grace at the office when I told HR I was taking a month leave of absence. They said I could do it on my own dime."

"That's raw. You gonna protest?"

"Naah. My momma took care of this trip. I can afford the time off." She watches him put a small black case on the coffee table, enjoying the beauty of his graceful body. "Glad you could get here tonight. I'm headin' out tomorrow for Nairobi, then on to southern Sudan.

"Into the fire." He exhales loudly. "If that's your idea of quality time away then I need a beer."

When she returns from the kitchen with a bottle of Heineken, she finds him poised above the open black case, grinning slyly. "You wanted spy gear. Check it out." The interior foam padding cradles a peculiar collection of items. With his thumb and index finger, he picks up a wafer-thin black square the size of a thumbnail. Affixed to one side is a miniscule turret, capped with a black button. "This is the camera and lens. You get an eighty-degree angle of view and clean color images even in low light. You got four different button sizes and a couple of lapel pins to conceal it." His large hands move with delicate certainty. "It's wireless transmission. You put the video recorder in your pocket." He lifts a short thin pen from the foam crib and holds it up. "Microphone. Also wireless."

"Damn! I get audio too?"

He eyes her with feigned indignation. "Ain't we pros?" He positions his hands on the recorder. "Just slide this switch with your thumb and the whole system is good to go." He faces her, his eyes prospecting. "You got no buttons."

"Often not."

"No worries." He pinches off the button on the camera and substitutes a miniature pin in the shape of a sunburst. "Here, find a spot to park this."

Reaching beneath the fabric, she pushes the pin through lapel of her sweater and docks the camera to it.

"Now turn it on."

She nudges the recorder switch with her thumb and slides it into her pocket.

He puts on a stern expression. "Passport! Monro, Zora." His accent sounds oddly like Mr. Senoja's. "American. You will tell me the reason for invading our country." He backs across the room. "This is about the limit of your range for clear images." He smiles so his dimples come out. "You're kinda sexy when you're plannin' somethin' dangerous."

"Dawg don't mess with me," she pretends to warn, admiring his full pouty lips. Her impending trip has not yet incited an itch for an emergency fuck. If it does, she wants it to be with him.

"Wanna see what you just recorded? Hand me that bad boy." He touches a button and his customs-officer scene plays on a tiny monitor.

"I got you an extra card and battery. You got a terabyte of memory. That should be plenty. Unless you end up shooting an epic." He pats the case tenderly as she removes the camera from her sweater "You gotta put everything back in the *right* place."

"Yeah, I know."

"For real," he insists. "Lemme see you do it."

She gently sets each component in its appointed slot. "Okay?"

Again, the dimpled smile. "Perfect." He swigs his beer.

After a knock and a short pause, Bert lets herself in. "Oh, sorry, I thought you'd be out on last-minute errands. I'm interrupting?"

"Naaah," RayJ drawls. "Jus' finished."

Bert appraises them, shooing away speculation of a tryst. "Zora, my dear adventurous niece, there are ongoing bombings, pillaging militia, and cholera outbreaks, just to mention a few red flags flying at your destination. And this guide of yours—"

"Mr. Senoja. Background checked by the Congressman's staff."

Bert scowls. "Now that's as reassuring as a wiretap." She sets her jaw, flutters her hands in lieu of words, finally training her attention on RayJ. "Can *you* talk her out of this?"

He rolls his eyes. "Too late, Miz B, she's already grippin' the throttle."

"Wheels up tomorrow late morning," Zora confirms, pleased with her confident tone. She's wrestled through too many days of second-guessing her need to find the stranger, her mother, who could be dead, and wondering if she's tough enough to cope with the physical demands of the mission. And with the peculiar Mr. Senoja.

Bert waits as if she expects a reversal, a laughing, "Gotcha!" Searching Zora's face, she surrenders a sigh. "Well then." She reaches into her purse. "If you insist on this journey—as I expected you would—then you should have this." She fastens something on Zora's collar. "If you think it's corny, I don't need to know."

Zora pulls the fabric to get a look. It's a tiny golden angel, wings outstretched.

"I believe in guardian angels." Bert states, pure faith in her eyes.

"She's beautiful." Zora sees tears welling. "Hey, I'm coming back."

Bert surrenders stiff-backed to her embrace. "Your momma and I agreed that whoever survived longest would look after you."

"I'm a big girl now." Zora touches her cheek. "The angel's your stand-in on this trip."

"She'll be jus' fine," RayJ declares. "I'll track her down if she doesn't check in." Finishing his beer he says: "ZoMo, whatcha doin' tonight?"

"Been invited to a house party. Either of you wanna join me?"

"Can't," he says. "My lil sis dropped into town. But I'll run you to the airport tomorrow."

"Thanks, but I'm getting picked up by my fearless guide."

RayJ had expressed some doubts about this guide. That he was vetted by the State Department didn't mean much to him. His distrust of government institutions ran chasm deep. He'd thought Zora's did as well. She had surprised him with a dismissive response.

Bert unbuttons her coat as if she will take it off, then moves to the sofa as if she will sit but does neither. "Who's hosting the party?"

"A Sudanese man, Ahmed. I found his name in Momma's address book. Called him a couple weeks ago. Momma's death really threw him. Seems a bit random, but I've given up trying to understand Momma's web of acquaintances."

Bert circles the sofa. "It's smart to get a feel for…the people you'll be dealing with."

"B, will you *please* sit down and relax!"

"I can't. I can't stay!" She glances helplessly at Zora. "Leave-taking is a small torture for me." She drifts for a moment in a silence. "Even after all this time, separation feels like a funeral waiting to happen." Zora reaches for her hand, but Bert turns for the door. "Stay safe, *kochanie*."

Following her, Zora realizes that nothing she can say is likely to stanch her distress. "I'll be back before you know it. I'll call when I can."

"I'm counting on it." Bert descends the stairs without looking back. Zora waits in the doorway until she drives off.

RayJ slides into his jacket. "Gotta go too." Grabbing his chunky ring of keys from the coffee table, he tosses it in the air, makes a show of catching it behind his back. "ZoMo, get your fine self back home safe." He busses her cheek and meets her eyes. "And bring my gear back same." She salutes him.

RayJ's stayed in her corner, a reassurance she needed. *Unlike Mookie.* But that issue will have to wait. After he's roared off on his motorcycle, Zora rests against the door. All the anchors of her life soon will be eight thousand miles away. Everything will be unfamiliar, everyone a stranger speaking another language. She breathes slowly to dispel a flash of panic.

Two days after giving the go-ahead for the trip, she'd nearly derailed Senoja's calm preparations by telling him, on Ahmed's advice, that she wanted to enter Sudan unofficially, across the southern border with Kenya. That would involve a liaison with a representative of the Sudanese Peoples Liberation Army, who controlled the border with its neighbor. Senoja had protested, cajoling her to go "the safe and proper way." She'd been adamant about avoiding interactions and scrutiny that would legitimize, even in a tiny way, the murderous regime in Khartoum.

Incredulous, agitated, but eager for the trip to proceed, he'd bowed to her wishes. Thinking about their dust-up makes her wonder, not for the first time, just where his loyalties lie.

As the hall clock ticks toward eight, she considers begging off the party, turning in early. But being alone will only leave opportunity for her anxiety to ratchet up. "For christsake, you can sleep on the plane," she chides herself, heading to the bathroom to reapply her makeup. Gazing at the tired woman in the mirror, she begins rehashing her motives for this trip. People scattered as warring troops and militia swept through their villages. The odds of finding her kin were abysmal. Would seeing their shattered lives up close somehow provide a bit of vindication for the work that consumed the best of her? Had she allowed her energy to be sucked into a black-hole fascination with brutality? *Was this just fuckin' crazy?*

As she locates the walkway to Ahmed's suburban split-level, an ethereal song wafts from the open door. Ahmed greets her with a robust handshake. He is a lean man except for a slightly rounded belly. His skin is ink black; his wild crest of hair mostly grey. His dark eyes gleam. "Come in! Come in!"

Tall people as dark as shadows crowd the living room. Ahmed squires her through them. "I want you to meet everyone, but first, my special guest." He ushers her to a seated man in a dark blue business suit wearing black-framed glasses. His bushy white hair and deeply creased face imbue him with a magisterial aura. Ahmed introduces him as Abel Adam Alier, a representative of the rebel Sudanese People's Liberation Army,

"You will travel soon in my country," Abel says in gently accented voice. "I am sorry that you will see our nation on its knees."

"You waste no time, sir, with idle pleasantries."

He nods, allowing a small upward curve of his mouth. "We have a saying: 'After God created Sudan, He laughed.' We do not yet understand His sense of humor."

She half-smiles. "I don't expect it will be an easy trip. I'm looking for relatives around Fangak."

He seems to ponder this information. "What will you do if you find them?" It's an obvious question that she's stubbornly skirted. "You realize," he continues, "they will see you as a savior."

She feels pinned by his steady gaze. "To be honest, I don't know what I'll do."

He offers a sad smile. "Ahmed will be able to guide you in this." He extends his hand. "We will meet again, *Insha'Allah*." He turns to a young man who leans to speak in his ear.

Feeling a light touch on her knee, Zora looks down at a chubby toddler. Her cornrowed hair is tipped with tiny shiny beads that match her frilly pink dress. "Hello, sweetheart," she says, kneeling beside the girl.

The toddler's smile reveals stubs of incoming teeth. A ruddy-faced woman, petite and sandy-haired, moves beside the child. "This is Safaa, my daughter. I'm Janice."

Zora shakes her hand and introduces herself. "She's a beauty."

"Just turned fourteen months," Janice says as she sits on the floor. "I found her when she was just over three months old."

"In Sudan?"

"Yes, she's from the Dinka tribe."

The toddler, serene and undemanding, snuggles against the woman. "When her village was bombed, her mother and some other women ran from their homes to hide in the bush. They ended up in a minefield. An explosion killed all of them." Her voice catches but she tamps down a swell of emotion. "Except Safaa. She was slung on her mother's back."

The child sways charmingly and lurches off.

Zora releases the breath she's been holding. "Who got her out of the mine field?"

Janice follows the child with eyes that seemed to take little for granted. "When the bombing stopped, a woman heard her crying. She was terrified but couldn't ignore the baby. She told me she wept the whole time it took to crawl ten meters through the field. But she made it to Safaa and carried her out to the road."

Safaa tumbles into friendly arms. Her life had dangled on the thread of a woman's courage, and here she is, sweetly unaware of the miracle. "Why did the woman let you have her? It seems—"

"Unusual?' Janice nods. "In better circumstances, she and the other women would have found a way to care for orphans like her. But they had nothing for themselves. The war had left them destitute. I'd come to their village with a medical team. Safaa was so malnourished—" Her voice falters. "We all knew that if she stayed, she'd die."

Zora exhales sharply. The same cruel logic could have been the pivot of her own fate. The idea assails her, and she pushes back from the thought, unwilling to let it leave her exposed and helpless among strangers. "How did you get her out of Sudan?"

"Oh God!" Janice sighs. "It was a long, complicated process. I would not wish it on an enemy." She explains protracted negotiations with immigration officials and the U.N. refugee agency. All the while, Safaa's quiet play holds their attention.

"She's so calm, so…dignified," Zora observes. "I've never thought of a toddler that way."

"Her life is a miracle," Janice affirms. "It's as if she knows the grace of it."

"Come, come," Ahmed beckons his guests. "Please. Food is ready for you to enjoy."

A large table has been set with a banquet of smoked fish, roasted chicken, and bowls of steaming rice and vegetables. As other guests fill their plates, Zora peers into a nearby room filled with teenagers watching a movie. At the door, a young man stands wolfing food with his hands from a bowl. "I'm Zora," she says.

"I am Zachariah." He points to his bowl. "This great thing of America. Eat any time! Much food!" His unabashed glee makes her smile.

"Do you go to school?"

"It is my dream." He wrinkles his nose, "First, I find work for money."

"And your family?"

His eyes drift away. He slowly finishes chewing his food, his face drained of expression. "I do not know if they live."

Ahmed touches her arm. "Please, let us talk in private."

She hesitates, pinioned by the young man's naked sorrow. Leaning close to his ear, she says: "I will pray that you find them alive and well." It's a meager offering, religious in a way that is not hers, but it seems necessary and right to add her name to his silent petition that they survive, somewhere.

Ahmed escorts her to the empty kitchen. "When you are in Nairobi, you must call this number." He hands her a slip of paper. "Tariq is like a brother to me. I trust him with my life. He can help you in your search." He glances over her shoulder into the crowded living room and then meets her eyes. "Zora, you must be *very* careful. Few things will be as they appear."

CHAPTER EIGHT

Zora'd packed methodically from a list of clothing. She'd filled her backpack with notebooks, maps, power bars, a desert hat, and sunblock. Senoja arrives at the promised time in a black Land Rover. Dulles delivers none of the usual airport hysteria. The start feels promising.

The flight from Washington is delayed by foul weather in Frankfurt. After twenty hours in transit with a brief layover in Schiphol Airport in Amsterdam, Zora is relieved to get the hell off the plane at Nairobi's Jomo Kenyatta Airport. Through a hall hemmed with trinket shops she strides beside Senoja to the baggage claim. Night has settled; the airport terminal is uncomfortably humid. Face beaded with sweat, Senoja consults a notepad as they stand in the customs line.

"I've arranged a car to take us to a private residence in Loresho. It is a relatively safe area west of city center. Tomorrow, we will procure the necessary travel passes. It will take time. The rebels who pretend to run border administration are known for their inefficiency."

She catches the exasperation in his tone. "Listen, Senoja, if you've still got your back up about this arrangement, then we should rethink –"

"Ms. Monro—"

"Will you drop the formal crap?"

"Zora." He wipes his forehead with a white handkerchief. "The travel documents will not be legitimate with the government in Khartoum."

"But they keep us off the official radar. We get to travel to Fangak. That's all I care about."

He wipes his brow again. "We are both tired." He offers a conciliatory smile. "Everything will be as you wish."

They move easily through customs and out to a waiting Land Rover. As they leave the airport chaos, she rolls down her window, eager to get her first sense of Africa beyond what she's read. The congestion on the highway seems odd for the late hour. The driver assures her that Nairobi traffic is always bad, but at least there is movement. Young men in white dress shirts and raggedy t-shirts hawk odd bits of merchandize from pools of light etched by yellow street lamps. The air feels undemanding with the coolness of the city's lofty elevation. She'd read that "Nairobi" comes from the Maasai phrase *Enkare Nyorobi,* "place of cool waters." The Nairobi River runs through it. She would like to see it.

The lighted skyline, a mishmash of boxy towers, rises into view. The Rover spins through a roundabout, neatly avoiding a man pissing at the side of the road. A group of women with bulging sacks balanced on their heads trudge along the dusty shoulder.

The main road skirts a large park lined with blooming jacaranda trees, the scent musky in the night breeze. Their young driver, perfunctory in his heart-stopping maneuvers, speeds past knots of pedestrians. Loud reggae beats pour from an open-air bar. Zora thinks she'd like to try the local beer. They cruise through a bright commercial area. Senoja finally pipes up: "This is Westlands. Many expats live here." She guesses from the number and ethnic variety of restaurants that those folks eat well.

They enter a dark stretch of road fringed by crude, dark shacks. As they crest a hill, the moon glints off a fantastically vast mosaic of tin and tarp roofs. "That is Kibera," Senoja says. "It is as desperate a place as it looks." Zora'd read about a plan to rehouse people from this slum, but intractable controversies moved one government official to remark that, at its current pace, the project would take nearly twelve hundred years to complete. Zora's eyes sweep over it, and she wonders what future can be built in so desolate a place.

Further on, the entrance to a road is blocked by a white wooden pole. The driver honks to wake up a guard, who ambles out of a tiny shack. After a quick word with Senoja, the sleepy man in uniform raises the barrier. Up a rise past several walled compounds, they turn into a driveway, the tires loudly scattering gravel. Another guard opens a tall creaking iron gate and they enter the lush grounds of a large dark house.

After the driver offloads their bags, Senoja unlocks the door and escorts Zora into a dark foyer. "This is the home of a friend who is out of the country. Your room is just there," he points. "The electricity is off tonight. I apologize for the inconvenience." He hands her a flashlight.

"It's okay," she murmurs. "I'm going to sleep." Off a narrow hallway, she enters a small room furnished with a single bed covered with a leopard-print blanket. She perches on a bamboo stool and lights two candles left with matches on a small bureau. Senoja enters and sets her duffel beside her. "I will sleep in the adjacent room. The WC is just across the hall. The housekeeper will prepare breakfast whenever you wish."

"I appreciate all you've arranged," Zora says. "It's much better than a hotel." He nods, impassive in a disappointing way. She smiles at him. "Oh, and just one more thing. I need to make a local call in the morning."

"There is no landline here. You are welcome to use my satellite phone."

"Good." She offers another smile. "I hope you sleep well." Senoja says nothing. He quietly shuts the door as he leaves.

Grateful for solitude, for a respite from his unpredictable moodiness, Zora sprawls on her back on the bed. A light breeze through the jalousie windows carries a pungent, marijuana-like scent. She dozes.

In a dream, she is soaring high over a desert. Her flying body knows how to play the wind, catching updrafts, warmed by a benevolent sun. Below her, a girl, as black as midnight, stands alone and naked on barren land.

Vicious barks and yelps jar her awake. Somewhere in the neighborhood, dogs must have the upper hand on a would-be prowler. As peach-hued dawn bleaches away the night, she lies awake, unstuck from time. Everything familiar lives on the other side of the planet. She hears Senoja's heavy footfalls in the hall, listens as he quietly gives instructions to someone. The front door opens then closes with a click of key in the lock. The Land Rover rumbles to life, tires spitting gravel down the driveway. No one could arrive here by vehicle unnoticed.

Shrugging on a T-shirt and shimmying into jeans, she emerges from her room to find a sweet-faced woman in a yellow *kanga* bustling around a spacious kitchen. The woman smiles, says *"Karibu"* and points at the dining table. Senoja left a note: *Mama Gitau will serve you breakfast. I have gone to secure the travel permits. Please do not leave the compound.*

Mama Gitau, a thin woman with stray bits of dark hair curling from the edges of her head wrap, carries a large bamboo tray to the table. As if in practiced performance, she delicately sets out a white teapot and a china cup, a covered sugar bowl, and a plate of sliced mango with several small rolls of crepe-like bread. She grins shyly at Zora's "*Asante sana*" and returns to the kitchen. Despite her usual aversion to breakfast, Zora eats with relish, pleased to enjoy a soft landing. Sipping the spicy, milky tea, she peruses a two-day-old copy of *The Nation* newspaper. Various political antics and scandals fill the first page. Outside the open window, unseen birds trill *ki-trrr, ki-tirrr* in the sun-bathed garden of diligently tended roses flanked by vigorous banana trees.

When she finishes eating, she steps out into the greenery. Near the door, pendulous yellow trumpet flowers festoon a large unruly bush. A mango and a papaya tree, thick with ripening fruit, shade a pair of wooden lawn chairs in a private corner. Promiscuous with its heady scent, a jasmine vine along the fence hosts the frenzied attention of hummingbirds. It is a swath of heaven offered, and savored, before a plunge into hell.

During the winding drive through the dark neighborhood the night before, she could see little but high walls and guarded gates. Her restless energy begs to be burned until she can meet Ahmed's friend. The gatekeeper looks alarmed as she approaches. "Madame, good morning. Please, you will wait for Mr. Senoja."

She flashes her best smile. "I just want to see the neighborhood. I won't go far."

He glances through the gate as if seeking instruction from a hidden source.

"I'll make it right with Mr. Senoja," Zora assures.

As if on cue, the Land Rover rumbles up the driveway. The guard, clearly relieved, salutes professionally as he opens the gate. Senoja eases the vehicle beside Zora. "Madame, you are looking well and rested."

"Good morning, Senoja. "Do I need permission to move about freely?"

He chuckles. "No, no. I'm merely interested in keeping you safe."

"With all the guards around, how could I not be safe?"

"Please," he sighs, "get in, and I will tell you what I have arranged."

She slides into the seat beside him, aware of his eyes on her. She has not decided if this is a friendly habit or the leading edge of flirtation.

"We fly to Loki tomorrow morning," he says, handing her a hand-printed itinerary. "Then on to Malakal. I will be able to pick up the travel documents this afternoon. In the meantime," he waves his hand through the air as if conjuring magic, "I will escort you on a tour of the city center and the markets."

"Excellent! But before the tour, can I use your phone?"

With a flash of disappointment, he unclips the phone from his belt and hands it to her. "Dial 882, then the number."

Tariq answers after one ring. She greets him and identifies herself. While they work out a time and place to rendezvous, she's aware of Senoja fidgeting in his seat. When she rings off, he clears this throat. "May I know the purpose of this meeting?"

She shoots him a surprised glance. "Senoja, you are *my guide*, not my chaperone."

Unfazed, he chuckles. "Yes, of course. Where shall I drop you?"

Java House, Nairobi's version of Starbucks, attracts a mixed crowd of home-sick Westerners and well-to-do locals. Scanning the customers, she sees that Tariq, "the bearded man in a white shirt," has not yet arrived. She takes a table near the window to watch the flow of people on the street. Aggressive drivers force pedestrians to dart for the narrow sidewalks. Two street boys in filthy clothes hustle a well-dressed couple for a handout. A young boy, head nodding like a junkie's, begs passersby for money. A man in a white *jellabiyah* loiters outside a storefront across the street.

"You are ZoMo?" The voice startles her.

She looks up at a lanky, cinnamon-brown man with stunning green eyes. He wears the short-sleeved dress shirt and dark trousers that seem to constitute the workday attire of Kenyan men. "I am Tariq, Ahmed's friend." He smiles, his teeth bright against sensuous lips, and extends his hand.

"Yes, I'm Zora Monro." She accepts his firm grip. "How did you know—"

"About ZoMo?" He surveys the room. "Let us move to that table in the rear."

"Why?" She picks up her bag.

"Just a prudent precaution in an unpredictable city."

After they are seated, he smiles again. "I am a journalist who loves research. That is how I know about ZoMo."

"That nickname's—"

"From one of your colleagues who likes blogging."

"Do you always finish other people's sentences?"

"Only to impart information." His voice flows with gentle Arabic inflections.

A waitress wearing a green apron appears with a faux smile. Tariq orders coffee for them. "You will find this Kenyan blend a treat." Resting his hands on the table, he gazes at her. "So, you have come thousands of miles on an errand of the heart."

She feels his eyes conjuring a spell too fast, too soon. "Yes, I suppose that describes my first trip to Africa." She looks away at a menu board on the wall. "Tell me why Ahmed felt it important we meet."

"He knows what I can do to assist your mission."

"What would that be exactly?"

"I know the Malakal area well. I understand the…political tensions. I speak Arabic, Dinka, Swahili, and English." His smile is wickedly charming.

"And do you share his commitment to the rebel cause?"

He leans close, his breath on her cheek. "What person of conscience would not?"

Dazzled by his intimacy, she waits for her stuttering thoughts to steady up. The waitress brings a tray with a large ceramic pot and two mugs. Tariq primes his cup with a generous amount of cream, fills it with coffee and adds three packets of sugar. The ritual occupies his full attention as she fills her own cup. He stirs and sips the brew, savoring the taste. Then he trains his eyes on her. "The Khartoum regime is well armed. The resistance has to respond with more cunning." As with many Sudanese she's met, he launches first into politics. She wants personal details, a lighter tone to give her instincts a useful reading.

"And you," she injects during a pause, "Who are you really? What were you before? What did you do, and what did you think?"

He shakes his head, confused.

"Humphrey Bogart, *Casablanca*." She props her chin on her hand. "Come to think of it, those lines didn't work really well for him either."

He laughs, three rich notes that seem to vibrate in her head. "You want to know about my *background*?"

"Well, yeah."

His expression drifts from amused to somber. "I grew up in Khartoum, the only son of a government minister and his Dinka slave. In Sudan, the father's bloodline defines identity. But among both sides of my family, I am an outlier, a half-breed." He says this without shame.

It pleases her, this confession, as if he has offered a promise of emotional common ground.

"I was schooled," he continues, "by a private tutor through secondary school. Then I came to your country to attend the University of Iowa. After graduation, I returned to Khartoum and was given a job as a reporter for one of the government-owned newspapers. And here I am." He spreads his hands and shrugs.

It's a baffling history of contradictions that could not be invented. "You live in Nairobi?"

"I live in many places, as suits my assignments." He relaxes his shoulders and sits back in his chair. "Some believe this city is a nest of drug traffickers, arms dealers, and real estate speculators." He smiles at her soft chuckle. "That is sadly correct. But Nairobi is also a transit point for people with information that is useful to my work."

"I want to hear more about your work."

Again, he gifts her with his dazzling smile. "I like your style of interviewing."

"And flattery deflects a question," she parries with a grin.

"My work interests you?"

She nods.

He draws a long breath. "I report on Arab League and East African politics. By clear but silent mandate, my articles can provoke neither the Sudanese Foreign Ministry nor the National Security apparatus." He spreads his hands. "With so much provocative activity occurring, I always learn more than will be published."

"It frustrates you?"

"On the contrary. My father's influence ensures that my position is secure and that I have access to many sources. Information is power."

"So, you are a well-placed opposition mole?"

"I wear the robe that suits the day's purpose." He sips his coffee, regarding her with a glint of attraction. "Ahmed told me you came to look for relatives in Sudan."

She reaches into her bag and hands him the photo.

For a long while he examines the image, glancing at her and back at the face in the photo. He sips his coffee then places the photo on the table between them. "She is your mother. A Dinka."

His guileless verdict incites a dark thrill. "She is *probably* my mother."

His eyes remain on the photo. "Do you know her clan name and village?"

"Kiir. Somewhere near Fangak."

He frowns. "The Arab tribes in that area have a tradition of taking slaves."

She stares blindly at her hands on the table. The idea of her living kin in bondage inflicts a wound that she cannot see, but it stings like a paper cut.

"I have upset you," he says quietly, tapping the photo gently.

'You've given me a scenario I did not want to imagine." She tamps down a quivering sorrow. "It makes me want to run home and end this crazy expedition. But I can't."

He runs his hand through his dark curly hair. "What drives you on this search?"

Her hand trembles beside the cup, so she slides it beneath the table. "Some empty part…of my soul."

"You are afraid of that emptiness?"

The warmth in his eyes feels like forgiveness for a failing. "I'm afraid of doing nothing about it," she answers.

"Then you must prepare your heart for what you will find."

"How do I do that?"

His beautiful eyes invite her to rest, to know she is understood. "Take me with you on this journey."

She gapes at him.

He folds his hands on the table. "Zora, the trip you are planning is dangerous. I know the area well. I am known among the Dinka. I speak the language."

She sips her coffee to control her surprise. "My guide is arranging a translator."

"Then he is not a native speaker. What do you know of your guide?"

"He's Ugandan. He's made many trips to Sudan. He was vetted by people I trust." She catches the challenge in his eyes. "He arranged the trip in about ten days, so he evidently knows how to get things done."

Tariq sniffs and rubs his chin. "Ten days to organize travel in Sudan is a suspicious accomplishment. And the minder outside? Is that for your benefit?"

"What minder?"

"The man in the *jellabiyah.*"

She remembers noticing him. "Why do you think he's minding me?"

"You, a new foreigner, come here, and he appears. It could be coincidence; except I know he is often hired for such work. Perhaps you will need protection *from your guide.*" He leans close. "Listen to me, Zora. Sudan is a land of terror. You need strong allies. I present myself as one you can trust."

She senses no bravado in his tone. She wants to linger in the intimacy he has fashioned with his body and voice. But it's no trivial request. "What's in it for you?"

"A plausible cover for my real work."

"With the opposition?" She shakes her head. "Tariq, I did not come here to enable a political agenda that could get me killed." She begins to rise.

"Please," he says, touching her arm. "Please, hear what I have to say."

She perches on the edge of her chair, poised to flee from his wondrous presence and sonorous voice, knowing, in the more rational brain she may have left in DC, it could be a very dangerous decision to trust him over Senoja, or Senoja over him.

"You will understand, when you see the desolation of my people, of *our* people. I gather sensitive information." He touches her hand, "Nothing I do will jeopardize your safety."

His eyes calm her. He seems the perfect counterpoint to Senoja, whose misogynist tendencies already are beginning to annoy her. Zora imagines gaining sustenance in his resolute company, his confident beauty. Like her, he lives in the rough landscape between two identities. They'd have notes to compare, new insights to work into the complicated puzzle. And, political or not, he could enable conversations with ordinary people, the ones trapped inside the horrors that confounded her at work, the ones she's only read about.

"You'd have to pay your own way," she says.

"Of course."

She regards him, drawing secret pleasure from the perfect palette of his face, sensing a momentous alliance. "The flight leaves tomorrow morning at seven from Wilson Airport. Can you be there?"

He nods, delight in his eyes. "You have blessed me greatly." He rises, his gentle grasp of her hands an invitation to intimacy. He pays the waitress, nods a smiling goodbye, and disappears into the throng of passersby.

A few minutes after he leaves, Senoja arrives in the Land Rover as if on cue. Climbing in, pointing to the white-robed man, she asks, "Is that your guy over there?"

"Only a precaution."

"I don't like being followed," she warns. "Let's dispense with the parental monitoring,"

His face remains impassive.

"We'll have another traveler joining us."

Senoja swerves, narrowly missing a pedestrian. "But Madame—Zora, all arrangements have been made."

"His name is Tariq. It's a done deal."

Senoja drives in silence, lurching through late-afternoon clots of vehicles and careless pedestrians. As they idle at one of the few working traffic signals, a young woman approaches Zora's window. She carries a crying infant swaddled in a dirty blanket. Rapping softly, she holds her palm near the window.

"I advise you," Senoja says, "to resist the impulse."

Zora opens the window and hands the woman a hundred-shilling note. Senoja speeds away. "You may do as you wish. But you should know that car-jackings start with that kind of shill."

Chastened by this explanation, she admits to herself that she doesn't know much about daily life on this continent. She resolves to end her resistance to his instructions: she will not allow her ignorance to screw up the trip. She is too proud to tell him this.

Much later, after they've both retired to their rooms, she studies a map of Sudan. With a red pencil, she traces the long route from Nairobi to Lokichokio to Malakal, wondering briefly if Tariq will become her lover. As the candles flicker in a breeze, she draws a red circle around Fangak, near Malakal and Bentiu and the contested oil fields. From a pouch, she takes the beaded necklace retrieved from her momma's safe and puts it on. Yelping dogs chorus in the jasmine-scented night.

CHAPTER NINE

As the sun struggles up over the haze of the city, Zora and Senoja arrive at Wilson Airport. A convoy of battered pickup trucks queues in the dusty parking area, idling under loads of baled *khaat*. The restive Somali drivers banter loudly as they wander around drinking tea served from a grimy kiosk. Diesel exhaust fouls the spreading lavender sunrise. The airport buildings' weathered facades are patinaed with grime and look as though they've had long wearying years concealing nefarious activities.

Senoja hefts their bags from the Land Cruiser. Outfitted in a tan vest and cargo pants, he is calm, all business. Tariq arrives in a taxi. His black hair and dusky skin conspire with his long white tunic in rakish elegance. He carries a brown canvas satchel and a small black hardcase.

"Mr. Senoja," she says, "please meet—"

"Tariq Taha," he says, offering his hand. "I am honored by this opportunity to be of service."

Stoic, Senoja responds with a perfunctory handshake. He turns to Zora. "The aircraft will be fueled shortly. We must proceed through the administrative section."

A gaggle of Somali women and children surrounds the entrance, steeped in the odor of sweat and piss. When the dour guard unlocks the doors, they surge forward. Small children whine in the crush of bodies. Zora follows Senoja as he uses his bulk to clear a path. A baby-faced official in a pristine uniform examines their travel documents, appraising them as if he hopes to make them nervous. He deftly pockets the currency folded in Senoja's passport and waves them through.

On the tarmac, three jump-suited men scuttle around a small twin-engine aircraft that is unmarked except for a string of numbers painted below the cockpit. One of the men stows their bags as they climb aboard. Tariq settles next to Zora. Senoja stands in the aisle beside them, explaining that the flight will stop for refueling in Loki, then continue to Malakal, three hours to the northwest. As the engines roar to life, Senoja studies them like a displeased parent before retiring to a seat across the aisle behind them. The plane taxies, lifts off, and noisily gains altitude. Zora watches the sprawl of Nairobi fall away.

"Zora," Tariq whispers, "is Mr. Senoja always so unfriendly?"

"Only when his plans are messed with."

"I believe it is the will of Allah that we should make this journey together." His bold malachite eyes suggest he is happy about more than a pre-arranged flight. He holds out a white envelope. "I trust this will cover the cost of my passage. Two thousand U.S. dollars." He places it on the armrest between them. "Perhaps money will be the least of your concerns. I do not know how to prepare you for what you will see."

She glances at him. "Are you trying to frighten me?"

"I would rather shield you. But that would serve neither of us." He shifts, craning his head to see out the window. "There on the eastern horizon is Kiringyaga: Mt Kenya, the spiritual home of the Kikuyu people. They believe, or used to believe, that the supreme spirit Nagai apportioned his gifts to all the nations of the Earth." She watches mist fondle the mountain. "As you know, the Europeans had their own plans for the wealth of this continent." As the plane banks to the west, the cloud-wreathed mountain slides from view. "And now," he says as though sharing a confidence, "others have come to plunder in their place."

Below, lush escarpments jut like fists from a verdant plain. "This is the Rift Valley. You will not see such magnificence anywhere but paradise." Dazzling light glints off silver lakes scattered like confetti to the horizon. "Lake Bogoria," he says, reaching across her to point, as flamingos rise like a cloud, washing the sky pink.

.   Zora'd seen photos, but that thrill pales beside the experience of being in this fabled place. Like a dreamscape, the Earth seems to thrust up and pull her back to a primordial time. She wants to plant her feet on the ancient rocks and learn their mythic secrets. A sudden weight on the headrest dissipates her reverie. Standing in the aisle, Senoja speaks in Arabic to Tariq.

"Hey, guys," she chides. "Could you refrain from talking as if I'm not here?"

"He is asking my intentions," Tariq says, a mischievous smile stealing over his face. "Sir, I am planning to ravish this beautiful woman when you are asleep."

A twitch escapes Senoja's flash-frozen scowl.

Zora chuckles.

"Mr. Senoja," Tariq begins again in formal tone. "My apologies for not properly briefing you."

"I am listening." Senoja crosses his arms over his chest.

"A mutual acquaintance led me to Zora. She invited me on this journey because I speak the Dinka language and know the Fangak area well. I am also a journalist. This trip allows me to visit an area of professional interest."

"What I told you last night," Zora prods. "I think he'll be an asset to our search." She lifts the envelope. "He's paying his way."

Senoja recovers his courteous persona. "It is your arrangement, and I will honor it." He leans toward Tariq. "I ask only that you follow my directives if we should encounter problems."

Tariq dips his head. "Exactly as you say."

Senoja returns to his seat. With merriment that surprises her, Zora imagines their triad will produce some fascinating face-offs. The journey will never be boring.

Below, the cliffs flatten into a sandy plain flecked with clusters of grass-roofed huts. An enormous lake of shifting colors glimmers in the east.

"Lake Turkana," Tariq says. "In the midst of a desert, a jade sea fed by rain from the Ethiopian highlands. This is the birthplace of mankind." His awe, his eagerness to share it, adds one more jeweled piece to the tempting puzzle of this man.

As the aircraft descends, a herd of zebras, spooked by the noise, sprints away. A line of camels winds from a village, moving on an ancient route, the kind of trek that had sealed the fate of her ancestors. A rocky promontory to the east signals their arrival at Loki, the last Kenyan stopover before Sudan. The plane lands hard on an asphalt strip in blowing sand.

Senoja readies himself behind the cockpit. "I will see to the loading of a few necessary supplies. You may wait on board or deplane, but please stay near." As soon as the pilot opens the hatch, Senoja steps off to his duties.

"Stretch our legs?" Zora invites. They step into molten sunlight that seems to burn scent and oxygen from the air. Zora puts on a canvas hat. "How do people survive this godawful heat?"

Tariq grins. "One grows accustomed to it." He points at a nearby building. "Allow me to show you something." He leads her to a warehouse lined with rows of pallets heaped shoulder high with sacks of grain. "This shipment of wheat and rice has been grounded for ten days, waiting for the regime to decide if it has starved enough women and children." He surveys the dark warehouse, empty of people. "To move this food, the aid managers sometimes resort to creative misinformation."

"Meaning?"

"If access to certain villages is denied, they simply change the names on their flight requests and fly there anyway." He examines the grain leaking from a chewed hole. "Rats love these places. This backlog probably means the misinformation strategy has provoked official displeasure."

Zora runs her hand over a sack stenciled *USAID From the American People*. "Has any food made it where we're headed?"

"We will see."

Senoja calls them back to the aircraft. As they settle in, a new co-pilot brings them fruit juice in plastic glasses and cellophane-wrapped biscuits.

Senoja sits across the aisle. "Mr. Taha, I –"

"Please call me Tariq."

"This journey takes you home?"

"No. My family lives near Khartoum. And your family?"

"A few survive." Senoja picks at his fingernails. "We Africans have great difficulty staying close to our own people."

Tariq wrinkles his nose. "We Africans are broken and scattered *by* our own people. Here the government *attacks* its people."

"It is known," Senoja parries, "that violent incidents are the work of bandits and rebels."

"Bandits and rebels do not use helicopter gunships."

"And you know firsthand of such things?"

"I know this from many sources," Tariq shoots back. "Perhaps you neglected to include reliable situation reports in your planning."

Senoja sniffs. "I am very thorough in planning—"

"You've ignored the—"

"Stop it," Zora breaks in. "I don't need a pissing contest here."

Tariq glares at her. "A virtuous woman does not tell men how to behave."

Zora stares at him, astonished by his rebuke. "Well, you must have me confused with a virtuous woman." She turns away. "Why don't you just haul your butt over to the boys' side?"

Engine drone envelops them. Outside the window, a yellow haze of wind-blown sand burdens the sky. The landscape far below, stubbled with scrub and rock outcroppings, stretches to the horizon like a weathered carcass.

Tariq clears his throat. "Zora"

"Don't say anything."

Senoja sniggers.

For the rest of the flight, she sits alone reading *Islam Unveiled*, fingering her angel pin, pissed that she'd been stupid enough to let her heart go prospecting over a handsome macho African.

On a dirt tarmac in Malakal, the heat assaults Zora. A Land Rover, its roof rack loaded with cases, eases beside the cargo door. Sweating profusely, Senoja barks out instructions to two men arranging bags in the vehicle's rear compartment. A thin young woman appears with a covered plastic bin. She's wearing a green wrap skirt and a T-shirt advertising *Need to Lose Weight? Ask me how*. At Senoja's direction, she puts the bin on the front seat, all the while pointedly observing the preparations. Catching Zora's eye, she waves like a shy schoolgirl then walks with a slow, graceful gait toward the hangar.

"We must have the petrol *now*," Senoja shouts at the helpers. Wiping his face with a towel, he approaches Zora. "Our extra fuel tank is on its way here. Please, cool yourself inside the vehicle. There is food in the bin."

"Calm down," she says, climbing into the back seat.

Tariq follows her. "In Sudan, everything moves in its own time."

Senoja slams the door.

"He has the temperament of an American businessman," Tariq observes.

"And you," she challenges, "seem to have the temperament of a Muslim cleric."

Tariq sighs. "The beliefs that have guided me since childhood do not blend neatly with the...*perspective* of a Western woman. But I am willing to be educated."

"Are Sudanese women so different?"

He considers the question. "They are less overt. More deferential. But in everyday matters, they rule men's lives."

"Not so different then."

He chuckles. "I am not afraid of what you have to teach me." The statement is more than she'd hoped for.

A battered truck arrives. With a round of grunting, the men hoist and fasten a large fuel tank to the rear of the vehicle. Senoja bounces into the front passenger seat. A young man opens the driver's door, arranges a cushion and eases behind the wheel.

"This is Adam," Senoja announces. "He will be our driver, mechanic, and cook."

"*Salaam allekum,*" Adam says in greeting. His narrow, swarthy face has a boyish insouciance. He wears a long buff colored tunic over loose-fitting black sweatpants.

"*Wa allekum salaam,*" Tariq answers.

"Adam speaks little English. He is trustworthy and skilled in his duties." Senoja consults a map. "We will cross the Nile south of Malakal and proceed west-southwest toward Fangak. Adam, *yella.*"

Along the banks of the muddy Nile, mighty banyan trees rise like sentinels, buttressed by serpentine black roots. A rusty steamer ship languishes against a decayed dock. Curious islands of matted papyrus clot the river upstream. The road quickly disintegrates into a rutted dirt track. Tariq resumes his commentary. To the south, is the Sudd, a great swamp where early explorers either died miserably of disease or were blocked by impenetrable vegetation and gave up their expeditions. To the north, a rugged plain of tawny scrub and hardwood trees stretches to the distant brooding Nuba Mountains where the Nuba people have suffered government predation for a generation.

As a teenager, Zora'd pored over Leni Riefenstahl's book of photographs of the Nuba people. Their ebony nakedness, frozen in the passion of dance, had jolted her Catholic idea of modesty. She'd stared fascinated by the breasts and legs and asses greased and ornamented for display. To her amazement, her mother had not banished this provocative gift from Bert. The women of her family, what she'd assumed was her family, had been always unpredictable in their interpretation of sinfulness.

The road opens into a clearing. Bushes partially obscure the charred remains of huts. Animal carcasses litter the ashy ground.

"Wait, stop!" she orders. "What is this place?"

"It was a cattle camp," Tariq answers.

She jumps out of the Rover, stepping around a five-foot crater studded with glinting bits of metal. Nearby, a curved horn protrudes from a half-buried skull. A human ribcage, clinging to shreds of faded blue cloth, arches from the red clay. A pelvis gnawed by scavenging teeth joins a trail of half-buried human bones that disappears into the surrounding dry grass. Zora walks slowly, touching nothing. Inside the blackened circle of a hut, the half-clad skeleton of a child curls in fetal position. An eerie silence roars in her ears. Tariq moves beside her. "Only the government has aircraft capable of bombing. These were their targets of choice."

She shivers, covers her mouth with her hand.

"The dead wait for burial," he says. "But no one will return for that."

Zora meets his eyes, dark with rage. "We are here. We should at least bury the child."

She pulls a shovel from the truck, ignoring Senoja's protests. They take turns digging in the dry hard earth, sweating under the hot sun. When they've finally made a small deep hole, they carefully lift and carry the little skeleton, laying it to rest in the earth. As she pushes the heavy dirt over the bones, Tariq murmurs in the Dinka language. "A short prayer," he tells her.

They drive on. The track takes them through two small encampments, one empty and cratered by bombs, the other inhabited by a few stick-thin people too old or too young to leave. Tariq's inquiry about the Kiir clan turns up no information. Zora has nothing to leave for the people but a bag of fruit and nuts. Their desolation mocks her "errand of the heart."

Senoja chooses a campsite at a clearing skirted by abandoned *tukuls,* not far from a dry creek bed. As Adam wrestles bins off the roof, Senoja tells Zora, "We have two tents. It was too late to add another for our guest." He arches his eyebrows, letting the question of sleeping arrangements dangle among them. Without comment, Tariq helps him pitch the domed tents. Adam starts a cook fire, pulls food from the bins. As darkness enfolds them, they gather at his fire to eat, using their fingers to gather bits of roasted goat, boiled greens, and rice, salting the quiet mealtime with brief exchanges in Arabic.

When they finish, Senoja opens a bottle of whiskey. Surprised but not disappointed, Zora allows him to pour a shot in her tin cup. She stares at her dusty boots as the alcohol loosens her thoughts. "I'm ashamed that my country has done so little to stop this misery."

Tariq pokes at the fire. "The survivors fear they've become invisible, that no one will come to end this suffering."

"They have plenty of reason to feel that way," she allows. "They are trapped in a perfect storm of denial."

Senoja sniffs, frowns dismissively, but says nothing. They sit for a while, enfolded in the heat of the night.

Tariq peers at her. "Zora, what will you do if you find family?"

She throws a stick on the fire, watches it ignite. "Anyone I find will have something to say about what oughta be done."

"Yes, they will." He drinks water from a metal cup. "Are you ready to hear them?"

The question nettles her. *The misery so crisply quantified in situation reports at work will soon have faces and names and the smell of fear and filth. What puny remedy can she offer in such a vast wasteland of need?*

Senoja rises, dusting off his pants. "We should rest now. We continue at first light. Good night." He ducks into the tent he will share with Adam.

"Zora," Tariq says quietly, "I will sleep beside your tent."

She is keenly aware of the grit that coats her skin, the odor of stale sweat that permeates her clothes. Fatigue has shredded all want of intimacy. "Tariq, I don't –"

"I am not searching for an invitation."

She unlaces her boots. "Good. I'm not making one."

He unrolls a sleeping mat. Settling on his back, he links his hands behind his head. "*Numi ques.* Sleep well."

She memorizes his face, eyes half-closed, lips curved in a gentle smile. When she extinguished the lantern, she feels the night vibrate with the cacophony of insects.

"Before you go in," he says, "look up."

A riot of brilliant stars bejewels the blackness above.

"I will tell you some of their names," he offers, "one night during our journey."

CHAPTER TEN

In a vivid dream, Zora watches from a muddy bank as a roiling river sweeps away a black bag containing her clothes, her shoes, her useless kit of creams and makeup. She awakens eager to escape a withering helplessness. Rising stiffly from her mosquito-netted mat, she wets a cloth with water from a plastic jug and wipes her face. Slipping on a clean shirt, she remembers the spy cam. Addled by yesterday's discoveries, she's already missed recording the cattle camp. Chastising herself, she retrieves the kit, fumbling to place the receiver and connect the cable. Finally, she nests the lens in the angel pin, pins it to her collar, powers on the unit, and ducks out of the tent.

Vermilion bands of clouds thread across the coppery dawn sky. Hunched near the campfire, Adam whacks off the top of a pineapple with a machete. Seeing her, he hurries over with a slip of paper, waiting expectantly as she reads Senoja's cramped printing.

I have gone to a village with Tariq.

PLEASE wait with Adam. We will return soon.

She nods. Adam smiles, evidently relieved to have completed his assignment. He is a lean young man with almond brown skin and hazel eyes that avoid engagement. His dark blue t-shirt bears the legend *Billy Bob's Auto Repair Amarillo Texas.* Perching on a nearby case, Zora watches him fry up tortilla-like bread. "*Kisra,*" he explains, sliding it onto a metal plate.

She takes a bite. "Good,"

"*Kisra,*" he repeats, as if speaking to child.

"Yes, good *kisra.*" Waving her hand at the sky, she says, pointlessly, "Hot day!"

"*Allahu akhbar,*" he proclaims.

Their lack of shared language does not seem to trouble him. She finds it vaguely amusing and presses on, pointing at herself. "American."

He thumps his hand to his chest. "Rizeigat."

At least they can confirm tribal affiliation.

A branch snaps. With stunning speed, he draws a pistol from his belt and positions himself as her shield. Senoja's command in Arabic precedes his appearance. Adam returns calmly to his cook fire. She stands with her heart racing.

"Ahhh," Senoja says, approaching her. "I trust you slept?"

She nods toward Adam. "He's twitchy with a gun."

"As he was trained to be," Senoja assures.

Tariq stalks into camp. Grim-faced, he accepts a piece of *kisra* and sits on the ground in silence. After serving Senoja, Adam goes to tinker under the hood of the Land Rover.

"Not much to report," Senoja announces. Rivulets of sweat course down his face as he eats with quick bites. "The people here are moving north. One man knew of a Kiir clan, but not its current whereabouts." He gulps at his cup of tea. "Tariq is a most cooperative translator." His tone is patronizing. Tariq says nothing.

Senoja glances at the heat-washed sky. "Armed units are moving to our west. We must be especially alert today. And we will need to ration our water. The people told us that many *wadis* are dry because the rains ended earlier than usual." After a final swig of tea, he stands. "Time to move."

Tariq helps Zora take down her tent, glancing over his shoulder as he works. "Senoja is not African," he whispers. "But he is very good at pretending so."

"How do you know?" she whispers back.

He shakes his head to warn her into silence. Continuing her task with distracted hands, Zora wonders what clue Tariq has seen that she's missed—and what his observation means.

They travel southwest on a rutted track. In the back seat next to Tariq, Zora consults her map, noticing for the first time a small cautionary legend: *In Africa, distances can rarely be given with absolute accuracy*. Their route roughly follows the Bahr el Zeraf, a tributary of the Nile. Villages dot the river's flood plain. Feeling Tariq's eyes on her, she glances at him. "I'm a map freak. I like to see the lay of the land." She leafs through a set of plastic overlays, choosing one that delineates tribal areas. The day's journey will take them from Shilluk territory into an area shared by the Dinka tribes.

Tariq tells her that the tribes' neighborliness left much to be desired: they were proud to the point of insufferable arrogance and prone to cattle raiding. Over the tribal map, she places an overlay of oil tracts. He leans closer to look at it. "Many thousands of people have been driven from these ancestral lands."

Adam clutches prayer beads against the steering wheel as he maneuvers around jagged rocks. Clumps of acacia infringe on the path, their thorny branches raking like fingernails against the side windows.

"I don't understand," Zora murmurs, "how anyone survives here."

"No one will," Tariq answers, "if the genocide continues."

Senoja huffs impatiently. "You must stop this chatter about genocide."

"You deny what is obvious to so many?" Tariq raises an eyebrow at him.

Senoja flips his hand as if shooing a pestering insect. "You are too partisan to understand the realities of counterinsurgency warfare."

Zora cuts them off to avert a disruptive duel. "Try asking Adam what he knows about the locals."

Tariq looks surprised. "Why?"

"He is Rizeigat. This is his clan's territory."

Senoja shakes his head. "Adam understands our mission. He would have given me any pertinent intelligence."

Zora reaches over the seatback, holding her photo of the mystery woman and her baby for Adam to see. Tariq speaks to him in Arabic. He stops the vehicle to study the image. After a moment he waves it away, distain in his voice as he answers Tariq.

"He says," Tariq translates, "All Dinka look alike. His people no longer learn their names." Adam cannot know that he has waved away the image that brought Zora here, but the stab of pain she feels is unexpected. Ella, the only mother she knew, would expect her to keep going. She pushes the pain to the side with a deep exhale.

The Rover lurches on in second gear. Around a curve in the track obscured by a rock ledge, five horsemen, rifles slung on their shoulders, march toward them. Adam brakes. The horsemen's white *kufiyas* frame their dark solemn faces. Their white *jellabiyas* ripple in the wind.

"Wait inside the vehicle," Senoja instructs. He and Adam get out and approach the men slowly. Senoja hands one of them a paper.

Tariq fidgets, slouching in his seat. "At the very least," he leans toward Zora, "these men should rob us. If they bring us no grief, then Senoja is protected by a powerful patron."

Zora opens her door and stands where her spycam has a clear shot. "You sure of that?"

"These militia take orders from the government."

One of the horsemen dismounts, unslings his rifle. Senoja produces the Glock from his vest. Adam follows suit with his weapon. They stand examining their arsenal, gesturing, and talking with animated faces.

"What *is* this?" Zora whispers. "A damn gun show?"

"A strange warrior ritual," Tariq answers. "It means we are safe—for now."

Zora slides back into the rear seat as Senoja and Adam return. The horsemen salute with their rifles and trot away on an intersecting track.

Senoja grins. "We are lucky today," he says, wiping his sweat-sheened face with a towel.

"Tell me about it," Zora prods.

"One never knows how these militia will behave, even with clearances."

"How did you get a clearance?"

He faces her, incredulous. "Madame, it is *my job* to expedite your journey."

"With friends in high places?"

He allows a slight smile. "I know how to make money work."

Zora leans against the window, miffed by his seamless stonewalling. The thought comes that what she doesn't know might somehow protect her. She squints at the passing landscape, an unbridled experiment with the color brown. Tawny grasses. Burnt-amber shrubs. Terra cotta earth. Rocks shellacked with ocher mud. Even her three companions present in various hues of cocoa. She thinks brown might be the color of misery.

Two more days drag by under the wicked, omnipotent sun. Their clothing reeks and has become obnoxiously dirty. The camp routines vary only in the accompanying music selected by Senoja. He is working through a collection of Ugandan music. Tunes by Sarah Zawedde and Mr. Nice entertain them for a while, but Zora believes that one more auditory assault by Bacha Man will make them mutinous. Encounters with people along the track are invariably wrenching. Once-prosperous villages have been bombed or torched into ruins. In their desolation, the scattered survivors can provide no information to assist their search. Often it seems too much to ask.

Zora had vowed to keep a journal but the best she has been able to muster is a note of day and place. Now they are "Day Five, east of Fangak." Adam maneuvers the vehicle into a wide barren flat edged by several grass-roofed *tukuls*. The structures appear to be abandoned. Then a tall, wizened man emerges from one of them, wearing only a loin cloth, grinning as if he expected their arrival. A bony old woman in a faded wrap follows him. Two little girls in dirty dresses crowd against her legs. A naked toddler lurches behind them. The old man smiles broadly, displaying prominent yellowed teeth, and firmly shakes hands with each of them. He indicates that they should sit on the stumps assembled around the entrance of his home. Tariq speaks with the man, offering a packet of dried beans that he accepts with a nod. The girls hover nearby. Zora crouches before them. "Zora," she says, pointing at herself. The girl in a blue dress giggles and answers "Aguil." The other hangs back. Aguil elbows her. "Dut," the girl murmurs. Zora rummages in her bag for trinkets that might interest them. She finds a note pad. With a red pen, she draws a sunburst on one page and offers the pad and pen to Aguil. The girl eases to the ground beside her to scribble on a blank page. Zora gives Dut a tiny soapstone elephant she'd purchased from a street vendor in Nairobi. The girl fingers the animal as if trying to coax it to life.

Tariq touches Zora's arm. "This man is Bol Majok. He says he is related by marriage to the Kiir clan. Some of them were about two days walk from here."

"Our first lead!"

"But he doesn't know if the bombing has driven them away."

"We'll find out." Zora's mood ascends on a flimsy scrap of information.

"He also welcomes us to stay here for the night."

Senoja grunts. "We have about an hour of daylight. Perhaps we should move ahead. There is nothing here for us."

Aguil nudges Zora's arm, displaying her drawing of a stick figure reaching skyward, an eerie rendition of her own dream image. The girl examines the red marker as if she suspects magical power.

"We won't make much progress before dark." Zora says. "Besides, I think I like the company. Let's camp here."

"As you wish." Senoja's strained expression belies a deferential tone. At his instruction, Adam begins unloading the truck. The girls watch the spread of stuff with wide eyes. When Zora begins to pitch her tent, Aguil sidles over to study the operation. Zora hands her an anchoring stake, shows her where to place it. They make the chore into a miming game punctuated by furtive giggles.

Adam sets up a spit to roast a hunk of goat meat. Senoja slouches nearby, headset plugged into his iPod, cleaning his gun. The old woman brings a small bag of grain and sets it beside Adam's fire. He flashes a look of distain, as if the offering offends him. She has turned to lift the toddler and does not see it. Bol Majok sits quietly beneath a bamboo lean-to, surveying the scene with a faint smile, smoking a pipe crafted from a cattle horn. By the time the tent is pitched, Zora's face is running with sweat. The girls grab her hands and lead her down a dusty trail.

"Stay strictly on the path," Senoja calls. "There could be landmines. Don't go far."

The little ones hurry her along until they arrive at the bank of a shallow stream. They shuck their dresses and scamper in. Stinking and grimy, Zora decides that a bath of any sort is well worth the price of modesty. The three of them bound to the center of the tepid stream, laughing as they splash each other. The girls throw themselves backward into the water, screeching joyfully. Reluctant to submerge in water laden with silt, Zora cups water over her long-unwashed hair, vowing never again take clean water for granted. Suddenly Senoja appears on the bank. Helpless under this gaze, Zora reflexively folds her arms over her breasts.

"I was alarmed by the screams," he says. "You must come out. The water is filled with parasites that will do horrible damage to your body." He turns and retreats up the path.

His warning drives her out of the water. She dresses quickly as mosquitoes seek their meals. The naked girls follow her back toward the scent of roasting meat. Tariq and the old man are immersed in conversation. Adam and the old woman squat near the fire, tending steaming pots. Senoja shoots Zora a grin. She subtly flips him off. Kneeling on the ground, she helps the girls on with their dresses.

The horizon devours the sun, bloodying the sky before night erases the engine of a vicious-hot day. Unseen birds strike up a harsh chatter. They gather to eat. The firelight dances on the weary faces of their hosts, sculpting them like masks.

"Bol tells me," Tariq says, "this is the first meat they've had in many months." The family eats with their hands, intent on each bite. "Bol says the bombing has deprived them of bush meat. The war has no dignity."

Zora considers this pronouncement. "Does any war have dignity?"

Tariq's expression turns pensive. "In times past, war was a ritual arranged by the elders to resolve a dispute. Only a select group of warriors could engage in battle. The place and time of engagement was mutually agreed. It was considered a grave dishonor to injure non-combatants."

"The old ways," Senoja says through a mouthful of food, "have no place in this world."

"You're wrong," Zora retorts. "Think of all those pompous men claiming for years to be negotiating a peace deal. If they had to leave their cushy hotels and spend their nights out here, on short rations, they'd come to an agreement right quick, don't you think?"

Tariq translates. Bol laughs loudly.

"And maybe," she continues, "A few grandmas with sick, crying babies could keep them company, help them stay on task."

Tariq's quick translation brings more laughter. Senoja rises and ducks into his tent, much to Zora's relief.

She regards the faces peering into the fire. "Tariq, please ask them why they are here alone."

He poses the question, listening for some time as the old man speaks. "He says that the children's parents, his son, and daughter-in-law, were killed by a bomb that landed near the stream. The few others that lived here fled in fear, though they did not know where to go. He says they are too old to travel, and there was no one else to care for the children."

The old woman quietly addresses Tariq. He listens and translates for Zora, "She says you should stay. With so many dying, they will need strong women to rebuild." Implicit in her words to Tariq is the knowledge that she will not live to see that time of resurrection. She seems to gather herself then, inhaling deeply, and begins to sing. Her resonant voice flows from a place much grander than her frail body. In the flickering light, her gestures appear eerily animated; her eyes flash and tear up, as if submitting to a fierce vision. Her keening song cuts the night with sorrow and longing. When she finishes, abandoning them to hard silence, she touches Zora's cheek with a callused hand. Bidding the two girls to follow, she vanishes like a shadow into their *tukul*.

Zora sits stunned, aching as if she's survived a harsh initiation.

"Dinka women sing of their hopes," Tariq says softly. "Her song was a wish for a death with no fear or pain." The din of insects fills the void between them.

Unperturbed, chewing the tip of his empty pipe, Bol points at the sky. "Nhailic's jewels," Tariq says. "The great spirit keeps the stars as his treasures." He peers into the darkness above. "Do you see the Hydra?"

"What am I looking for?"

"Four bright stars in the shape of a zigzag, just above the horizon." He points.

"There are too many!"

"Try," he coaxes. "It is a worthy effort to learn the map of the heavens."

Her fussy reluctance embarrasses her. "Okay, let me sight along your arm." She rests her head against his shoulder. The fine hairs on her neck happily rise to attention at the scent of him. "Yes, I see."

"And now," he says, "follow up to four bright stars, three as a head and one jutting like a beak. That is Corvus."

"The Raven," she whispers. "My totem." She turns her face close to his. The firelight prances in his curious eyes. "The American Indians believe that a mystical animal can become a spiritual guide."

"You are also from the American Indians?"

"It's one of my mother's—my American mother's—ancestral ties. A remote one."

"And the Raven?"

"The Raven is a clever shape-changer, a powerful messenger."

"You admire these traits?" He gazes at her, seeming to know his provocative effect.

"I aspire to them."

Two explosions thunder in the distance. She bolts to her feet.

Senoja emerges from his tent. "Maybe thirty kilometers to the west," he says, unruffled.

"What?"

"Antonov bombers," Tariq answers. "If we hear them approach, we must shelter in the crater near the stream."

Flashes from scattered explosions tear up the horizon. The family has not emerged from their *tukul*. Perhaps they've learned how to read a routine nuisance, but Zora struggles for calm. The sky glows white, orange. The thunder stomps west and then stops. The drone of mosquitoes settles around them.

"They probably are finished for the night," Tariq offers. He spreads his mat and bows in prayer.

Unnerved, she slaps a mosquito on her neck, catching the edge of her angel pin. The camera has been on all day. She switches off the unit, wondering how many of the day's events were decently recorded.

Retreating to the tent, Zora lays awake considering the fate of their hosts, alone and abandoned by their clan. *They have no room in the Rover to take them. They will die out here. Which deaths will be first and worst: the old or the young?* Her mind wrestles through the night with the unforgiving calculus of the invisible genocide.

CHAPTER ELEVEN

Just after the sun breaches the eastern sky, Zora unzips the tent flap. Two grinning faces bob into view. Her greeting inspires a riff of giggling from the girls. Sweet smoke wafts from Adam's cook fire. Senoja sits nearby studying a map spread on the ground. He grunts a greeting as she approaches. The girls follow like shadows. Cheerful as usual, Adam hands her a mug of tea. He spoons thick, dark porridge into three bowls. Senoja refuses the offering, unwraps a package of beef jerky. The girls eagerly accept a bowl, filling their mouths rapidly with their fingers. The glutinous mush makes Zora gag. She wants to fuel up but perseveres only through two mouthfuls. The girls happily consume the rest.

Tariq returns from washing at the stream, his tunic clinging to his body. She returns his greeting, tamping down a stray fantasy of caressing his fine body. She sips her tea and tries to force order on her unruly thoughts. *They will be leaving five people here to die. That reality will haunt her. She's traveling with men who increasingly test her trust. Tariq has given little evidence to support his suspicion about Senoja, just the observation that Senoja "did not communicate well" with the people they met. She doesn't know if this has anything to do with African-ness or lack of it.* The question buzzes like a suddenly pesky fly: *what might Tariq be concealing?*

When they finish breakfast, Senoja issues his daily order about rationing water. They can filter bad water they collect from the stream, but they will not survive without any water. If local sources remain in short supply over the next day, he will require them to return to Malakal. Zora does not want the search ended, *not for this reason.* Intuition, however irrational, tells her that a breakthrough is coming.

When the last bag is secured in the Land Rover, Bol rises stiffly and shuffles over to bid his visitors farewell. The girls clutch Zora's hands, their eyes clouded with disappointment. She hugs each of them. At a word from Bol, they scurry toward the *tukul*, seeking solace against the skirted legs of their grandmother who cradles the toddler. As the vehicle shudders onto the track, Zora returns their goodbye waves.

Senoja mops his brow. "What a relief to be getting out of that miserable place."

Zora taps his shoulder. "Could you at least work on being civil? They were hospitable. And they'll die there. And we could do nothing about that."

He ignores her.

Zora grips his shoulder, not willing to be ignored. "I'm not feelin' good about what's happenin' here."

Senoja swivels to face her. "I'm not feeling good about traveling in a war zone."

She blinks in disbelief. "Wait, isn't this what you *do*?"

"My other clients did not find it necessary to camp in the bush."

"Oh, heloed in and out? Quick and dirty?" Zora narrows her eyes. "Then they missed what they should have seen."

Tariq rustles beside her, maneuvering his hardcase under the seat. "What's in there?' she asks.

"Personal items." He sits up, turning his attention out the window. She wasn't expecting a rebuff. Tariq's stonewalling makes her want to dump him on the side of the road.

"Senoja," Zora turns back to him, "how many kilometers is the two-day walk Bol mentioned?"

"Perhaps fifteen or twenty. We will cover it in less than two hours. If there are no obstructions." He glances at her. "You may not ask, 'Are we there yet?'" Facing forward, he chuckles. She represses an impulse to smack him hard. As usual, Adam's hand works his prayer beads astride the steering wheel. Senoja is pawing through CDs. Tariq snores softly beside her. Their predictable habits are fraying her last nerve. *It's been bad enough to be in this hotbox of a country at war with itself. Ignorant humor and unspoken agendas raising their pointy heads doesn't help.* Flipping down the brim of her hat, she isolates herself against the window to think.

Solitary trees, splayed like flattened umbrellas, rise defiantly green from the ocean of parched vegetation. They cross a dry *wadi* littered with stones and branches from a past flooding. A few long-horned cattle, dusty hides taut against ribs, languish in the shade of a rock outcropping. An empty footpath hemmed by scorched sorghum offers the only hint of human habitation. If the windows could be opened without garnering the rebuke, "The AC is on!", she would smell the withering dryness. *It would be easy for anyone to die here, savaged by sun and stupidity. How profoundly unlucky*, she muses, *to be born in this desolate land to which the world has turned a blind eye.* A sharp thought slices in: She *might be from this place and escaped against ridiculous odds.* With her eyes and nose in this parched tableau, her errand of the heart gains some needed grounding.

With a sudden metallic whine, the vehicle jolts to a stop. Adam sucks noisily at his teeth. Senoja slaps the dashboard. They jump out to investigate. Adam slides into the dust beneath the vehicle. Zora opens the door, stands in the heat shading her eyes. Senoja tells her: "Adam thought he heard the axle break but it is not so serious. A sprung strut. Fixable."

Turning, she peers up the track. "Looks like we've got company."

A group of gaunt people, like onyx statues, stands about fifty feet away. She pulls her backpack out of the rear compartment, remembers to switch on her camera "Tariq, I need you now."

"Wait here," Senoja vehemently warns, "until the repair is complete."

Zora strides up the track, Tariq hurrying to catch up. "Please let them know we are friendlies," she says to him over her shoulder.

A tall young man steps forward, hand extended. Tariq greets him; a rapid exchange ensues. "I know this man's uncle," Tariq announces. An elaborate handshaking, shoulder-slapping ritual with a mantra of greetings expands to the entire group. Senoja approaches, his face tight with anger.

"We're going on to the village," Zora tells Senoja. "They ain't gonna 'go Baghdad' on us." The slang prompts Senjoa's micro-flash of recognition. He turns abruptly and stalks back to the vehicle. Her suspicion about his real identity has found a new puzzle piece.

As the group ambles forward, Tariq falls into animated conversation with the young man. The others in the group surround them like true believers in a religious procession. Occasionally Tariq remembers to translate. "He says he will take us to an elder of the Kiir clan."

Zora stumbles and rights herself, uncertain if the heat or the news makes her suddenly woozy. The track opens into a clearing. Large craters smolder amid a cluster of blackened mud foundations. Two bloodied corpses sprawl in the dust as if an unseen hand had thrown them carelessly from above. The stench of putrefying flesh assaults her.

"There are many dead," Tariq says. "The grain stores have been looted. The survivors are hungry." He holds her arm as she retches. "You have not seen death before?"

She wipes her mouth with her sleeve. "Not like this."

"Come," he takes her hand. "The dead will be buried in time. The living have urgent needs."

They approach a lean-to sheltering an old man. Tariq squats before him, speaking quietly. The man gestures for them to sit. A tracery of wrinkles frames his dark eyes, the most striking feature of his ebony face. A thatch of silver hairs crowns his finely sculpted head. Six prominent angled scars ornament his forehead.

"Zora Monro" Tariq gestures with his hand. "Meet Luk Jok Kiir."

She shakes Luk's outstretched hand. He holds on, his rough skin rasping hers, while he studies her face.

"He says they cannot be as hospitable as he would like," Tariq tells her, and Luk smiles, revealing outsized front teeth and a gift for irony.

She returns his smile. "I'm grateful for his welcome." She corrals an impulse to pick his brain *right now*. "Tell him we brought food."

Luk nods. He instructs two young boys to follow them to the truck. Ignoring Senoja's petulant disapproval, they carry back two food bins. Zora inventories the stock. "We've got rice and beans, really questionable goat meat, and the last pineapple." She set out two kettles. "How many are we feeding?"

As if materializing from the air, a young girl squats beside her. More startling than her sudden appearance are her eyes. like shards of coal. Her skirt and ancient t-shirt are stained with blood. Tariq comes close as the girl speaks. "She says twelve people are alive."

"Tell her everyone will eat." Zora stands among the supplies, shielding her eyes from the sun. "What's her name?"

"Abuk."

The girl's plaited hair zigzags across her dark scalp. Her finely arched cheekbones and pouty lips conspire in a fetching kind of beauty despite her obvious distress. Her dirty pink t-shirt reads *Listen to Bob.*

Abuk speaks to Tariq who says, "She will prepare a place for a fire. She asks you to collect some wood."

"Glad to be useful."

"Mind where you walk," he cautions. "There might be unexploded ordnance." She shoots him an anxious glance. He waves her on. "Avoid metal objects. You will be fine." Two boys come to him. "I told them I would help dig graves."

"I got the better chore," she answers.

As Tariq and the boys move off to hack at the hard clay with poles, she ranges around the edge of the clearing, lashed by the sun, gathering sticks into a pouch of her tunic. Sweat runs in rivulets down her body.

When she returns with her load, Abuk has dug a shallow pit and set three large stones inside. As Zora hands her the dry materials, the girl arranges a conical pile over the stones. Zora rummages in the bin for matches. The convenience draws a perfunctory smile from Abuk, as if she restricts facial effort to compulsory courtesies. A smoky fire sputters to life.

"*Piu*," Abuk orders, indicating the jerry can.

"Water?" Zora lifts the container. "Here, I'll pour it."

Abuk allows her the task, slicing her hand in the air when the kettle is sufficiently full. They repeat the operation with a second, smaller pot. Abuk accepts the bin of rice, measuring the grain by handfuls into the pot. "*Lop,*" she says.

"Rice," Zora answers.

"*Lop*," Abuk insists.

She hands the girl another plastic container. "Beans."

"*Akuem*," Abuk corrects her, measuring them with her hand into the kettle.

Zora opens the cooler and fishes a packet of meat from the tepid water. The girl unwraps the soggy bundle, takes a whiff and shrugs. "*Apiyem*."

"Goat," Zora says. "It's been on the road a while."

Abuk arches her eyebrows, not understanding, then expertly skewers the gray flesh and mounts it on stakes beside the pots. She sits away from Zora, watching the food cook. Light-headed from the heat, Zora covers her face with her hands. She hears Abuk rise and walk away.

A short while later, the girl returns dragging several thick branches, balancing a sheaf of dry grass on her head. She quickly lashes the branches together with strips of sisal. After framing a simple lean-to, she roofs it with the grass. Wordlessly, she sits in the square of shade it casts, motioning for Zora to join her. Zora feebly scoots over, grateful for a reprieve from the sun's flogging.

Abuk sits with her knees to her chest, tapping her feet on the ground. She points at Zora's neck, "*Dheng.*"

"She says your necklace is pretty." Tariq appears above them, sweat streaking the film of red dust that covers his skin. "*Yin apath* means 'Thank you.'"

"Abuk, *yin apath.*" Zora tries to meet her eyes, but the girl resolutely stares at the ground.

"It is considered impolite," Tariq tells her, "For a young Dinka to look into the eyes of elders." He fills a small basin with brown water delivered by a young boy and briskly washes his face and arms. From her patch of shade, Zora watches. His lean arms are finely veined, his biceps mounded like rain-sculpted hills. The water beads like diamonds on his hair. He catches her eye. She does not look away.

As if a dinner bell has sounded, six mostly naked children follow four women wearing elaborately beaded necklaces as they assemble around the fire. The young man they first met, and Luk, wearing an elaborately beaded *malual,* shamble to the gathering. Nobody wears shoes. An older woman sit near Abuk as she arranges a motley collection of bowls. Senoja stalks into the clearing and circles the group. "We cannot feed all these people. We will have no rations for the rest of our trip."

Zora spoons rice into the few bowls. Abuk adds mushy beans and bits of meat.

"This is a *big* mistake," he insists.

"They have no food." She regards him, annoyed by his bluster. "What? We supposed to chow down with them watching?"

Senoja reaches impatiently for a filled bowl. Glaring at her, he retreats from the group to gobble his meal. She feels too weary to fight over his noxious attitude.

Luk chews slowly, closing his eyes with each mouthful. At length, he speaks to Tariq, his voice husky like a smoker's, and Tariq interprets. "Luk says they used to have a prosperous village with many cattle and goats. Their fields produced all the food they needed. Then the soldiers came, and everything was spoiled. In the good times, there would have been feasting and singing to celebrate your visit."

"Tell him I'm happy to have found them."

The old man nods and continues. "He says he has lost many of this family. All his sons and nephews have gone to fight. He believes that most of them are dead." He pauses, sorrow overtaking his calm expression. "His wife was taken in a raid and never returned."

Zora bows her head. "I am sorry for his terrible losses."

Luk leans forward, his voice composed, tender.

"He says of his blood relatives, only Abuk remains. She is his granddaughter."

At the mention of her name, Abuk smiles for the first time, a lovely brightening of her weary face.

"He says she is special. They call her 'the one who knows the way.'" Luk glances around the group, his face drooping with fatigue. "He thanks you for your gift of food. He says we should rest in the heat of the day. They will leave this place tomorrow."

Startled, Zora asks where they're going.

"He says they are traveling north, toward the city, where no bombs drop from the sky."

The old man regards her as if she is an apparition, but not an unexpected one.

"Luk says you resemble his sister."

Zora's breath catches in her throat. Luk closes his eyes. She wonders if he has seen her fear and been disappointed.

"He says we will speak of this when darkness comes." The old man rises with Abuk's help and shuffles to the shelter of his lean-to.

"But—" Zora rises to follow.

Tariq gently grasps her hand. "Leave him. He has only the comfort of his habits."

"But I've come so far for an answer." She hears the whine in her voice and regrets it.

He squeezes her hand. "Then let him gather his strength to give it to you."

A woman screams. The children scatter. Adam stops abruptly at the edge of the clearing, the loose end of his *keffiyeh* fluttering like a foreign flag. Tariq calls to the villagers, halting their flight. Advancing with wary eyes, Adam accepts a bowl of food.

"What just happened?" Zora asks, a thread of fear in her voice.

Tariq gestures to the children dodging away from Adam as he marches back to the vehicle. "They were frightened to see a Rizeigat. They know them only as raiders."

Zora nods. She had not realized her own traveling party would provoke fear. *Another troubling piece of a puzzle presented by this motley assemblage of men.*

Like a gloomy Buddha, Senoja settles beneath a stunted tree surveying the scene with his gun in his lap. The villagers rest in seated positions in jerry-rigged shelters of thatched grass. Zora lays down on a mat under the lean-to Abuk constructed. Facing sideways at ground level, Zora finds herself inspecting a column of red ants marching to the duties of a supply caravan. Foreboding slips into her thoughts. *What will she do now that her 'mission of the heart' has probably found its mark? What will be asked of her? Will she muster the courage to do what's necessary?* She dozes fitfully.

The splash of pouring water awakens her. Abuk has begun cooking. Zora has no energy for it, nor any appetite. She craves being home in her own bed, clean and safe. A small unworthy thought, given the horror of this place. She rises to lend a hand to "the one who knows the way."

As night steals over them, the haggard women and grubby children gather again to eat. They receive the meager porridge with the same reverence she has seen on the faces of elderly Catholic ladies taking Communion. Luk, his expression serene with pleasure, licks his fingers for every trace of food between each bite.

When every bowl is fingered clean, Luk rests his back against a food bin padded with bunched dry grass: another bit of Abuk's handiwork to care for his comfort. He quietly says words to her. She disappears outside the firelight, returning a moment later with a battered tin box. Luk nestles it in his lap, stroking the lid. His voice comes low and soft.

"He says," Tariq translates, "the necklace you wear helped him know who you are."

She touches the beads. Her eyes begin to burn.

"He says that no Kiir woman would give up her child willingly."

She covers her face with her hands.

After a long pause, Luk speaks softly. "He asks if you want him to go on."

She wraps her arms tightly around her knees. "I came a very long way," she says softly, "to find out about my family." She meets Luk's eyes. "Yes, I want him to go on."

Luk nods and continues as Tariq translates. "He says that many seasons ago, a band of *jellabiyas* attacked the village. They killed most of the men. He was wounded and left for dead." Luk parts his tattered *malual* with two fingers, revealing a ragged purpled scar across his right chest. Then, as if to drive home the price he paid, displays another granulated crest of skin traversing his left calf.

"He says his wife Atong and his sister Nyabiel were returning from the stream when the raiders ambushed them." Luk stares into the fire. "The *jellabiyas* roped them together like goats and drove them from the village with their horses." His eyes flash with angry pain. "He laid in his own blood, hearing their screams. But he could not go to save them."

Tears course down Zora's cheeks.

Luk is silent for a long while, his face battling an onslaught of emotion. He clears his throat. "Two seasons pass. A miracle happens. His sister Nyabiel returns." A lone tear skims down his cheek. "But only her body. She is dead in her soul. Her master had beaten and raped her. He had put a child in her belly."

Strange judders rise and overtake Zora's eyes and jaw. Abuk abruptly leaves the circle. Luk watches her disappear, his face pinched with grief. With a great sigh, he continues in a raspy voice, Tariq translating. "Nyabiel gave birth in great pain. She almost died." Bowing his head, Luk opens the box. He lifts a photo and hands it to Zora. From the yellowed curled paper, a thin woman stares back at her, cradling a naked infant in her arms. It is the same as the photo she carries in her pocket.

"Her baby caused memories of her terrible master." Luk goes silent, staring at Zora as she examines the photo. Tariq waits with a stricken expression until Luk speaks again. "He says his sister wrapped that necklace in the swaddling cloth when she gave her baby to the missionaries." Luk coughs as though his throat has gone dry. He glances in the direction Abuk has gone. "The missionaries gave Nyabiel that photo. She wanted to burn it. But he took it and saved it." His grizzled hand strokes the tin box.

Swatting tears, Zora fumbles for the photo she's carried. Luk examines it, working his lips between his teeth. He smiles. "We named you Nyaring even though you would not grow up in the clan." Zora wipes her face with her sleeve. "The name means 'running'" Tariq adds quietly.

Running has been the nature of her life: frantic motion seldom with clear purpose or destination. Fingering aside new tears, she speaks in an unsteady voice. "Can you ask him what happened to my mother?"

Luk shakes his head. "He says that after the missionaries took you, Nyabiel would not eat. A fever sickness finally took her."

Palms hard against her face, Zora weeps. No one speaks. The bright fire crackles and hisses, an aberration in the gloom.

After a long while, Luk raises his bowed head. He gently taps Zora's hand and meets her eyes. His voice moves in fluid cadence, like a preacher delivering a sermon. Tariq continues to relay his words, "He says you are part of his family. He is your uncle. Abuk is your kin. So many of our clan have been lost."

The night birds strike up a call-and-response, an eerie vesper from the windless dark. Luk's voice catches, and Tariq touches his hand. "Our god has sent you to save the last of our clan. Abuk must have a life." Tariq clears his throat, his voice now a whisper. "He wants you to take Abuk with you."

CHAPTER TWELVE

The circle of faces dissolves into the night. Luk rises stiffly and retreats into his makeshift shelter with Abuk, again his shadow, his comforter. Zora sits alone at the rim of the fire's glow, aware that the men are pitching the tents, but unwilling to join their effort. Luk's story seared her. His request upturned her.

When her tent is up, she ducks inside. The night presses upon her like a heavy quilt. She weeps, pounding a fist in the dirt, over the depraved violence that had produced her. She weeps for the woman who endured it, the mother she would never know, the victim who would not survive. She weeps that she'd been thrust away, no matter that her new unchosen world surpassed anything her mother could have dreamed. Nyabiel's choice ravages her with sharp sorrow. She curls around her pain like an abandoned child.

When the tears run out, when she is hollowed out, she stumbles out of the tent, unable to endure confinement. She spreads her sleeping mat on the lumpy ground and yields to her fatigue. Tariq rustles nearby. He places his mat next to hers. She watches him settle on his side, prop his face near hers. "Your sorrow is shared by many," he whispers.

She shakes her head, forcing her eyes toward the night sky. "That's the saddest thing you could say." She covers her eyes with her arm. "A whole army of raped slaves. And right in there's my momma. How does that leave me with anything good?"

He gently lifts her arm from her face. "You have *life*."

She pushes his hand away. "My life was her *shame*."

He edges closer. "An infant does not choose the circumstances of her birth." His breath caresses her cheek. "Your mother's soul called you back to know the truth."

She gulps air to keep from crying out. "And what do I do with this ugly truth?"

His eyes are bright in his dark face. "Gather it as fuel for what you must do now." He strokes her arm. "Abuk will show you the way."

She peers again at the stars, the trails of tears drying on her cheek. "I don't know how to be her…auntie."

He huffs gently. "No woman knows how to nurture a child. Until she must."

"Oh, just stumble forward on instinct." She turns her face from him. "She and I don't even speak the same language."

"The girl is young and teachable."

"She's never *seen* a city or—"

"So, you would leave her in this hell?" He touches her chin, guides her face toward his. "She *will* adapt."

"You make it sound simple." Even as she says it, Zora is ashamed to hear herself whining again.

"It will be complicated." He strokes her cheek. "You and she are Dinka, with a gift for adapting."

She breathes in the musky scent of him, surrenders to the strength of his arms as he embraces her. The fretful desire that had hijacked her during their days together dissipates like vapor. He offers refuge, solace, uncomplicated gifts she cannot refuse. In his arms, she falls into dreamless sleep.

An explosion shatters the night. She bolts to her feet. Tariq is gone. Two more thunderous detonations light the sky, too close, too loud. Silhouettes run screaming across the camp. Abuk pulls her arm. They fall to the ground. Zora knows instinctively to follow her crawling shape. They roll into an old bomb crater. Abuk shimmies against her body. More people fling themselves into the hole. Blind in the dark, Zora hears their whimpers. She clutches Abuk's trembling body. The odor of piss stings her nose. They wait.

The eternity of silent blackness gives way to soft gray. In the frail dawn light, she can make out the forms of her crater mates. Four children and two women curled together, still as corpses, except for their wild blinking eyes. The sun advances a ruby glow, laces it with tangerine. The dazzling colors vanish in a cerulean sky. The sun ascends to terrorize the day.

Zora gently disengages from Abuk. The spy cam in her pocket grazes her chest. She checks to see it is powered up, inching her head above the lip of the hole. She sees Adam carting his bins toward the Rover. A shadow falls across her. She peers up at the broad shape of Senoja. "What the hell happened?" she demands.

He gives her a hand up. "The explosions were to the west but I'm not sure what caused them."

"And where were you?" She faces him. "You smell like a damn drunk."

"Zora, I have been fully functional."

"You leave me and these *children* scared shitless in a hole while you get bent?"

His face remains untroubled. "The good news is that the vehicle is now fully functional."

Tariq strides into the clearing followed by the young man who'd greeted their arrival the day before. He approaches, swinging the hard case at his side.

Zora reaches in her pocket to check again that the recorder is powered on. "Where have *you* been?" she demands.

"Completing a mission."

"A mission?"

He squares his shoulders. "A loud protest against the predatory regime."

She grabs his arm. "What did you *do?*"

He regards her with hostile surprise. "You see these people." He gestures at villagers. "Forced from their homes because *here* is where the oil lies. Oil transported on a road—"

"About two kilometers to the west?" Senoja cuts in.

Tariq nods. "There is a section with a new bridge. Last night, we blew up that bridge."

Incredulous, she stares at him.

"It is the only effective way to—"

"Are you out of your mind?" She rakes her hair with her fingers. "You terrified this entire village!"

Tariq glares at her. "In the battle for our people's survival, I must use every weapon available."

His stubborn scowl reveals a deviousness she had not imagined could be so well concealed. "You *used me* to make this trip!" She pushes her face inches from his. "I should leave you here."

"I support that idea," Senoja says.

"Shut up!" Zora snarls.

Abuk tugs her arm, speaking in an urgent tone. Zora glances at Tariq for translation. He dismisses her with a wave of his hand. "You should learn the language of your clan." Turning, he heads toward the track.

She watches him disappear, horrified that she had been so trusting. *Why hadn't she insisted he open that damn case? What warped, needy part of her had allowed* a crush *to muffle her instincts?*

"One less problem to concern us," Senoja mutters. "We are done here, don't you agree?"

Luk approaches with measured steps. Abuk scurries to halt his progress. He holds her shoulders and speaks close to her ear. With a gnarled hand, he points at Zora. Abuk hesitates. It seems she cannot accept that her own grandfather is giving her to a stranger, that his decision is final. Batting away a willful tear, she walks away from him.

Zora sits in a small patch of shade cupping her hands over her face. She feels Abuk's presence beside her, smells the odor of her sweat. She peeks through the side of her hand. The girl's sorrowful eyes lash her like a whip. She uncovers her face. "I'm sorry," Zora says. "I don't know how this should work."

Suddenly, the villagers are running in panic as a thundering sound rises like a wave. Horsemen in *jellabiyas* burst into the clearing, their faces swathed in black *kufiyas*. Zora pulls Abuk back into the crater. Two gunshots crack the air. Senoja shouts in Arabic. The trample of hooves slows and then dies. A harsh voice responds. A heated exchange ensues. She hears the metallic clack of clips loaded into guns. Close by, a horse snorts, paws the ground. She shades her eyes. Above looms the fierce figure of a robed man, his rifle aimed at her head. He shouts in Arabic.

Senoja steps toward them, his hands raised. "He orders you to come out."

Zora rises on unsteady legs. Together she and Abuk clamber out of the crater. The rider slaps out his words.

Senoja clears his throat. "He says the terrorist action during the night requires punishment. We must hand over the saboteur."

They will murder Tariq. Zora knows this as she searches Senoja's eyes for his intention, warning him with a subtle headshake. He purses his lips as if calculating a complex equation then exchanges words with the horseman. "This man says that if we do not know the whereabouts of the saboteur, he will take this *abid* girl instead."

Zora circles her arm around Abuk. "Over my dead—"

"He will surely oblige you."

"Tell him I'm an American. I'll give him one-hundred U.S. dollars."

Senoja translates. The man sets his rifle across his saddle. With a quick jerk, he reins his horse's head against Zora, shoving her off balance. He spits out words. Senoja hesitates.

"What?" she pleads.

"He says an American woman is stupid to be here with these worthless dogs."

"Two-hundred dollars," she answers. "He leaves all of them unharmed."

Senoja relays the offer, evidently adding his own thoughts on the situation.

"He says that is not enough."

The raider's horse pitches its head, knocking Zora into the dust.

"He refuses to negotiate with a woman. He wants all your money." Senoja watches as she stands up. "I recommend you do as he says."

Zora eyes him, furious that he won't defend her. But resisting this group seems a poor choice. She fumbles in her tunic for a small pouch, one of three in which she's hidden money. As she withdraws it, the horseman skewers the strap with his rifle barrel, flips the pouch and grabs it in mid-air. Ripping it open, he thumbs through the bills, grinning. His horse skitters backwards. At his command, the horsemen trot to the edge of the clearing. Suddenly he swivels, firing a single shot. Senoja bellows, collapsing to the ground. The raiders gallop away.

"Goddamn muthafuckin' son of a *bitch*!" Senoja yells, clutching his left leg. Zora gapes at him as if he were a stranger in sudden crisis. "Fuckin' shit," he howls. "I'm hit! You gonna just watch me bleed?"

Zora scrambles over and pushes up the leg of his pants. Blood oozes from a wound on the side of his calf. "Flesh wound. Doesn't look serious," she says, eyeing his angry face. "What the hell are you up to?"

"Girl, I'm *bleedin'* here!"

She pulls a first-aid kit from her pack. "Here, hold gauze on it. You're gonna live." She stands above him, bristling. "Will they be back to harass these people?"

Nearby, the villagers begin to shoulder their meager belongings. Hefting a small satchel over this shoulder, Luk holds up his hand and catches her eye. He approaches, holding up his tin, the Pandora's box of family's secrets. He mimes that she must contribute something. Obediently, she fishes in her pack, retrieving an extra passport photo. She has to search for a pen, wondering as her fingers work blind if Luk will even be able to read a simple note. *But how else might they connect?* Withered and sweating under the blast-furnace sun, she turns the photo over and writes her name and phone number. She presents it to him with both hands, bowing her head in respect. He sets the photo carefully among his few treasures. Closing the lid, he extends his hand. She grasps it tightly. His eyes roil with a grief so sharp she has to look away. She understands with bitter certainty that neither staying nor leaving will afford these people any safety, that *casual brutality poisons this godforsaken place.*

Luk points at Abuk then at Zora and clasps his hands together. It is not an entreaty but a statement of duty: Abuk is now in her care. Of the possibilities Zora had imagined and feared before this journey, she had avoided the terror of this one. Now it head-butts her into submission. She wants to howl against a choice that feels irrevocable, but instead bows her head in numb acquiescence.

The Land Rover roars into the clearing. Senoja raises himself from the ground with the aid of a long branch. Unexpectedly, Abuk hurries over to help him into the Rover. At Luk's signal, the villagers file onto a trail. Abuk shields herself behind the vehicle, hands covering her face. When she allows herself a glance, her people have disappeared into the bush.

"We'll be okay," Zora murmurs, hoping a reassuring tone will compensate for words that mean nothing. The girl produces a tiny sack tied with sisal, evidently the sum of her earthly possessions.

Senoja scowls as they climb into the back seat. "Girl's not comin' with us."

Zora resists the urge to cuff him, instead stating, "It's all gonna work out."

"A Dinka girl ain't gettin' into the US with no ID papers."

Zora shuts the door. "Dog, you do just fine foolin' people about *your* ID. Let's see what you can do for hers."

The Rover turns onto the track. Steeped in the odor of unwashed bodies, they isolate themselves from each other, nursing anger and grief, leaving this hell, going home, light years away.

CHAPTER THIRTEEN

Pressed against the vehicle's door, Abuk stares at her fisted hands in her lap. Zora fumbles with her paltry Dinka vocabulary, sharply regretting that she was not a diligent student when Tariq was a willing teacher. The girl does not respond, even stiffens at her touch. Zora abandons her awkward attempts to connect. She watches Senoja, head bobbing to the music in his headphones as if nothing has happened. His wounding, which Zora regarded as a well-deserved punishment, jarred him out of his Afro-Brit charade. The expletives he shouted, his inflection, were undeniably American to her practiced ears. It makes no sense to Zora that he had scammed her and, *incredibly,* Jackson's people, about his credentials. Zora cannot see how her journey could be of consequence to him, beyond the money he's been paid. Zora calculates that his contempt for the rebels puts him in the government's corner, but the raiders chose only him as a target and inflicted no more than a slight wound. *A well calculated shot or dumb luck?* She realizes that even as he had not shielded her from the shakedown, he'd spared Tariq from capture. *None of it makes sense.*

The vehicle suddenly smells of cooked beans. Evidently Adam had prepared a meal before the chaos and has lifted the top of the pot. Senoja hands it to the back seat. Abuk quickly pushes the mush into bowls and distributes the meager breakfast. Hunkered defensively over her share like a feral creature, she devours it quickly.

Weary and disoriented, Zora surveys her companions in their wheeled lifeboat, navigating a potentially fatal hotscape. With luck they will survive the trip back. Bert would seize this moment to pray. Zora welcomes the familiar mental image of her aunt: prim and loyal. *She's probably worked herself into a bog of worry after seven, or what is it eight?, days without word.* She taps Senoja's shoulder. "I'd like to use your sat phone. Please."

He turns to her, his face impassive. He takes the phone from the console. "Time to phone home, ET?"

His stupid grin annoys her but she nods, takes the phone, dials the long string of numbers and waits. She hears Bert's 'Hello.'

"It's me, B. Everything's okay."

Bert releases a deep sigh. "I'm so relieved—"

"Can't talk. Just a ping to let you know I'm alive."

"Kochanie—"

"I'll call you in a day or two. Love you." Zora ends the call, certain she could not say what was needed in Senoja's presence. She touches the angel pin, wondering how the recorder battery is holding up.

They lurch along the pitted track. The men seem oblivious to the psychic turmoil that haunts the ladies in the back seat. Zora decides to find handholds on the mountain of unanswered questions. "Must have been a strain putting on your bogus accent," she says.

Senoja coughs out a chuckle. "Had you believin', didn't I?"

She suppresses an impulse to strike him. "You're American."

"Yeah, came up in the Baltimore projects."

"Where'd you learn Arabic?"

"In prison, after a hitch in the Army." His tone is matter of fact, as if he suddenly has nothing to hide.

She leans forward. "So, you're a military-trained ex-con who speaks prison Arabic. Who you workin' for?"

"That's my business."

"How long you been workin' this gig?"

He laughs. "Couple a years."

"What *is* the gig?"

He throws her a defiant glance. "I don't discuss my business."

She huffs. "Looks like your business is mixed up with mine." She pokes his shoulder. "You put us in danger. Tell me what I need to know."

He turns in his seat. "The less you know, the safer we all be."

She holds his gaze. "What else is comin'?"

"Runnin' outta food or water cuz you gave out most of it back there."

She wants to be anywhere but in this filthy vehicle trying to decode his motives. As they round a bend, a trudging figure comes into view. "It's Tariq!" she cries.

"Turnin' up like a bad penny." Senoja spits out the words.

The Land Rover draws alongside Tariq. Zora leans out her window. "Hey, you wanna make things right between us?" She hates that she needs him. "Or would you rather die out here?"

He keeps walking, allowing no sign that he's heard. Zora jumps out, slamming the door just as Senoja begins to complain. She strides to catch up with Tariq. "Don't you walk away!" she shouts. "Let's settle this. We got nothin' but time and space right here."

He stops but remains silent, his face half hidden behind a flap of towel.

"What is it with you?" she gripes, shading her eyes. "You'd die out here to *make a point?*" She steps in front of him, backhanding sweat off her face. "After you left, militia showed up to avenge your revolutionary statement. They wanted a few slaves. It cost a lot to make them leave."

He pushes back the towel and stares at her. She closes the distance between their faces. "Listen, I *agree* with the cause. But you acted like a thug. Just like the people you claim to hate."

He dusts his sand-crusted cheek. "What gives you authority to judge my behavior?" He pulls the towel from his head, his green eyes as hard as glass. "You come here *a visitor.* You know nothing of resistance to government brutality. You speak of threats to a small group, but you don't see how *entire tribes* are being destroyed."

The ravaging heat makes her lightheaded. The anger that launched her out of the Rover collapses under a load of fear. "I didn't think I'd have to protect myself from both you and Senoja."

"You are fortunate to have a limited view of your dilemma."

She squints at him, nearly blinded by the harsh sunlight, grasping for the grace of humility. "You can rework my politics later. Right now, I need your help with Abuk."

They stand eyeing each other like boxers unable to go another round. "I don't know where you were headed." She pushes away sweat dripping into her eyes. "Call me crazy, but I think the truck offers the best alternative to dying out here."

He nods. They climb in on either side of Abuk. She smiles when he greets her in Dinka.

"Senoja," Zora says, "the man needs water."

"I ain't no waiter. Can's behind you." He directs Adam to drive on.

Zora wrestles a container over the seat from the rear compartment and pours a mug of water. Tariq guzzles it. When he's finished, he shoots a questioning glance at Zora, canting his head toward Senoja.

"Senoja's no African," she explains. "When he got shot in the leg, he collapsed into his American self."

Senoja turns with a sullen expression. "Don't talk 'bout me like I ain't here."

"Don't listen."

Tariq offers a small nod of understanding. He sniffs. "Do you notice a bad odor?"

"Which one?"

"The one associated with, ah…female problems."

"Damn right!" Senoja complains. "Fuckin' nasty."

Sniffing, Zora leans toward Abuk. "How about a pit stop? A shady spot."

They come upon a stand of acacia trees. Adam stops and cuts the engine. Zora guides Abuk behind one of the larger trunks and mimics raising her skirt. The girl reluctantly complies. Her sparse pubic hair is crusted with blood. Her vulva, laced shut with crude stitches, oozes bloody pus. Zora has never seen a female circumcision but there can be no other explanation for this appalling wound.

She signals Abuk to wait. When she returns from the truck with the first aid kit, Abuk is crouching behind the tree, hands covering her face. "Abuk," she whispers, opening an antibiotic wipe. "Let me help you." After quiet coaxing, Abuk raises her skirt and closes her eyes. Zora daubs the wound, grasping Abuk's hip when she pulls away. After wiping the wound clean, she fastens a gauze pad into the crotch of a panty and motions for Abuk to put it on. She complies, then smoothes her skirt over her legs. She bats away a tear and follows Zora back to the truck. Predictably, the men say nothing. She knows Abuk will need medical treatment for the raging infection. Senoja will have to be pressed into finding a doctor. They drive on in silence.

Abuk gradually drifts to sleep, her head dropping onto Zora's shoulder. Propped against the opposite window, Tariq begins to snore softly. Even ever-alert Senoja nods off. Adam, working his beads, drives in first gear, zigzagging around the biggest holes, jouncing through the rest, never seeming to mind. *The smart folks*, she decides, have allowed exhaustion to carry them into the temporary oblivion she craves. Her stomach churns from the constant jostling. Her thoughts roil with the implications of "saving" Abuk. *How will she get her home to Washington?*

After a long day of slow going, wispy clouds begin to scutter across the western horizon, marbling the sky peach and lavender. As the sun rests beneath the rim of the world, they camp for the night near a dry *wadi*. In the lantern night, they shuffle about their usual chores like weary invalids. When Senoja withholds water for cleaning Abuk's wound, Zora barks an insult, but then makes do with the last of the hand wipes. He offers an appeasement: a packet of beef jerky he'd been hoarding. She gives it to Abuk. They're too exhausted to bother with conversation. The girl obediently beds down next to her in the tent, shutting her eyes tight. As a rare breeze ruffles their canvas cocoon, Zora wonders at the secrets in the soul of this stranger, a child of her clan. During the night, a dust storm rakes across the camp, drilling through the gaps in the tents, coating everything with grit.

In the morning, they towel off before emerging from the tent. With no water to spare, nothing can be done about their smelly clothes. Senoja sits by the cook fire, bitching about the apparent ruin of his satellite phone, their only lifeline if they get stranded. He disassembles, cleans it, tests for a connection, swears loudly. It's the first hint of fear he's revealed, and it alarms Zora.

Asida is all that can be made of their remaining supplies. The ache in Zora's empty belly tames her revulsion for the pasty mush; she swallows a few globs, daydreaming about a full meal of *spicy roasted chicken, creamy mashed potatoes,* then shoves aside the images. She will plan a magnificent buffet if they make it back to The World. She's allowed "if" to enter a side alley of her fear.

She forces her thoughts in another direction: imagining Abuk's reaction to American food. And to the miracle of clean water from a tap. And to a soft bed in a safe place. Perhaps embracing these comforts will be easy after all the deprivation she's known. More difficult will be the grief of losing her people, of not knowing their fate.

Abuk touches her shoulder, points at the Land Rover. The others are packed and waiting. After filling the tank from the reserve, Senoja announces that to conserve fuel, the Land Rover's air conditioning will be shut off. They will drive with windows open. Within five minutes, the cab turns oven hot, blooming with dust. Abuk slumps between Zora and Tariq, arranging folds in her skirt, eyes downcast.

"Tariq, I'd like to know about Abuk's life in the village."

He frowns. "You would start the day by stirring harsh memories?"

"I need to know about this girl I'm taking home. I have you here to translate, and I don't take that for granted."

Wiping sand from his eyes, he gently questions Abuk. She stares into her lap, answering in brief murmurs. "She says that her village and people are gone. She wants to know where you are taking her."

Senoja swivels in his seat. "Probably a refugee camp—unless some magic happens."

Zora soft slaps his head. "Magic is your job. And excuse me, this is a private conversation." With a scowl, he turns away.

"Tariq, tell her that I'm taking her to my home in America."

"I doubt that will mean much."

"Then say my house has a good bed and lots of food."

He translates. Abuk musters a dubious smile. "She says the time she was taken away, the people made her work all the time."

"Who took her away?"

Abuk speaks in anxious fits and starts. "She says *jellabiyas* took her. They made her a servant in the house. At night they kept her in a shed with goats and gave her spoiled food. Sometimes she was so hungry, she crept out at night looking for something to eat."

"But she escaped. How?"

"She says white people came. They paid money and took her back to her grandfather's village." He brushes sand from his lips. "Slavery abolitionists made a cause of Sudan." He grimaces. "Their efforts to 'free the slaves' have created a profitable new business for traders."

She gazes at the woman-child beside her. "Who circumcised her?"

Tariq waves his hand as if to bat away the question.

"I saw her wound. It's infected. I want to know what happened and when, so I can get her medical treatment. Please, ask her."

He draws a deep breath and speaks quietly to Abuk. She wraps her arms around herself, holding so tightly that her ragged fingernails bloom like pink petals against her black skin. "She says her master's wife forced it on her. Many days ago. She told no one because of her shame." Abuk shuts her eyes hard, as if closing off the memory.

"I will take care of her," Zora says quietly. "I will keep her safe. Tell her that." She frets that the heat has addled her brain; she's making promises to a dark-skinned girl about a safe life in Washington, DC.

As the vehicle jolts over a rut, Abuk fists away tears. Raising her head, she speaks with prickly fervor. "She says her grandfather calls her 'the one who knows the way.' He taught her to respect this gift."

"As will I," Zora says. *Another promise, one that requires knowledge the girl does not yet possesses. In her new life, Abuk will have no familiar references to find the way. That will be her job.*

The blistering day merges with the next. The dirt-crusted Land Rover protests the constant abuse with a rash of broken parts. Abuk studies each repair effort with rapt attention. Adam's ingenuity with duct tape and odd bits of wire earns him exalted status and an extra ration of water.

They pass the place where the two young girls had taken her to the stream. There's no sign of them. They and their grandparents finally must be on the move north, toward the illusion of safety. She refuses to think of them dead.

Senoja allows Abuk to listen to his iPod. After wide-eyed shock at the big sound in the small box, Abuk becomes possessive of the device. When Senoja irritably demands it back, an argument erupts. In no mood for the squabbling, Zora requires them either to "share the earbuds or to stow the damn thing." Tariq develops a violent headache with a fever. Guessing a bout of malaria, Zora doses him with Doxycycline from her dwindling stash.

Two more days grind by. The last bits of dried fruit are consumed; Senoja filters what little water they can find, and they munch pods from a plant that Abuk identifies near a *wadi*. Late on a sweltering afternoon, Senoja consults his GPS then powers up the phone he has fussed over since the dust storm, ordering it to work. When he connects with his advance man in Malakal, the travelers whoop and clap, shamelessly relieved that they will not die in the metal shell that's carried them through one of Death's favorite neighborhoods.

CHAPTER FOURTEEN

Dry grass and acacia trees cede to Dottlieb palms along the banks of the languid Nile. The heat persists, but the river's moisture softens its grip. The road improves enough to speed along in third gear. In the front seat, Senoja packs up his electronic gadgets. "I told my guy to have the plane ready to roll with food and water. Don't wannna spend even one more day in this piss-poor excuse for a country."

"I'm with ya," Zora admits.

"Damn straight." He turns to her. "Now here's what we're lookin' at. Ain't gonna be much problem movin' our little girlfriend into Loki. But I wanna avoid any trouble mulin' her into Nairobi. I need time in Loki to score some travel papers."

"Do what you gotta."

Tariq chuckles softly. "This kind of English is … entertaining." He slowly straightens from the slouch his illness had imposed on him.

"How you feeling?" she asks.

"Weak. But able to function."

"We'll get you to a doctor in Loki." She glances at Abuk. "Is there any way you can prepare her for the plane?"

His ashy face registers the effort of thought. "There are few Dinka words to capture the experience."

As they skirt the southern flank of Malakal town Adam speeds up, throwing clouds of red dust that bring protests from the locals trudging along the shoulder. He jams through every gear, smiling like a freed prisoner, and corners sharply into an unmarked dirt road. A weathered twin engine Cessna is parked at the side of an airstrip. The Land Rover lurches to a stop behind the wing. Senoja opens his door. "Grab your personal stuff and get on the plane pronto. We're losing light. I hate flyin' in small aircraft in the dark."

Adam sits in the vehicle watching impassively as they offload the cargo. When they are finished, Zora barely has time to say *"Shukran"* before he races away. Grasping Abuk's hand, she steps to the aircraft's door. Tariq moves slowly beside them. "One day, you will come back and see Sudan resurrected from misery."

.   Zora scans the rough land, inhaling the acrid smoke-scented air. "I doubt either will happen any time soon."

"Then I am the optimist." He reaches for her arm to steady himself on the steps. Zora'd been uncertain if the tenderness of his only embrace had been an illusion. This gentle touch telegraphs that he's been waiting to show her more.

As the plane's engines rev, Zora guides Abuk to a window seat and buckles her in, repeating the words Tariq has given to quiet her wild-eyed fear. As the engine roar mounts, Abuk curls in her seat like a cornered cat. The Cessna turns, gaining speed as it bounds over the clay airstrip, straining for lift. Abuk grips the armrest fiercely. With a hard shudder, the craft is airborne.

As the earth falls away, she coaxes Abuk to uncoil by pointing out the window. Guardedly, she watches the scruffy *tukuls* shrink and disappear from view. The clotted green river dwindles to a thin ribbon as they fly southwest in a pale ochre shroud of sand. The fractured Jonglei Canal sprawls below in the dusk. Sketchy cirrus clouds steal violet tints from the setting sun. The drone of the propellers, the steady vibration of the aircraft, seem to lull Abuk into provisional calm.

A cheery co-pilot emerges from the cockpit to distribute juice and biscuits. Abuk picks with uncertain fingers at the packaging. Zora nudges her, demonstrating how to grasp the edge and tear. She does as shown, then allows herself a suspicious nibble of the contents. Zora consumes her biscuits in quick bites, overjoyed with the return of edibles with taste. The juice carton resists opening where a green arrow directs; she rips apart the top seam, splattering orange juice on her shirt. Abuk looks away to hide her amusement.

They ease into a game of naming body parts in English and Dinka, prompting the first giggle Zora has heard from Abuk. Far above her familiar world, a place of belonging and misery, Abuk seems to submit to this new experience like a dog chowing down, heedless of what had been swallowed, looking only for more.

A yellow full moon ascends over the darkening landscape. Though exhaustion gnaws at her, Zora considers the problems that have arrayed themselves before her. Practical problems like finding a doctor, and travel papers, and decent clothing for Abuk. Existential problems like re-mapping her life in the wild wakes of a traumatized girl and a provocative man. Wrenching sorrow tethered to crazy exhilaration. *Surreal. What will follow*, she muses, *cannot possibly be boring.*

The silhouette of a jutting ridgeline announces their arrival in Loki, the place where they'd begun the trek nearly two weeks earlier. Two Buffalo aircraft squat on the tarmac, their rear doors yawning before pallets stacked with white sacks. Some Sudanese would eat today. The Cessna thumps and rattles to a stop at a small hangar.

Senoja limps to the hatch. "I got a vehicle to take y'all to a guest house up the road. Just let the driver do his thing. I got business to handle."

A freshening breeze blows from the east as a dust-covered truck pulls alongside the plane. Their unloading drill proceeds with practiced efficiency. A dark, silent man with a blue baseball cap drives them to the customs station where an official waves them through. They continue on a dirt road flanked by tin-roofed *dukas*, most shut for the night.

The driver turns at a small white sign with "748" painted in black. The sturdy whitewashed walls of the compound promise a serious upgrade from conditions in the bush. Reggae music greets their entry into a courtyard with green canvas safari chairs clustered around dark wood tables. A young man smiles from a well-stocked bar. They continue into a large room, passing a buffet table set with trays of grilled fish, roasted meat, and a stew of vegetables. Abuk gapes at the sight. A Kenyan man in a polo shirt and chinos approaches. *"Karibuni!* Welcome! You are with Mr. Senoja, yes? You had a long journey. You are tired."

"We are," Zora confirms. "And desperately need showers."

Their host smiles knowingly. "Yes, and laundry. Let me show you your rooms."

Abuk sidles toward the buffet table, staring at the food with wonder. She turns to Zora with pleading eyes.

"Looks like we should eat first," Zora informs their host.

"As you wish, Madame." The man gestures toward the buffet. "Please, enjoy."

She hands Abuk a plate and holds up a serving spatula. "Check this out," she says, demonstrating how to lift out a serving. Abuk frowns, muttering in Dinka.

Behind her, Tariq chuckles. "Abuk says hands work better with food."

"Maybe so," Zora answers, picking up a plate for herself, "but not so much where we're going."

Across the room a huge flatscreen TV beams a soccer match. "Ghana versus Nigeria," Tariq notes, smiling at the prospect of viewing the game. The three of them carry their plates to an empty table with an unobstructed view of the screen. Abuk eats with both hands.

"Child," Zora chides, "you need to use—"

"I think," Tariq intercedes, "it will cost nothing if you allow her this feast in her own way, just for tonight."

"But—" Zora catches herself. "Already I'm sounding like an irritating auntie."

He rests his chin on his hand, a disarming fondness in his eyes. "It's a path of discovery. You probably are more suited to it than you realize."

His smile warms her. In their days together, he's provoked more anger and longing than she'd imagined possible with one human being. His risky sabotage stunned her, but the passion that fueled it draws her like a flower to sunlight. *Being with him, being his lover—how could that work?*

"*GOOOOAAALLL*" blares the TV. At a table across the room, four men hoot and down their beers in a haze of cigarette smoke. As if reminded suddenly of the environment, Tariq's face tightens.

"You okay?" Zora asks.

He shakes his head. "I feel too exposed here. I'm going to my room." He leans and whispers, "I will wait for you later on the patio."

She nods. Watching him leave, Zora feels the creep of anxiety, but she returns to eating, forced to coddle a fitful stomach. Abuk devours chunks of fish and potatoes, clearly the first substantial meal she's eaten in a long time. Zora has never experienced that sort of hunger. When she was coming up, Ella had pretended to complain that Zora's friends descended on their kitchen like locusts, routinely eating enough to "put us in the poorhouse." But she found a way to feed them all, feed them enough, usually with grace and humor. Ella's rituals of eating would be reinvented by her now, undernourished Abuk in tow.

When they finish the meal, the host brings their key and directs them to their room. They walk along a covered veranda. Bird-of-paradise plants grow densely in a central courtyard; a thicket of flowering shrubs screens the rear wing where they find number twelve. The whitewashed room she is sharing with Abuk is furnished with two twin beds and a small cheap bureau. A vague odor of disinfectant lingers in the cramped space. Zora ushers Anuk to the bathroom, laughing in spite of herself at Abuk's surprise when she turns on the shower.

Abuk quickly sheds her filthy t-shirt and skirt. Her thin body is mottled with small dark gnarls, the scars of injuries or abuse, Zora cannot guess which. The sight grieves her. She holds out a bar of pink soap, rousing a grin from Abuk, and then Zora motions Abuk into the flow of water and pulls the curtain shut. Abuk begins loudly gargling water and splashing her feet in the puddling water. Soon the giggles blossom into song. Her voice, much bigger than her body, races through a torrent of incomprehensible lyrics. The riff enchants Zora. For a moment, she believes all will be well.

After that sweet moment out of time, she surveys the small room, canting her head at a brash painting of a Kenyan market scene with the perspective oddly bent. Opening her duffel bag, she piles her smelly clothes on the floor, then adds Abuk's few things to the heap. She unpacks a tube of mascara, an eyeliner pencil, pot of blush, and two lipsticks, all unused since departure, and wipes each clean of sand. She empties sand from a floral makeup case she'd once thought cute, then repacks each frivolous item within it. Her small backpack receives the same treatment. With a small cloth, the wipes down the flashlight, the Leatherman, the camera, its case, and the pockets of the pack.

Finally, unwilling to find another distraction from the rankness of her body, she marches into the bathroom, pulls back the shower curtain and turns off the water. Abuk blinks at her. "My turn," she smiles, handing Abuk a towel. The girl relinquishes the stall with a flash of annoyance.

Zora peels off her clothes. Standing in the flow, she watches rivulets of brown grit cascade down her body. Liquid amnesia pools in her hands, a balm for her sun-ravaged face. Sweet relief flows over her breasts and belly, laps at her callused feet. Even as the tepid water runs cold, she revels in its curative magic, a pleasure she pledges never to take for granted. The flow turns cold, peters out. But she's gotten what she needed.

Wrapped in a towel, she emerges to find Abuk curled naked on the bed, asleep. She covers her with a sheet. Ella had had a goodnight ritual: a favorite book, a prayer, and a kiss on the forehead while tucking the blanket around her. She wonders if Abuk has known any comforting intimacy. In the dim light, she studies the girl's face. Cleansed of dirt and fear, her young skin glows like burnished night. Her plaited hair glistens with jewels of moisture. She is a black angel at rest.

Tariq would be out there waiting. After stuffing the soiled clothes in the hotel's laundry bag, she dresses in the least soiled dress, hand-combs her hair into the best version of unkempt, sets the bulging bag beside the door, and hurries out.

A man she does not at first recognize sits at a patio table nursing a cup of coffee. He's wearing a green Oakland A's cap, a black t-shirt emblazoned with the Red Hot Chili Peppers logo and faded blue jeans. He looks like an expat on mission.

"A new fashion statement?" she says, sitting across from Tariq. He gazes at her, a new sadness in his eyes. "You won't sleep if you keep drinking that stuff."

He offers a small smile. "No rest for the wicked."

"Wicked indeed." She signals the barkeep who comes to take her order, a whiskey, rocks.

Tariq regards her with somber eyes. "I regret endangering you without your knowledge."

She allows a grin. "You would have endangered me *with* my knowledge?"

He moves his face closer to hers. "With full understanding, you would have been my co-conspirator."

"You don't—"

"I know what you have seen." He leans further forward, his lips near her cheek. "You cannot deny, as so many have, that the evil ruling this land must be stopped."

A waiter delivers Zora's drink, and she sighs. "I'm one person in the middle of a big invisible war. What I've seen is the reason I'm bringing Abuk out."

"A worthy start," he says. "She may help you see your duty with new conviction."

She fingers the short hairs at her left temple. "I didn't come out here to argue politics."

He appraises her. "Why did you come?"

She meets his gaze. "I wanted to find out if we … if we could have something…*more* between us."

He turns away. "Zora, we can have nothing beyond this."

She feels she is toeing an emotional cliff. "You don't feel the attraction I feel?"

He screws up his face as if in pain. "Zora, you dazzle me."

"You're married?" she presses, wanting to stop.

"When I was very young. She died in childbirth."

"I'm sorry."

"It was a long time ago." He shifts in his chair. "Now you are torturing us both."

She covers her mouth with her hand.

Gently, he strokes her fingers. "Zora, you have come into my life like a splendid gift. I did not see that until it was too late."

His touch makes her tremble. She lowers her hand. "What are you saying?"

He draws closer. "When I destroyed the bridge, I interfered with something of great value to powerful men. They *will* have their revenge."

She draws back. "But your father's influence?"

"To protect his position, he cannot intercede in this matter."

She shakes her head. "You can leave the country. Disappear."

"I *am* leaving. Tonight."

Senoja limps into the patio, unsuccessfully affecting a strut. "Now *this* is what I'm talkin' 'bout," he says loudly to no one in particular. He approaches their table. "Ladies, got some news. Found a guy to make travel papers *and* a doctor." He beams with self-satisfaction. Tariq sips his coffee. Senoja glances from him to Zora. "I'm not hearin' 'pull up a chair'." He raises one eyebrow and waits.

"Good work," Zora offers.

With a pouty glance at Tariq, Senoja turns and limps to the bar.

"I think," Tariq whispers, "that man is in love with you."

Zora sniffs dismissively. "He's a devious son-of-a-bitch."

"An asset on this journey."

"Let's not talk about him." She sits in miserable silence, staring at the floor. A little chaos of longing and disappointment overtakes her. Letting her heart out to play feels as naïve to her as having a schoolgirl crush. "Please stay," she asks. "At least until I sort out Abuk with the doctor."

"Zora," he sighs.

"Just one more day." She moves her hand from his reach. "Give me time to accept this." She rises and heads down the path to her room. She wants to yell, *"Fuck! Fuck! Fuck!"* and kick her own ass, as if that were possible. A diesel truck rumbles by on the road, piercing the oppressive quiet. She pauses to take a few breaths and opens the door to her room. Abuk is as she'd left her, hard asleep. Zora flops on the empty bed, her thoughts like leaves in a churning stream.

From their first meeting, she'd imagined him as her lover. He provoked astonishment, as if she were seeing, smelling, touching a man's body for the first time. She'd judged him magnificently fuckable and fantasized a passionate seduction, fueled by sparks of danger, with no one to notice or to judge. Then he'd begun to *intrigue* her with his travel stories, his knowledge of myths and science, his graceful rapport with the people they'd met. He'd been a willing interpreter; he knew how to set Abuk at ease. He'd walked beside her among bloody corpses with eyes that did not blink—and found no fault when hers did. He'd pushed her forward on a journey that wrenched her from all the trivial trappings of her Western life. She could not accept that there would be nothing more between them.

Abuk cries out. Startled, Zora rises to her feet. The girl begins to thrash and moan. Blind in the dark, Zora trips over a bag on the floor, landing on her knees beside Abuk's bed. She reaches out as a flailing arm strikes her shoulder. "Abuk," she says, catching the girl's hands, "I'm here.

Shhh, shhh. You're safe." Cooing this mantra, Zora embraces her. Abuk's labored breathing evens out. The tension in her body ebbs. In a few minutes, the soft purr of sleep-breath returns. Zora sits beside her bed, keeping vigil. She adds 'night terrors' to the list of Abuk's cargo, along with an obscure language and a festering wound that means she will never know sexual pleasure, taken from her before the possibility even reared its lovely head. During the long night of watching and thinking. Zora comes to realize how much she needs Tariq's help with Abuk. She finds herself believing she could ask for and receive it without losing herself.

CHAPTER FIFTEEN

At dawn, Abuk awakens. In the meager light she lies motionless, eyeing the unfamiliar objects around her. She strokes her belly that aches from the strange food she'd eaten the night before. The painful wound is leaking between her legs. She finds Zora sleeping on the floor beside her bed. Rolling silently off the other side, Abuk drops onto her hands and feet. She creeps toward the door. When she pushes down the metal latch, the door pops open. A large bag falls into the doorway.

"Abuk," Zora calls.

Abuk stops, her naked body washed in sunlight. Zora rises stiffly, exhausted from the fretful night. Padding over to the door, she pulls the bag into the room and shuts the door. "Clean clothes," she says, emptying the bag on her bed. Abuk snatches her skirt and t-shirt and quickly slips them on.

"You still got that funky smell," Zora says. She wants to ask, "How you feeling?" but lacking the vocabulary, reaches to feel Abuk's forehead. The girl pulls back. In no mood for finesse, Zora firmly places Abuk's hand on her own forehead. "No fever." She reaches again toward Abuk's forehead and meets no resistance. "Fever," she confirms. "Today we see a doctor." She rummages through the stack of laundry, aware that Abuk is watching her. She realizes that getting this relationship on track will have to feel like a harmless game.

Zora pulls two T-shirts from the pile. "Green or blue?" she offers, displaying them in turn, repeating the words.

Abuk regards her with arched eyebrows. Zora wags her head in turn at each T-shirt. Abuk gives a small smile. "Green" she says. Zora hands it to her. "Put it on."

Abuk shucks her ragged shirt and pulls on the new one, her face emerging with a tiny smile. "O-kaaay," Zora declares. "*Dheng,* pretty.*"

"O-kaaay, pretty," Abuk echoes.

Zora removes her own stained shirt and slides into the blue T-shirt. "I'm gonna wear jeans. Do you want this?" She shows Abuk a brown and green patterned skirt. "Skirt."

"Skirt." Abuk nods and accepts the garment.

They finish dressing. "Now we go *eat*," Zora says, putting cupped fingers to her mouth. "Eat?"

Abuk shakes her head.

"No eat? How about *drink*?" Zora lifts an imaginary cup to her lips. "Drink?"

"Drink," Abuk agrees.

"Let's go see what we can find." Grabbing money from a stash in the duffle bag, Zora stuffs it in her small backpack, then opens the door to hot dazzling sunshine. On the restaurant patio, she settles for coffee and a *mandazi*. Abuk dallies over a glass of milk. Her eyes are dull; she is lethargic. Zora had roused Senoja for a trip to the doctor he'd found. When Tariq strides into the courtyard, Zora straightens from a slouch, relieved that he's stayed.

"Abuk, *ci yi bak*," Tariq calls.

Abuk returns his greeting, regarding him with curiosity as he sits next to Zora.

"Good morning, Zora." He orders tea from the waiter who appears. "How was your night?"

"Long. Abuk had bad dreams." Zora tries to avoid his eyes, but they call her in.

Tariq touches her hand. "We have this day together, *Insha'allah*. We should enjoy it." Abuk speaks to him, and he translates. "She wants to know if we are to be married."

Zora shoots him a quizzical glance.

"She says our eyes talk."

Zora looks away to hide the attraction she knows will not stay hidden, not from this girl with dead-on intuition nor from this man.

"Ladies!" Senoja booms as he limp-marches to their table. "Time to saddle up."

"Senoja," she warns. "I don't like this alpha-male 'ladies' crap."

"Oooh, somebody had a bad ni—"

"Show some respect," Zora scolds. "Be professional."

Senoja deflects the reprimand with a shrug. He scrutinizes Abuk. "After we hit the doc's office, she's gettin' her picture taken. Glad you found her a clean shirt." He waves toward the exit. "The Rover's hummin'."

The sun metes out its usual torture as they cross the crowded lot. Senoja maneuvers the vehicle along a littered track, his iPod kicking out Bob Marley's "Sun is Shining" loud enough for them to hear through his headphones. Loki presents itself as a tawdry encampment splayed around the World Food Program's warehouses and hangars. A Buffalo transport aircraft thunders overhead. Women in brilliant purple-plaid wraps amble along the roadside, herding children and goats. The air is pungent with wood smoke.

They arrive at a squat building. Hardened splatters of red mud apron the dung-colored walls. The tin roof sags under a patina of rust. The metal door, industrial blue and pocked with dents, squeals as they open it. Senoja stoops to lead them inside through a rough curtain.

The small room is dim and burdened with the odor of medicinal alcohol. Two rooms adjoin it, their doorways covered with dark, rug-thick curtains. A wizened woman cradling a fever-limp child slides over to make room on a low wooden bench. A wasted man with yellow eyes sits on the floor across from them, struggling to hold his head up. In the next room, a murmured conversation ends with the sound of a chair scraping the floor.

"We're here to see Dr. Josephine Kamau," Senoja calls.

A stout coconut-brown woman in a white coat pushes aside the curtain. "*Karibuni*. Please, take a seat." The musical inflection of her voice does nothing to conceal no-nonsense authority. "Others came before you. They also need care." She pats the arm of her departing pregnant patient.

"Dr. Josephine," Senoja insists. "I was assured you would be quick to tend to—"

"Sir, I will see to your needs in due course." She beckons the old woman into her surgery.

"Senoja," Zora whispers, "let's not do the Ugly American thing."

He rolls his eyes. "I ain't hangin' here. I'll be back."

Tariq sits next to Zora. His ease at creating intimacy gives her a quick shiver.

"What would you like me to tell Abuk?" he asks.

Zora avoids his eyes. "Tell her that the woman is a doctor who will clean her wound and give her medicine."

Tariq's translation provokes a look of horror from Abuk. She speaks rapidly. "She says she does not want a stranger to look at her. She wants to leave."

"Tell her, "Zora answers, 'that she has a bad infection that must be treated. I'll go with her, and you will stay outside."

When Tariq translates, Abuk rises, shaking her head.

"Tell her," Zora insists, "I am her elder, and I know what is best."

Tariq smiles. "An excellent time to—"

"Pull rank?"

"That is the American phrase for exercising authority?" He speaks again to Abuk. She wrinkles her nose and nods reluctantly.

They wait in silence. The airless space becomes oppressive. There is a calendar hanging crookedly on the cinder-block wall. Smudged and discolored, it features a portrait of former Kenyan President Moi with 1998 printed in red letters beneath it. Those were the bad old days of Moi's cleptocracy. Between the doors, a framed diploma, hanging from a length of sisal, declares that Josephine Wanjiku Kamau earned her MD from Johns Hopkins School of Medicine.

The doctor pushes aside the curtain and the old woman departs, clutching her child. At the doctor's beckon, the yellow-eyed man rises with a groan and shuffles inside.

A young woman, her neck encased by beaded necklaces, enters the clinic with two runny-nosed toddlers. Abuk flashes them a brilliant smile. Leaning toward the boys, she extends her right hand, palm down, scratching the air. They wobble toward her, grinning as if she were a favorite sister. Abuk begins a song with the cadence of a nursery rhyme. As the boys compete for her lap, Zora mentally catalogues the possible viruses and bacteria voyaging between the participants in the happy exchange. She rebukes herself for this suburban-mom fussiness. Abuk has managed to survive much worse.

The curtain parts. Dr. Kamau assists the ravaged man as he wobbles with a new cane to the door. Turning, the doctor appraises Zora with frank curiosity. "Please," she says, "come in."

Zora motions to Abuk. With a fearful glance, the girl gently disengages from her mini fans. The curtain whispers shut behind them. Dr. Kamau peers over tortoise-shell glasses. "I seldom see Americans in my practice here. As you surely have noticed, we cannot offer a Western standard of care."

"It's a blessing to find you," Zora says. "This girl Abuk needs your help."

Dr. Kamau regarded her new patient. "She is Sudanese, a refugee?"

Zora hesitates. "Do you need the whole story?"

Dr. Kamau smiles. "No Madame, I am not concerned with immigration matters, if that is your worry." She rummages in a box for latex gloves. "I need to know the nature of her illness."

"Yes, of course." Zora clears her throat. "I have never seen a female circumcision, but I believe that's what happened to her. The wound is infected."

Facing Abuk with calm solicitude, Dr. Kamau massages her neck, locating swollen nodes that make the girl wince. She deploys her stethoscope like a magical object, coaxing Abuk to relax as she places the metal circle on her back and chest. When she pats the wooden table, Abuk sits but refuses to lie down.

"Madame," the doctor says, "I imagine this girl has no pleasant memories of lying on her back in the presence of strangers. Please help me comfort her."

Zora sits at the head of the table, easing Abuk back into her arms. As the doctor gently works the skirt up her legs, Abuk tenses. The doctor frowns. "It is a serious infection." As she assembles gauze and instruments on a plastic tray, Zora searches for something to distract Abuk. The melody of "People Get Ready" noodles from her memory and she begins to sing softly. She strokes Abuk's arm as the doctor works. Suddenly Abuk yelps, straining against her.

"Forgive me, child," Dr. Kamau murmurs. "I am almost finished." When she finally pulls off her gloves, she says: "I am sorry. I had only a topical anesthetic. There was an abscess that I drained." She helps Abuk sit up, smoothing her skirt. "Without treatment, she would have died of sepsis, perhaps within a week."

Zora groans. Though they have been together only a short time, losing this girl would wound her deeply. She knows this without understanding why.

Dr. Kamau bundles a handful of soft leaves in a latex glove. "I use many medicinal herbs. These leaves are from *magutui.* Break them open and apply the fluid to the incision. Twice every day until it is healed." She measures powder into a small plastic bag. "This is from the castor plant. Dissolve a teaspoon in a glass of water once a day. It will strengthen her system."

Abuk winces as she stands up. Dr. Kamau pats her cheek. "Hers is a badly performed Sunna circumcision. It is not the most radical type, but damage has been done. The infection may have harmed her reproductive organs." She removes her glasses. "You are taking her to America?"

"To Washington, DC."

She writes on a slip of paper. "This Baltimore practice specializes in the health problems of circumcised women. I'm sure they can advise you and treat her."

Zora pockets the note. "You've given us both great relief. I hope this will give you some relief as well." She hands Dr. Kamau two fifty-dollar bills.

"*Asante sana.*" The doctor smiles broadly as she folds the money. "Life brings wondrous gifts every day. This will buy medical supplies enough for a month." She pushes aside the curtain. More patients have crowded into the waiting room.

Zora pauses. "Doctor Kamau, forgive me if I'm out of place, but why are you *here?*"

The doctor grins. "Did you not say that it was a blessing to find me?"

"Yes, it was! But with your credentials, you could practice anywhere. You chose *this* place."

Her cheeks dimple as she purses her lips. "These people have great needs. Outsiders lament that someone must help them. *I* am that someone." She rests her hand on Zora's shoulder. "Perhaps the same understanding has led you to this girl."

Senoja appears at the door. "We done here?"

"In a minute," Zora answers. "Doctor, I would be grateful if you would also take a look at my friend, Tariq. He spiked a fever. I gave him Doxycycline. He seems better, but I'm not sure what's wrong."

"Of course." The doctor beckons Tariq.

"I am fine," he demurs, hefting one of the toddlers into his lap.

Zora lifts the boy away and hands him to Abuk. "You have the opportunity for professional care. Don't pass it up." She gestures him into the exam room.

Senoja's face twitches with impatience. "I'm waitin' outside."

"Hold on, we got a doctor here. You wanna have her look at your gunshot wound?"

'Naah, I'm good." He pushes through the curtain to the outside.

With a sidelong glance, Dr. Kamau sighs.

"Tariq," Zora orders, 'You're up."

He rises like a man facing punishment. As he disappears behind the curtain, Zora rests against the wall, watching Abuk entertain the children. Her face seems already to have recovered a bit of shine. She has not lost the impulse to be playful.

Tariq emerges from the exam room with a sullen face. Dr. Kamau follows him with a forbearing smile. "I have never met a man willing to submit to a doctor's care until death seems imminent. Your friend is no exception. Without testing, I cannot confirm malaria, but that is my preliminary diagnosis. Your medication will help. I recommend another assessment when you locate a clinic with laboratory services."

Zora nods. "*Asante sana*, Dr. Kamau. God bless you."

Tariq mumbles "Thank you." As they get into the truck, Zora tells Senoja that everybody's gonna be okay. She knows he doesn't really care and will inquire no further.

After a brief bouncing ride, Abuk sits for a photo in a cramped seedy shop that reeks of photographic chemicals. "Tomorrow," assures the photographer with a grin that reveals brown-stained teeth. He adjusts the *imma* on his head. "You come tomorrow. I give document. You give money now."

"I give money tomorrow," Senoja retorts.

As they drive back to the "748" compound, Tariq asks, "How do you *find* these people—the doctor, the photographer?"

"Trade secret," Senoja replies. "My business."

"He doesn't talk about his business," Zora confirms.

"Gotta protect my livelihood." He corners quickly, nearly hitting a man leading a loaded donkey.

"Whoaaa!" Zora cries. "Stop! Apologize to that man."

Senoja shouts out the window and speeds on.

"That was cold."

"That was cold." Abuk mimics.

Senoja glances over his shoulder. "Damn, girl. You learnin' English!"

"English," Abuk echoes.

"So, let's keep it out of the gutter," Zora warns.

Senoja slaps the steering wheel. "Now you doin' like my gran. Sheee-it."

"Sheee-it," Abuk repeats.

Zora raps his shoulder. "Dawg, you hearin' this?"

"Maybe she can teach me Dinka cuss words." He ducks the paper cup Zora throws at him.

A large lunch and a long nap renew them. Zora feels giddy putting on a freshly ironed blouse and a clean wild-red-print *kanga*. Abuk prances around the room in a flowered sundress that Zora had packed in ignorant optimism. For the first time since they'd left Nairobi, Zora opens her make-up bag with intent to use its contents. She surveys her face with a small mirror. The sun has blotched her skin. The once-faint lines across her forehead have been carved a bit deeper. Her lips are chapped. Her eyes have country-girl plainness. She realizes suddenly that she hasn't called Bert. The poor woman probably has riled herself into debilitation. She feels Abuk's watching eyes. "We don't need any of this makeup, do we?"

"Do we?" Abuk repeats.

"Well, you don't. You look beautiful." Zora zips the bag and stows it in her duffel. "Senoja promised us a par-tay. Let's go see what he's puttin' on."

Tender breezes caress the evening. As they stroll along the veranda, Zora pinches two fragrant blooms from a jasmine vine. She nestles one into the plaited hair over Abuk's ear. The other she clips above her own. An electric guitar is tuning up. As they enter the patio,

Senoja limps toward them holding a Tusker beer in one hand and a joint in the other. "Lookin' fine, ladies," he says smiling, eyes half-mast, stoned.

"Can't take the 'hood out of the boy, huh?"

He takes a drag. "No worries. It's a *private* party."

Young Kenyan waitresses work the patio crowded with expats. Zora looks for Tariq.

"Pretty mamas," Senoja, croons, "whadaya havin'?"

"Your phone? To call home."

He unclips it from his belt. Leaning too close, he reminds her of the access code. After four rings, she hears Bert mumble "This better be good."

"B, it's me."

"Zora? Zora! You're alive!"

"Of course! I'm fine."

"I have just about worried myself insane." Bert's voice seems to reach over a vast chasm carved between six time zones. It takes a moment to understand what she is saying.

"And just tell me everything."

"B, I can't talk much right now."

"Oh *please,* throw me a bone," Bert wheedles. "Any little factoid."

"In a few days, I'm bringing someone home. Can you straighten up the spare room?"

"You found—"

"A niece."

Bert gasps.

"I'll call you before we cross the big pond. Miss you. Love you. Don't worry. Gotta go." She presses the END button. The sudden disconnect feels a bit cruel, but there's too much to explain.

Beside her, Abuk is watching the musicians. Senoja returns with two drinks. "A Jack Daniels for the lady, a Fanta for the girl. See, I know how to treat you right."

"Yeah, you clean up good," Zora teases. Abuk echoes her words, bobbing with the reggae beat.

"This girl's ready to dance." Senoja grabs Abuk's hand. Leading her to the dance floor, he begins to gyrate. Abuk remains motionless, glancing at Zora in confusion. Zora shimmies her hips and noodles her arms through the air until Abuk begins her own tentative effort.

Tariq has not shown up. Zora downs her drink and goes looking for another. At the bar, she squeezes in next to a middle-aged guy with dark receding hair and weathered skin.

"Name's Ruggins," he says, extending his hand.

"Zora," she answers. His grip is firm and sandpapery. She orders a whiskey. "And what brings you to these parts?"

"Hungry women and children," he drawls with a Georgia twang. "I'm loadmaster on food delivery flights."

"Hard work."

"I like hard work," he says. "But some days we're as nervous as sinners in a cyclone. Tight spiral landings. Airstrips all shot to hell. Blowin' sand. Then we sometimes get trigger-happy militia on the ground." He downs a shot and grimaces. "But let me tell ya what really cuts me. The little kids, five, six years old, pickin' bits of spilled grain off the ground like biddy hens. I don't look at their faces no more. Hell, those folks don't like handouts any more than we like riskin' our butts to deliver 'em." His eyes, crystalline blue, drift past her. "I figure we oughta send in the Marines, let 'em take out the bastards causing all this sufferin'."

"Ruggins, you might have a plan," she concedes. "Think you need some R&R?"

"Just got back from three weeks home in Valdosta." He winks at her and orders another shot.

Tariq, still in his expat ensemble, appears beside her. Looping his arm through hers, he leads her to the dance floor. The musicians kick up the beat, goaded by high-flying Senoja. Animated by a righteous buzz, Zora lets the beat take her. Tariq circles, his motions fluid, his arms inviting her. Senoja crosses between them, embraces her tightly, plants a hard kiss on her cheek and spins away. She wipes it way, glancing at Tariq who's stifling a laugh.

Nearby, Abuk bounces high, ululating in shrill bursts. She waves her arms above her head, then whirls low. She howls, spinning like a wild dervish. Her skin gleams with sweat as she bounds in a widening circle, chanting, feral-eyed, her arms thrashing the air. Zora watches her banshee energy dominate the space around her. The drummer pours on a fury of thunder. The guitar wails to crescendo, trouncing three final chords. Abuk groans and folds to the ground.

In the sudden silence, the crowd stands gaping at the limp girl. Zora kneels beside her. "Baby, you're crying," she whispers, lifting her head. "Come, I'll take care of you." She helps Abuk stand and leads her back to their room. She hears the rise of voices, calling the band to play on. The drummer offers a rim shot; the musicians slip into "No Woman, No Cry."

In their room, Abuk slips docilely under the sheet on her bed. "I want to understand you," Zora says softly, kneeling beside her. Abuk averts her eyes. Wrapping her arms around her torso, she curls in fetal position. Slowly, the quiver of her body fades. Her drooping eyelids flutter shut. Zora turns off the light and props herself against the side of the bed. Clutching her knees to her chest, she silently petitions the God she doesn't believe in to allow Abuk at least this night of peace.

Soft rapping awakens Zora from a doze. She feels her way to the door. Outside, Tariq stands in the dim yellow glow of a small light mounted above the door. "Come with me," he whispers. She glances at the sleeping girl then closes the door and follows him along the walkway to his room. Inside, a candle flicks their shadows across the wall.

"I want to stay with you," she blurts. "But Abuk ... I don't know what happened with her." She drops onto an armless chair near the bed.

"I have never seen such a dance," he admits. "She was like...an oil fire." He rests on the edge of the bed, his elbows on his knees. The candle's glow teases over the fine curve of his cheek. "Abuk has survived terrible things. Perhaps she was casting out demons, in the way only her body knew."

"Maybe so. Maybe. But how do I help when I don't have the words?"

"Not everything can be done with words."

She fiddles with her necklace. "Tariq, why do I have to lose you?"

He rubs his face with his hands. "Because I was blinded by my past. All my life, I have moved between my father's Arab kingdom and my mother's Dinka village. I have felt a stranger in both, but it is my mother's spirit I embrace." He rises abruptly and begins to pace.

"Go on," she coaxes.

He folds his arms over his chest, drops them, fists his hands together. "My mother was forced to be a wife. She was but a slave. It desecrated her spirit. It destroyed her body."

He falls silent, sits, then stands again, paces. "She was a good woman. Her misery, her death should not go unanswered." The candlelight plays lovingly on his face. "My own revenge is mixed with the bigger solution." He takes a folded paper from a pocket inside his shirt. "For a long time, I have collected information from many sources. What is written here…," he breathes out a heavy sigh. "What is revealed here could help bring down the regime."

She looks at the floor. "Tariq, I don't—"

"You have seen the horrors inflicted on our people. Surely you can find a way to hobble the perpetrators. To bring justice." He holds the paper between them. "Please take it."

She hesitates, wondering if anything, no matter how damning, could penetrate the government's firewall of impunity.

"Take it," he urges. "Pease. Then I will not have risked everything in vain."

She wants to fling away every memory of their journey. She wants to run from the room. Instead, she takes the paper and slips it into her bra. He kneels beside her, caresses her cheek, his eyes bright with longing. She trembles as he traces the curves of her lips with his finger.

The door crashes open. Two men in desert fatigues and black *kufiyas* rush Tariq and fling him to the floor. Another man with a pistol grabs Zora's arm and shoves her into the corner. Tariq struggles as they tape his mouth, then slowly surrenders as they cinch his hands behind his back. Jerking him upright, they force a black bag over his head. The gunman points his weapon at Zora, watching her as he collects Tariq's satchel and case. "If you follow," he growls, "I will kill you." They wrestle Tariq into the night.

CHAPTER SIXTEEN

Low sobs awaken Abuk. In the dark, Zora stands near the window. Rising from her bed, Abuk goes to her, but Zora turns away to hide tears that wet her face. "Tariq," she whispers.

Abuk hurries to slip on a t-shirt and skirt. Taking Zora's hand, she leads her out. They pause outside Tariq's room. The door hangs open on metal hinges loosened from the wall. Zora will not enter so Abuk steps inside. A candle on the table has melted to a hard pool of wax. The cover on the bed is messy, like a badly dug field. A shirt on the floor looks like a stain. There is no other sign of Tariq.

Continuing down the veranda, she hears Senoja snoring. His door is half-open. She knocks and they enter. His heavy man-smell permeates the room. Dim light on his dark sleeping face renders him like a helpless boy. His large hands hold the little music device. He breathes out a sour smell. Abuk prods him but he burrows under a pillow. She turns to her auntie and points up. Unable to decipher the gesture, Zora grabs her hand. They hurry to the hotel office. At Zora's urging, the manager sends a boy to fetch the local *askari* from his home. She further presses the bewildered man to find someone who can explain to Abuk what has happened. He pads to a small room at the rear of the hotel office and rouses a Dinka maid from her bed. She comes to sit with them. Her sleepy translation of Zora's account of the kidnapping incident provokes horror on Abuk's face. Meanwhile, the boy returns with word that the police official has not taken kindly to the off-hours intrusion. He will receive Zora at the station at ten in the morning for a full report.

Outside in the unyielding darkness, Zora paces the patio, muttering about what do. She sits stiffly in a chair, legs drumming like pistons. Abuk mirrors her posture, her movements, as if studying their feel and effect. Zora closes her eyes to reconstruct the event, to pull out details.

Just after sunrise, Senoja shambles onto the patio, and Zora hurries to him. He listens without expression to her account of the incident. When she finishes, breathing open-mouthed like a tired runner, he slips on his sunglasses. "Ain't no *askari* in these parts gonna chase down a military-style raid. They'll figure he's long gone across the border and they don't mess with the Sudanese."

She gapes at him. "You're not gonna *do* anything?"

"Woman," he gripes "what do you think I *can* do? I got no authority here."

"But you have connections." She can't see his eyes behind the dark lenses, but the hard set of his jaw tells her that he is done with the conversation. "Listen" she presses. "I know you don't like Tariq. But he doesn't deserve to be dragged off by a bunch of thugs." She searches for a reaction, for words that might provoke a reaction. She rests her hand on his shoulder. "It matters to me what happens to him."

Senoja seems to consider then dismiss a thought. "Write a report. Tell the manager to give it to the police." He glances pointedly at his watch. "We got a flight to Nairobi in one hour."

"That's it?"

"Uh huh. Unless you wanna hang here and organize a posse. Ain't no one gonna sign on unless you wave boku bucks." He wrinkles his nose. "Count me out. I had enough of this shit. I ain't dealin' with police. Not here."

Abuk appears at her side, anxiety etched on her face. They watch him walk away. Zora stares down at their shadows, fumbling for pieces of a plan. *Contact the embassy? Which one? The UN? What agency? A government ministry? Who would admit jurisdiction? Would she report a kidnapping? Claim detention of a political prisoner?*

It becomes clear that precious little can be accomplished from this outpost. She will have to take Abuk to safety in Nairobi and work channels there. It's an option with poor odds. She curses and tramps back to her room, shadowed by silent, stoic Abuk.

Flouncing on the chair, she pulls out a notebook and details the incident in neat block-lettered words. *No goddamn bureaucrat is gonna ignore this report as illegible.* She sends Abuk with the folded paper to the manager.

Alone in the room, she begins punching clothing into her duffel. "What is *wrong* with these fuckin' people?" she rages, drilling a handful of underwear into a side pocket. "What kind of assholes go around tearing up lives?" As she strips off her bra, the folded paper from Tariq drops to the floor. She stares at the white scrap on the brown rug, incredulous that she's forgotten what he'd entrusted to her. She bends and fingers the sweat-softened paper.

"Go?" Abuk has returned and lurks at the door.

Straightening, Zora pulls on a fresh shirt and tucks the paper into an inside pocket. Abuk takes a tentative step toward her. Zora reaches for a small bag and holds it between them, pointing at Abuk and then herself. "We go." Abuk says nothing but the tension in her face ebbs. She folds her few items of clothing into the bag. Zora is grateful that the girl is not practiced in hiding her feelings.

Senoja blusters in waving a paper. "Got the manager to copy your report. Just in case." He appraises Abuk. "I see you ready to go, girl."

They drive through a dusty neighborhood. Women are coaxing smoky fires to life beside squat shanties. Children in dirty clothes hover nearby, rubbing sleep from their eyes. Men wash their faces over buckets on the ground. The routines of living, the comforts they convey, seem no longer to exist for Zora. Life has tumbled into a black hole of uncertainty.

At a weathered shed beside the airport entrance, an indifferent customs official stamps their travel documents. Senoja grins as they walk onto the tarmac. "I was countin' on him not lookin' close at the girl's paper."

"Why?" Zora asks, peeved that he's taken a risk, again, without so much as a heads-up to her.

"It's got irregularities. Won't hold up in the big league. Anyway, we got to buy a passport in Nairobi."

A fraudulent passport. What else could she expect? "How long will it take?"

"Coupla days, maybe longer." He hefts their bags into the cargo hold.

As the plane taxies, Zora surveys the blighted landscape, realizing there will be no search for Tariq, no suspects, no information. If he is still alive, he will be in a prison or disappeared into one of Sudan's ghost houses. She takes Tariq's paper from her pocket and carefully unfolds it. The hand-drawn chart is crowded with Arabic script that she cannot read.

—

In Nairobi, they arrive at the lodging Senoja has arranged. Zora locks herself in a bedroom and sleeps through the day. In the early evening, she shuffles into the sitting room where Abuk and Senoja turn in unison from the TV with annoyed expressions.

"I left you in a lurch," she admits.

"Damn right you did," Senoja huffs. He throws a handful of Dots in his mouth. "You look like hell."

"Thanks."

"Food in the kitchen," he points.

"Not hungry." She slouches on the sofa next to Abuk, feeling Senoja's eyes on her. "You got something to say to me?"

"Hell yeah! If you wanna get home anytime soon—I sure as shit do —then this ain't no time for you to be droppin' out."

"Well, damn if I didn't just lose someone I love."

He flinches. "Ain't nothin' we can do about Tariq." He finishes off a bottle of Tuskers.

"I'm not gonna let it go."

"Fine, you hold on tight." He looks at Abuk. "Just remember you got this here girl to think about. I ain't no babysitter. I got problems to solve."

Angry that he's right, she wants to punch the crap out of him. Instead, she trains her attention on Abuk, who is mesmerized by a Clint Eastwood movie on TV. The collision of her life with Abuk's means she's got to be much more than a minder. Instead of this graceless, selfish luffing, she needs to tack with the prevailing wind.

"Okay," she says, glancing at Senoja. "What are we up against? Lay it out for me."

"I'm seein' only one good option. The girl gets a custom-made passport." He opens another bottle of beer. "With a Sudanese passport, we're talkin' sudden death at U.S. Customs. And a U.S. passport's too hard to forge. So, I got a guy working on a Kenyan passport and travel visa." He leans forward in his chair, "Plan B is gonna be your assignment. You gonna take our girl to the UN and see what refugee-type papers they can pony up. Long odds, but it'd clean up our arrival in DC." He gulps some beer. "Plan C, we put her on a cargo flight."

Zora groans. "As *cargo*? A stowaway?"

"It's Plan C for good reason."

Abuk is silently mouthing dialogue from the movie. Zora touches her hand. She half-turns, eyes unable to leave the screen. "Do you feel lucky?" she rasps, expertly achieving Eastwood's inflection. Senoja chuckles but Zora catches a glimmer of fear in her eyes. Grabbing the remote, she shuts off the TV. "Abuk, sleep." She folds her hands against her face.

"Sleep. Okay." Abuk seems to fling aside the business of TV viewing like a used tissue. Wrapping a thin blanket around herself, she nestles beside Zora.

A night on the couch is not what Zora had intended. There are perfectly comfortable beds just down the hallway, but Abuk's seamless divorce from wakefulness invites inertia. The choice of sofa or bed is probably of little consequence when her reference point is a grass mat in the dirt. She cushions Abuk's head with a small pillow, murmurs, "You're safe."

"Girl's a handful," Senoja observes. He hefts himself out of the chair. "We gotta be out the door by eight a.m." He flips a last Dot into his mouth. "If you wanna hang with me later...." He cocks his head, his eyebrow raised suggestively, then moves off to his room.

Zora is relieved he knows when to quit. She shifts to a semi-supine position, propping her feet on a small table. Abuk has fallen asleep with the ease of a tired toddler on a road trip. Zora drapes her arm over the girl's back, content with the gentle rise and fall of her breathing. The house is quiet. Far off, a dog barks. The scent of jasmine wafts through a jalousie window.

She can think clearly now about finding Tariq. So many questions arise. *Does his influential father know what has happened? Should she contact him? How can she find his full name? The Sudanese custom of triple names means the search could lead her down many potentially dangerous paths. The men who'd kidnapped Tariq possibly know who she is. Or perhaps they've written her off as Tariq's inconsequential dalliance. But, if she shows up on the diplomatic radar searching for Tariq's father, that could provoke suspicion about what she knows. It would be too risky. Can Kenyan officials help? Would a trip to the U.S. Embassy be helpful? Or even wise?*

Abuk suddenly writhes and calls out. Zora soothes her cheek until the dream demons retreat.

In the early morning, Zora and Abuk sit together in the back seat of an SUV on Chiromo Road as the rivers of pedestrians and *matatus* stream toward Nairobi's center. Senoja drives with a tight grip on the wheel. "Your business is gonna take time," he says. "I got people to see. Don't leave till I come back for you." He shoots a warning look. "For real. I *mean* it."

They arrive at the compound of the United Nations High Commissioner for Refugees. Ten-foot-high cinderblock walls topped with razor wire girdle the grim three-story building that looks like a prison. It's a troubling façade for a custodian of uprooted people seeking safe resettlement. They wait at the security gate while a guard copies their identification details. Inside, a queue of people snakes around the lobby. They take their place behind a tall young man. Turning to them, he flashes a look of recognition and greets Abuk in Dinka. Abuk responds with a tumble of words and gestures. The man nods, interjecting a question. He extends his hand to Zora. "My name is John Kennedy Eboul."

"Zora Monro. Pleased to meet you."

"Abuk tells me you take her to America. This wonderful fate!" His smile reveals large, crooked teeth. "She also wants to know why you not find Tariq and bring him."

The reminder of Tariq's absence feels almost as bad as having no explanation. She knows a lie will be cruel. "I do not know *how* to find him," she admits. "And no one will help me."

John Kennedy frowns sympathetically and translates. Abuk leans against Zora.

"I am true sorry," John Kennedy says. "This thing happen in my family. Also many friends."

"Then I am sorry for you as well," Zora offers. "Please tell Abuk I will find ways to look for him." The translation brings a flicker of skepticism to Abuk's face.

They stand together in silence like mourners at a funeral. The queue shuffles ahead. Zora gently grasps Abuk's hand. "John Kennedy, could you please tell Abuk that we are here to get documents for her travel."

He regards her with solemn eyes. "I am wait for two years. It is, how you say, 'long chance'?"

"A long shot." She sighs, "We have to try."

As he speaks to Abuk, her stoicism yields to a single raised eyebrow. Zora wonders what it will take to give the child a reason to smile.

Abuk glances from John Kennedy to Zora and speaks again. "She says," John Kennedy translates, "That your face lines deepen the way her grandfather's do when he is thinking about a hard problem. She knew he would protect her. They would be safe together."

Zora imagines that Abuk sees all the ways her "auntie" is not a Dinka. *Her skin is the color of wet sand, not their beautiful dark color. She is tall like them, but her hair is too straight. She doesn't know their language, or how to cook on a fire.*

"John Kennedy," Zora says." Please tell her I will do everything I can to keep her safe."

Hearing the words from him, Abuk nods but still sadness settles in her eyes.

When his turn comes, John Kennedy shakes their hands and wishes them luck. With a frown, Abuk watches him disappear. Soon, a short dark-haired white woman comes to them.

"You are Zora Monro with…" she consults a clipboard, "Abuk Kiir?"

Zora nods. "Thank you for seeing us."

"I am Helene Darcq. Please come with me." They follow her into a bright office that reeks of cigarette smoke. The woman sits behind a desk laden with files, gesturing to two chairs against the wall. "How can I help you?"

"I am American and Abuk is Sudanese, but we are blood relatives. We need documents that will allow her to travel with me to the United States."

Darcq sits back in her chair. "Refugee resettlement is a complex and lengthy process." She lights a cigarette and exhales a billow of smoke. "Tell me your situation."

Zora details the events that brought Abuk into her care. The woman listens with an expression that suggests she's heard many stories like this but is intrigued by the particulars. "How exactly are you related?" she interjects.

"Abuk is my niece."

"Her age?"

"Thirteen, I think."

Darcq stubs out her cigarette and lights another. "From what you have told me, I believe we could make a case for the need to resettle her." She jots a note in a folder. "Let me explain the procedure. Our staff meets weekly to review new cases. We refer a qualified applicant to the U.S. Embassy. The Embassy in turn refers them to the Joint Voluntary Agency. The JVA prepares the necessary documents in coordination with a U.S.-based resettlement agency. This requires a passport, a medical examination, a security check, a birth certificate, and affidavits from other relatives."

"I'm guessing that could take weeks," Zora says.

"Months to years, actually." Darcq takes a long drag on her cigarette. "Our rate of acceptance by the US embassy is about one percent. The fact that Abuk is a minor complicates everything."

"It could be more complicated?"

"You are not immediate family." Darcq ashes her cigarette with a delicate flick of her ringed finger. "Does Abuk have a birth certificate?"

"I don't think she's ever had any piece of paper with her name on it."

Darcq massages her chin. "You have a difficult situation. I'm amazed you got this far."

"I don't have the resources to wait indefinitely. What do you recommend we do?"

Darcq folds her hands on her desk. "I cannot tell you what to do. If you wish, I will initiate the process of her application for resettlement. Any other option is, frankly, beyond my purview." She fingers her lighter, revolves it in her hand. "The way you survive this process is by not minding the wait."

Zora gathers her bag. "If it were you, would you 'not mind'?"

Darcq lights another cigarette. "If I could, I would relocate this girl today."

Clasping Abuk's hand, Zora rises. "Thank you for your time. It's been enlightening."

Darcq nods. "Shall I put Abuk's case for review?"

"Couldn't hurt."

"Good luck." She places the new file on one of the stacks that crowd her desktop.

—

Two days drone by. The passport counterfeiter cannot be hurried. Zora makes trips to the American Embassy and the Kenyan Police Headquarters to file reports about Tariq. The American official points out that the US government has no diplomatic channels through which to pursue the matter. A Kenyan police clerk gives Zora's report a cursory review. He informs her that the entire missing persons unit has gone off to a colleague's funeral. After thumping the report with blue-inked rubber stamp, he says with perfunctory courtesy that they will contact her if there is any news. Zora drafts a list of people in DC she can prevail upon to make inquiries. She phones Ahmed, who'd connected her with Tariq, hoping he might know how to contact Tariq's relatives. Ahmed's voice message informs her that he's traveling and will not be returning calls until the end of the week. She leaves a message for Mookie, intentionally mysterious, about needing inquiries made. Mook's curiosity will compel her to call back.

Under Senoja's watchful eye, she and Abuk kill time wandering the city center. On Kenyatta Avenue, they rummage through racks of used clothing, selecting flowered skirts for Abuk. Smiling market women accost them with Maasai dolls and soapstone trinkets. "Make my day!" invites a young man as he riffles a sheaf of brightly colored scarves dangling from his arm. He bobs around them, flourishing a gauzy red one. A grizzled man kneels in front of Zora, trying to polish her sandals. She bribes him away with a few shillings.

At an Internet shop off the main square, Zora composes an email to Bert informing her of their impending arrival. She avoids details, finding it impossible to relate all the bizarre events of the journey. Abuk watches every keystroke as if snatching mental snapshots for analysis.

Unfettered by traffic signals, cars and buses roar past, trailing billows of acrid exhaust over begging children at the curb. The equatorial sun washes hot over the tawdry spectacle. Across a wide plaza flecked with piles of human feces, stands a large museum, its columned façade stained by soot. Hoping for a bit of relief from the tumult of the streets, she maneuvers them through street vendors to the entry. The cavernous, musty space is empty except for a security guard. They walk among the displays, discovering opulent silver jewelry arrayed in a smudged glass case. Abuk presses her face against the side, studying a tarnished bracelet as wide as her neck. Dusty ceremonial masks peer from the walls like discouraged observers. A collage of mysterious icons dominates one wall; another is crowded with vivid paintings of fabulous creatures, a mythical zoo. A legacy of vibrant artistry seems to languish here, ignored by a citizenry preoccupied with survival.

That night, as they watch BBC news over plates of Indian take-out, Zora tells Senoja about the experience at UNHCR.

"Then it's all about the passport," he grouses. "Officials at Kenyatta Airport are gonna know by lookin' at the girl that she ain't no Kenyan. But she's *leavin'* the country, and I'm bettin' they won't care as long as the papers *look* right."

"What are the chances they'll look right?"

"Decent," he says, massaging a bottle of Tuskers. "A few months ago, a dust-up about kickbacks chased out all the amateur passport forgers. My guy should be able to deliver good papers."

"So, the problem is?"

"U.S. Customs." His mouth is full of rice. He chews and swallows like a trucker in a hurry. "Since 9/11, they be hard ass. I don't wanna go down for child smugglin' or fraud." He swigs his beer. "I gotta make sure they get exactly what they want."

On the morning of the third day of waiting, Abuk primps for another excursion as Zora searches the phone book, jotting down numbers of private investigators. They hear a honk at the compound's gate. From a window, they see the guard admit the Land Rover. As it speeds up the driveway, Senoja waves a passport from the window. The vehicle skids to a halt at the front door. They hurry to meet him as he jumps out, displaying a set of tickets. "We leave tomorrow night," he announces proudly.

Zora throws her arms around him, squealing in relief. He tries to hold on as she pulls away.

"What say we celebrate?" he coaxes. "A little road trip to Lake Naivasha. Have a nice meal. Check out the hippos."

Unnerved by his breezy swing from covetous to casual, she hesitates, shakes it off. "Abuk probably would like a day trip," she allows. "Better than hangin' around here."

Zora sees that Abuk is watching them with a confused expression. Zora has never hugged or even touched Senoja on purpose. Possibly Abuk thinks Senoja has replaced Tariq in her auntie's affections. She will do nothing more to support that notion.

The road north of Nairobi traverses a ridge with astonishing views of the misty Rift Valley. The day is a gift of warm sun and mild breezes. Buoyed by Zora's attentiveness, Abuk plays a game of point-and-name: "market" where "trucks" bring "pineapples," "women" in *kangas*, a "bus" full of "children," a "trader" selling "sheep skins." Senoja loads a CD and cranks up the volume. As they cruise past vast fields of roses, he cajoles them into a sing-along of "Respect," with Abuk trying to remember the letters of what Zora thinks is probably the first word she's ever learned to spell.

In late morning, they turn up a shaded drive that leads to an elegant colonial-era lodge. Rainbow-hued starlings flit among flowering shrubs near the arched stone entrance. The mahogany-paneled lobby whispers of old wealth. A grey-haired Kenyan man in a white service jacket offers a deferential greeting and escorts them to a table on the manicured lawn. They sit in the dappled shade of an enormous ancient neem tree. Abuk fingers the white table linen and a large China plate with a tentative smile.

They idle over drinks, watching royal ibises promenade on the grass. A large one hovers nearby, displaying spectacular pearly plumage. Wheeling, it soars majestically into the clear sky. Zora imagines her worries flying away on its extravagant, black-tipped wings. In dreams, she has flown like this bird on invisible currents, her muscles relishing the triumph over gravity. The ibis hovers again, its wings gloriously translucent in the sunlight. Then it lands in a frantic flutter of body parts, ungainly beyond belief. She thinks it is another cruel witticism of nature. Perhaps an omen. She looks away. "Let's eat," she says.

"Let's eat," Abuk echoes.

The buffet offers an excess of European delights: prime rib, rack of lamb, roasted chicken, scalloped potatoes, assorted roasted vegetables, green beans with slivered almonds, pasta Alfredo, a tray of puff pastries and miniature fruit tarts. It's almost too much for Zora, the collision of abundance with the scarcity she has witnessed in her homeland.

Abuk loads her plate, dallying to investigate the source of heat under a silver chafing dish. Senoja hums tunelessly as they return to the table. He makes a flourish of arranging Zora's chair as she sits. "Nothin' like a fine meal with a beautiful woman."

Zora glances at him, wary. "What's on your mind?"

"You and me, girl," he answers pulling his chair to the table.

Hoping to deflect the overture, she says nothing.

He waves a fork over his plate, selecting a first bite. "When I'm workin', I don't mix in personal feelings so I can focus on the job."

Zora looks at her plate and decides he has been rehearsing.

"Now I can speak my mind," he declares, trying to meet her eyes as he chews a mouthful of prime rib. "When we get back in the world, I think we could have a thing together." He swallows and licks his lips.

"A thing?"

"Don't be messin' with me," he counters, the bravado gone from his tone. Abuk stops eating to watch them.

"Senoja," she says, "I appreciate how resourceful you've been—"

"Don't care 'bout appreciation." He stabs a chunk of potato with his fork. "Unless that's what you need to hook up with me."

Knowing she faces another day of travel with him, she carefully composes her reply. "Senoja, you have a lot going for you. But we're too different. I don't see that kind of thing with you."

He sets his fork across his plate, his face an ugly mask of defiance. "So, you the house nigger, and I be the field nigger—and they don't mix?"

"Nigger?" Abuk asks.

"Girl, shut up," he snarls at her.

"Don't talk to her like that." Zora throws her napkin beside her plate. "I don't feel the way you do. Not about us and not about your slurs." She slaps her hand on the table, trembling China. "Especially in front of this child. You gonna tell her what that word means?" She leans toward him. "Don't even think of puttin' me in a corner because you can't have what you want." Pushing back the chair, she rises. "When you're done eating, I'll be in the lounge."

Spooked by her sudden movement, the ibis lifts into the air. Starlings scatter as she strides across the lawn. In the lobby, a party of African Americans dressed in safari apparel is arriving for brunch. These days, blacks didn't have to be members of the service staff to enjoy this retreat. Senoja's dig has jarred her like a shovel striking rock, forcing her back into a world of ugly skirmishes in black and blacker. She wanders along a wide carpeted hallway. The walls are lined with framed photographs of the lodge's famous visitors, mostly white Europeans. She feels a sudden fury at the seemingly endless predations on ordinary Africans, first by foreigners, then by their own greedy and soulless leaders. Soon she gets to go home to steep in the American brand of racism. The trip has exhausted her soul. She sits in a large leather chair and closes her eyes.

Abuk and Senoja stroll into the lounge. "Like pullin' teeth," he quips as they draw near to Zora, "gettin' this girl away from the table." When Zora does not respond, he shifts on his feet. "Listen, I'm no good at this. I—"

"Please, let's drop it." She studies the two of them standing before her like mismatched bookends.

Senoja nods. His expression says he is discouraged but not finished. "I told the girl that 'nigger' is a fucked-up thing to say." He wipes his forehead with the back of his hand. "What say we check out the hippos?"

He is so raw Zora can only roll her eyes. She will not be the wet blanket on an outing that seems to be energizing Abuk. Senoja is showing himself capable of sidelining, at least temporarily, his own agenda. And she probably will never again be within a few dozen feet of hippos in their natural habitat. "Lead on," she says.

They walk across a vast lawn to a spit of land with a dock. A lithe young man tells them he can, for a fee, take them in his small launch to a part of the lake where the hippos usually spend their time. With arms folded across her chest, Abuk refuses to step into the boat. No amount of wheedling or demonstrating the comfortable seating can entice her from where she's planted herself several feet behind the dock cleats. Zora imagines Abuk wants to tell them that flying through the sky in a metal machine has been test enough, and that floating on water must be left to animals born to it.

The three sit on a weathered bench at the end of the dock, each cocooned in longing for someone they cannot be with, watching the wind furrow the clouds, the golden sunlight dance over the rippling lake.

CHAPTER SEVENTEEN

Their silence endures for most of the ride back to Nairobi. Abuk sleeps sprawled on the back seat. After a stop in Westlands for Chinese takeout, they sit to eat under a flame tree in their compound. Zora picks at an egg roll while Senoja and Abuk gobble spicy chicken. Between mouthfuls, Abuk glances pointedly at her. Zora imagines Abuk is trying to figure her out. Why does she argue with Senoja? Doesn't she know that men always have the last word, even when they are wrong. Does she even like Senoja anymore? Oh! Of course! She is worried about Tariq and wants to be with *him* again.

After they eat, Zora fills a white tub with warm water and lets Abuk sit it in for a while. She gives her girl more of the oily medicine that makes her face pucker. The pain seems less. The bad smell has receded. *It's a relief that she's feeling better before they fly.*

In their room, Zora carefully lays out each of Abuk's new skirts and blouses on the bed, watching astonishment grow in her eyes. Choosing the purple skirt and pink blouse, Abuk hurriedly slips them on her thin body as if they will vanish if not captured in this way. She turns to present herself.

"You look beautiful. *Dheng*," Zora says, dazzled by the play of bright fabric against her glowing dark skin. She opens the closet door, revealing a full-length mirror. Wary, Abuk steps in front of it. Her eyes widen. She touches the glass, stares at her reflection, looks away and then back at her image. She stretches her arms, laughing when her hands disappear, brings them back into view, turns sideways, examines herself, turns away and looks over her shoulder, grinning at her backside. She continues this ritual through a crimson and turquoise ensemble, an emerald wrap skirt with a long-sleeved yellow blouse, and a plaid dress with frilly white collar. As she poses in the last outfit, a giggle bubbles up. Senoja comes in with a pouty expression.

"We're doing girl stuff here," Zora tells him, suddenly caught up in Abuk's infectious giggling.

"Girl stuff," Abuk affirms. She drops on the bed beside Zora, claps her hands and begins to ululate loudly. Zora attempts the high-pitched keening but cannot move her tongue to the right effect, sounding instead like a wounded turkey. He sighs and backs out of the room, closing the door. They sprawl backward on the bed laughing until their energy sputters out. The TV in the other room blares louder than usual.

"Tomorrow we fly," Zora says. She glides her hand through the air.

"We fly," Abuk repeats.

"To my house."

 "My house?"

"Yes, a good house."

"Tariq?"

Zora shakes her head. She pats the pillow to signal sleep. Abuk obediently rests her head, serene. *It's a good thing that they laughed, though she didn't know what was funny. Maybe it had just been too long, and she needed to remember how redemptive it felt.*

Dogs bark and howl in the night but no evil phantoms disrupt their sleep.

Mid-morning, they dawdle over breakfast. Zora calls the Kenyan Police to learn that they have not initiated an investigation, but the case is "in the queue." She makes a few calls to leave voice mails for Bert and Mookie and Ahmed, who'd helped lead her into this quagmire. She sits with Abuk in the sunny garden, making a list of what she'll need to do in Washington to find Tariq. Then a second list of what's needed to get Abuk settled in. The cataloging of "to dos," once a mundane routine, crosses into surrealism. The details will determine the survival of two human beings. It feels like a higher calling.

Finally, as rush-hour traffic begins jamming the main roads, they drive to the airport. Gazing out the side window, Zora's relieved that the dreary uncertainties of this place will no longer assail her. They pass near the café where she'd met Tariq. It seems long ago, that strange, heady day when her life had been upended by his dangerous passion. She checks a second time that the spy cam and recorder are packed in her carry-on. She has not viewed any of the footage from the trip but intuits something there will be valuable to what she must do in DC.

A crowd presses around the entrance to JKIA international terminal. Zora grips Abuk's arm as they are jostled through half-open glass doors. A scowling security guard scrutinizes their tickets and waves them into a queue. Senoja's tailored gray business suit furnishes his bulk with executive authority. They've carefully rehearsed his plan, but Zora feels sweat rising beneath her blouse. Abuk stands quietly between them, an icon of innocence in her plaid dress. She watches the scene, her face intent.

At the ticket counter, a stout woman agent with close-cropped hair and eyes that seemed resigned to some bitter truth, receives them with the air of a magistrate. With an unnecessary flourish, Senoja presents their tickets and passports. The agent casts an appraising glance at Abuk. "This Sudanese girl has a Kenyan passport," she says. "Please explain the circumstances."

"She is going to visit her grandmother in Washington," Senoja answers.

"That is her *reason* for travel," the woman counters, "but how was she recently issued these travel documents?"

Senoja smiles. "I assure you that —"

"Madame," Zora cuts in, "her situation is complicated. She was a refugee in Loki." She pauses to cobble together facts and plausible fictions. Senoja kicks her foot.

"Go on," the agent prompts.

"Abuk's grandmother was resettled in the United States," she lies. "I am her aunt. Mr. Senoja and I have been working for months to reunite her with her grandmother. When we received word that Abuk was ill, we traveled to Loki to see about her care." She leans forward to speak in a confidential tone. "The girl was badly circumcised. She almost died from an infection."

The woman nods with a grave expression.

Zora presents the note the doctor had given her. "A Dr. Kamau saw to her care —"

"Dr. *Josephine* Kamau?" the agent asks.

"Yes. Do you know her?"

"She is my mother's cousin."

Zora smiles with unfeigned surprise. "Dr. Kamau saved Abuk's life."

"She is a great healer," the agent affirms.

"And trained at Johns Hopkins." She hopes this gleaned fact fuels her credibility. "Dr. Kamau referred Abuk for care in the United States. An official at the Ministry understood the urgency of the situation and approved Abuk's passport."

Senoja kicks her foot again.

"Eat," Abuk whispers. Zora circles an arm around her shoulders. "Soon, baby."

The agent again appraises them. "I do not know if all your story is true," she says, pausing for an interminable moment. "It is, however, a *good* story." She sighs. "It seems we both have enough difficulty in our days." She processes the tickets and returns their documents. "Good luck, Miss Monro."

"Thank you." She kicks Senoja's foot and smiles at the agent. "You've been very helpful." They gather their carry-ons and walk to the customs desk at the entrance to the departure hall to fill out the yellow exit forms.

"Now," Zora says, squaring her shoulders, "let's see about some food for this growing child." She buys Abuk a fruit salad and sits with her near a TV monitor, ignoring Senoja's forbidding silence. After a lengthy boarding process, after they're settled in their seats, Senoja turns on Zora with venom in his voice. "Never, *ever*, volunteer information to an official."

"You gonna rag me about how I saved our asses?"

"You got lucky."

"You just like raggin' me," she counters. "How about a drink to help you chill?"

"Listen up," he orders. "U.S. Customs don't know one African from another, so that cozy story won't buy you shit. At Dulles, let me do the talkin'. You *got* that?"

Abuk, sitting between then, chucks him under the chin. "You…Okay?" Zora has not seen her behave with such familiarity. Disarmed, Senoja surrenders a sheepish smile. "Yeah, nothin' to it."

"Nothin' to it," Abuk agrees.

Zora notices Abuk seems more at ease in the big cabin, as if its size insulates her from the sensory assault of smaller aircraft. During the overnight flight, she eats everything brought to her tray table. Fingering the empty plastic containers and packets for the last bits, she hides them in the seat pocket. When Zora presents her with headphones and powers on the screen, Abuk raptly watches a Flintstones movie. Then she fiddles with an aircraft safety information pamphlet and leafs through an in-flight magazine she cannot read. A trip to the lavatory produces her usual wide-eyed reaction to unfamiliar technology. Zora gently nudges her inside and motions for her to sit, with the usual mantra, "It's okay."

After several hours of amusements, Abuk wraps herself in a blanket and quickly drops off to sleep. Zora studies her face. In just the short time they've been together, she'd gained a bit of heft, fueled by a boundless appetite. The girl's curiosity, her inclination to lean into new experiences, are marvels to witness. The coming adjustments will not be easy, but their bond is beginning to feel like a kind of sustenance.

Zora reaches into her purse for Tariq's paper. Simply touching it triggers an upwelling of longing. She leaves it in place, knowing that its secrets require a trustworthy translator. That would not be Senoja.

The flight path takes them over the Sahara Desert, a void where points of light, dim and vastly separated, signal miracles of human habitation, or, perhaps, activities that can only occur in such isolation. For a moment, Zora wishes to disappear into that oblivion. She's exhausted from every new thing this journey has delivered.

As the rising sun struggles against the grey sky above London, Zora awakens from a fitful doze. The aircraft touches down hard and taxis for what seems like miles before parking at a jetway. While passengers wrestle luggage out of overhead bins, Abuk gathers the small collection of food service items into her bag. They stand waiting as a woman in the front row blocks the aisle with her two children, one of them shrieking, the other whimpering.

Abuk watches the scene with disapproving eyes. She wrinkles her nose at the smell of a fart released nearby. "We go," she says loudly. A few passengers turn to stare at her. "We go," she insists.

Zora puts a hand on her cheek and turns her face so they are nose to nose. "We wait," she says. "Soon we go." When the noisy children are finally carted off, they move quickly through the aisle followed by Senoja.

"No fly," Abuk declares in the jetway.

Zora cannot tell her they are in for another long flight. She hopes the three-hour layover at Heathrow will provide sufficient diversion to soften Abuk's irritability. Like lemmings, they trudge through a maze of beige corridors, arriving finally at a checkpoint to receive a perfunctory acceptance as transiting passengers.

When they enter the main hall, Abuk stops abruptly. Zora imagines the sight offers unknown wonders: hundreds of pale-skinned people wearing heavy shoes and carrying all sorts of bags over their shoulders. A loud voice garbled by the PA system provokes Abuk to cover her ears. Zora guides her into a place with pretty baskets and boxes. She gives a cheerful woman in a blue dress money for a box she tells Abuk contains "chocolates." They walk for a long time, stopping to look at silver jewelry in a box she can see through, and things Zora tells her are "books" piled on a table, and clothes on white bodies that are not alive.

At a place with thin red bands of light over the door, they eat a "pizza." After Abuk throws up in the room with toilets, they go back to sit by the big windows. Zora sees her smile watching the people outside breathing vapor in the cold air, throwing bags into the belly of what, to Abuk, must look like a painted metal bird. The girl inhales loudly to see the plane move away, and watches with rapt attention as another in the distance leaps from the ground and disappears into the low clouds, thundering.

Witnessing Abuk's wide-eyed, hawk-like, occasionally giggling, study of the new world around her makes Zora giddy. Relieved when Senoja wanders off in search of CDs, she sits with Abuk, enjoying the passing show until their flight is announced.

Plied with a bag of treats, Abuk surrenders with little fuss to another confinement. An in-flight movie keeps her occupied for the first couple of hours; then she begins to fidget. Zora roams with her around the cabin for a while. When she returned alone, Senoja rises brusquely to retrieve Abuk. He leads her back and orders her to sit down. She wrinkles her nose at him. After a brief standoff, she plops into her seat with a pout.

He glares at Zora. "Do something to keep her from prowlin' around makin' a scene. I'm gettin' a drink."

Zora can't decide if he is being condescending, protective, or just tired-grumpy, but his attitude disappoints her. Abuk squirms in her seat, clearly desperate for relief from what must feel like captivity. Zora opens her tray table and spreads open a coloring book she bought on impulse. Opening a box of crayons, she makes a show of choosing one. "Blue," she announces and sets about coloring the feathers of a large parrot.

As a young child, Zora had crayoned her way through many a lonely or sad time. When the coloring books had run out, she'd drawn her own crude creatures to color. The long-abandoned activity soothes her. She waits for Abuk's curiosity to kick in. Soon Abuk opens her tray table. Zora carefully tears out the page she is working on and passes the book over, setting the crayon box between them.

Abuk pages through the drawings of animals, settling finally on a monkey hanging from a tree. Pulling out a brown crayon, she curves her fingers around it and attempts to color the monkey. Her awkward grip suggests another piece of news: she has rarely, if ever, held a writing instrument. Gently, Zora adjusts her grasp, guiding a few strokes. Rather than resisting, Abuk continues slowly, glancing at Zora's inside-the-lines effort, frowning at her own.

"Do another," Zora says, turning the page.

Senoja returns and settles in his seat. "Coloring books?" he chuckles. Immersed in their activity, they ignore him. As they progress through the book, Zora names each color, each animal. She praises Abuk's skill as she rapidly advances from an elephant to zebras to a fabulously executed peacock. The Atlantic Ocean passes below as they fill the cramped space with a zoo of vivid pictures.

When the captain announces the final descent, the setting sun is struggling to make a place amid thickening clouds. Abuk methodically replaces the crayons in their box. As Zora gathers the finished pages from the seat pockets, her thoughts race ahead to the final official hurdle. Senoja awakens from a fitful doze. "Girl's gonna need a jacket," he grumbles.

"It's in my carry-on," she answers. "I hope you'll put on a happy face for customs."

"No worries, girlfriend," he says, adjusting his tie. "Just follow my lead and *don't* answer questions they don't ask."

"Yes, sir. Your show."

After a shuttle ride to the Dulles terminal, they are shunted into a cordoned maze with a long queue of arrivals. Senoja scans the customs stations. "Two brothers up there," he whispers. "We gonna make sure the line works us their way."

She stares at him. "What?"

"We gonna give a brother a chance to do right by his own." His wink tugs her back into the nervous embrace of American racial etiquette, back to the tacit assumption that color defines every interaction. Despite their different shades, she and Senoja will be seen as "black," or in correct parlance, as African American. But there will be no mistake that Abuk, the darkest of them, is a stranger, an African. Which tribe would accept her on this side of the Atlantic?

After a half-hour wait, Senoja presents their passports to a linebacker-sized inspector. They exchange the brother nod Senoja had counted on. The man scans his passport, inquiring on the purpose of his trip. "Business," Senoja answers.

He glances at Abuk, firmly gripping Zora's hand. "The minor is from Kenya?" he asks.

"That's right."

"You are her guardian?"

"She is," he answers, pointing at Zora.

He examines her passport and documents, then signals a supervisor. "This way please," the uniformed woman says, waving Zora and Abuk to follow her.

"We're traveling together," Senoja protests. "I am—"

"Wait over there," the inspector instructs, pointing to a seatless over-bright area. "If we need you, we'll call you."

Zora and Abuk enter a small white room furnished with a long metal table and two chairs. The inspector, a pudgy almond-brown woman with stylish weaves, regards Zora for a moment, then pages through Abuk's documents. "I see the young lady's Form I-94W and visa. And a notarized statement of guardianship. Do you have her return ticket?"

"That's required?" Zora keeps her voice even.

"For a non-immigrant, yes."

Zora silently curses Senoja for overlooking this detail. "This child has come here for medical treatment, so we are not certain of her departure date."

"I see." The woman again searches her face. Opening Zora's duffel, she paws through the clothing, runs her latex-gloved hands along the inside pockets, unzips the makeup bag and fingers it contents. Turning to Abuk's small suitcase, she gropes its contents, pauses, and withdraws a vial of oil. "What's this?"

"Castor bean oil. It's a traditional medicine to strengthen her system. The girl almost died from an infection."

The inspector uncaps the vial and takes a whiff. "Do you have a doctor's statement concerning this condition?"

"I have only her referral," Zora produces the note from Dr. Kamau.

The inspector claps her hands. "I know where I've seen you! You're that spokeswoman for Human, ahhh…."

"Human Rights Defenders. That's me."

"Haven't seen you on TV lately."

"I've been on leave, doing kind of a *Roots* journey."

The woman's expression warms. "I been wantin' to do that myself. Find out where my people came from, you know, before they were slaves."

"Some bad news there."

The woman looks surprised, "Like what?"

Senoja's warning about undue disclosure echoes loudly in her mind, but what she's started may produce a dignified way out. "My family in Africa has been almost destroyed by war and slavery."

The agent wrinkles her nose. "I've read about the HIV and the famines, and they always seem to be fightin', but I thought slavery was in the past."

Zora rests her hand on Abuk's shoulder. "This girl, my niece, was a slave."

The agent looks incredulous. Zora decides to press home. "Lots of brothers and sisters over there got *serious* problems. They need our help."

"I been wantin' to get my hands into something, you know, something big like that. Lotta people in my church would too." She hesitates. "Would you be willing, sometime soon, to tell me more?"

"Yeah, of course." Zora opens her purse for a business card. "Just phone or email me," She glances at the woman's name badge, "Agent Johnson."

"Call me Thelma." The woman receives the card with a slight bow. "I'll surely be in touch." She zips their bags shut. Gathering their documents from the table, she hands them to Zora. "Everything important seems to be in order."

To Zora's relief, the return ticket issue seems to have fallen away.

"I know you're doing the right thing." Thelma declares. "Welcome home. And lil' sister, welcome to the United States."

"She doesn't know much English yet. We're workin' on it."

Abuk echoes her last phrase. Thelma beams as if she has enabled a miracle.

As they leave the room, Senoja moves toward them. Zora nods and smiles, happy to have, once again, a victory to rub gently in his face. At the curb, he sweeps her and Abuk into a rough embrace. "Damn, girl, I thought we was busted."

She pushes from his grip. "Let's get outta here."

"Outta here?" asks Abuk.

"Baby, we're going home."

"Home…okay."

"Had one of my homies bring our ride," Senoja says, leading them along the crowded passenger pick-up area." He can't help but smile. To his vast relief, everything has fallen into place as planned.

With Senoja's friend Derrick at the wheel of a black SUV, they cruise onto the Dulles access road. In the back seat, Zora stamps her feet and hoots out the window. "Gotta score you high on this one," Senoja says over his shoulder. "What'd you say to that inspector?"

"I told the lookin'-for-the-meaning-of-life sister that we have to reach out to our people in Africa."

"No shit. Gotta remember that one."

"Dawg," she grazes his cheek with her fist, "I was *serious*."

He shrugs. She's accepted his way of breezily dispatching matters requiring moral discernment. His remark might be comical except for the undercurrent of calculated indifference. Soon she will be done with him, but there remains the unsolved mystery of his true mission. Since the mood is easy, she decides to probe for a chink in his armor. "I been meaning to ask: what's the deal with that dent in your head?"

He pitches back as if he were going to laugh. "Family souvenir. Got it the day my momma finally saw what a son-of-a-bitch drunk she married." He laughs harshly. "Sight to see! Momma dumpin' every drawer on the kitchen floor, screaming like a crack whore been ripped off. I was comin' in for a look-see when she got 'round to the dishes. Cleared the shelves with her bare arms. Pieces flying like shrapnel. Chunk caught me right there. Bled like a motha."

His casual tone surprises her. "I thought it was from prison or —"

"Combat?" He sniffs. "The joint, the army, my dad's crib, it don't matter. They all war zones—and I'm a survivor."

He punches up WHUR on the radio. "My man Snoop," he shouts as the base vibrates the windows. He picks out words, punching them with a throaty voice. Abuk joins his game. Zora bides time for another flanking maneuver.

Traffic jams up in Rosslyn as drivers jockey across lanes onto the Key Bridge. Though Christmas is weeks away, red ribbons wreath the bridge's antique light posts. In the early dusk, the murky Potomac glimmers with spikes of red and yellow light driven from the tiered buildings that line its bank. As they enter the Whitehurst freeway, the Kennedy Center comes into view like an icy white monolith. Abuk gapes at the sight. Easing against the headrest, Zora debates if Senoja's "business" matters. She wants ordinary time to flow again. Hot morning showers. A leisurely reading of *The Washington Post.* Regular meals with taste and texture.

The newest terrorist of her psyche, prickly guilt, rears up on its hind legs: she returns to comforts aplenty while the rest of the family in Sudan hangs on by their fingernails. There will be no reprieve from this knowledge. It will dog her, of this she is certain, until she finds a way to relieve their struggle.

Senoja pulls in front of Zora's building. Soft yellow light bathes the porch of her apartment. Potted, rust-colored mums nest on each side of the door. Bert's handiwork, no doubt. The black shutters and brick steps look opulent, foreign. She lets Abuk inside. Senoja dallies near the car, occupied with a task she cannot see. Finally, he marches up the steps and sets their bags inside the door.

She smiles at him. "We made it home."

"Like I said we would."

They stand side by side in awkward silence, watching a passerby in a hoodie stroll through a pool of streetlight.

"Thank you, Senoja."

He reaches for her hand. She avoids his grasp.

He shifts his weight. "Hell of a trip."

She faces him. "You said we'd all be safer out there if I didn't know what you were up to."

"Yeah." He stares into the sky.

"Well, we're home. Tell me now."

"Can't," he says, moving toward the steps. "It ain't played out." He moves quickly to the gate. "Hey," she calls, "What ain't played out?" He slides into the SUV and it peels off down the narrow street. Annoyed and bewildered, she goes inside and bolts the door. She'll pester him after jet lag subsides, when her anxious mind is clearer.

Abuk stands in the foyer surveying the living room. "Pretty?"

Bert has tidied up the place. *To her it feels unfamiliar, overwrought.*

"Eat," Abuk declares.

"Baby, you never let anything interfere with your appetite." She points. "Kitchen."

"Kitchen. Eat."

"Yes, baby."

A foil-wrapped pie has been left on the counter next to a stack of mail. A note in Bert's tight cursive proclaims *Welcome home!!!! Call me!!!!* Zora opens the fridge. It's stocked with juices and labeled Tupperware containers. She chooses fried chicken and mashed potatoes, and pops open the microwave. "Abuk, for cooking. Hot—no fire." Abuk nods, her eyes void of understanding.

"Microwave," Zora says.

"On TV?"

"Yeah, like on TV."

When Abuk sits down with a plate of steaming food, Zora wanders into the living room. On the coffee table is a vase of red roses with a white card impaled on a small plastic trident. It reads: *"Beautiful lady, welcome home. JS."* Jackson probably had heard from Senoja that they were headed back.

Their association troubles her as much as this fresh evidence that the congressman hasn't given up pursuing her. It has gotten undignified, like a smarmy private joke.

Abuk comes from the kitchen, wiping her mouth with the back of her hand. "Good," she says.

"Thank you," Zora says. She has already forgotten the Dinka word. There will be a confusion of courtesies for a while.

"Thank you," Abuk repeats.

"You're welcome. Come."

Abuk follows her down the hall. She switches on the light in the small pumpkin-hued room she's used as an office. The bed is covered with a fluffy russet comforter and too many accent pillows. Bert's hand, again. The room looks irrelevantly stylish. She glances at Abuk. "This is for sleep." She points at Abuk. "For you," and waves her forward. In mid-motion, she sees Abuk's puzzlement. The fit between girl and space is dubious at best. This can be remedied. She moves on to the bathroom, where towels have been rolled and stacked on the vanity, spa-retreat style. *Clearly Bert is reading too many decorator magazines.* Abuk inspects the space with frank amazement, gently touching everything. Sighing, Zora opens the door to her own room.

Bert knew better than to tidy up what she refers to as the "girl cave." The bed is unmade, the floor scattered with rejects from pre-trip packing, and books stacked on the floor beside the bed. Abuk walks in without hesitation and circuits the room, her eyes roving, pausing, roving again. Survey complete, she bounds down the hall and returns with her bag.

The phone rings. Zora leaves her to answer in the kitchen. "The lady is back!" Jackson exclaims. "How was the trip?"

She's in no mood for pleasantries. "Saw a lot of dying. Got revolution in my blood." She pauses. "I fell in love."

"Oh." He sounds disappointed.

"His name is Tariq Taha," she continues. "He's been detained in Sudan."

"Bad break."

"Jackson, I'm messed up over this" She imagines him with a snifter of brandy, his expensive tie loosened, custom-made shirt unbuttoned at the collar. He has never given any indication that his own junkets to Sudan rearranged his perspective, much less his soul. Maybe she's never asked the right questions. "Will you help me find him?"

He groans softly. "Girl, you know how to turn the knife."

"You and me been over for a long time."

He sniffs and says nothing.

"If you're still in my corner, help me." A niggling whisper in her logy mind argues for caution, but reckless, and knowing it, she decides to up the ante. "Tariq gave me some politically hot information. Need your take on how to handle it."

"So, I'm still good for something?" he pouts, insincere.

"It's information he was willing to die for."

"He told you this?" The slight upturn in his tone says his interest is self-serving.

"I can't say any more over the phone."

He is silent for too long. 'I got a morning hearing. I'll come after that."

She hangs up, alarmed by the nakedness of her need. She dials Ahmed's number, eager to learn his take on the kidnapping.

"My friend," he cries, "you have returned!"

"Yes, I—" She wants to be calm, but her voice catches. "Tariq was kidnapped. I want to find him."

"He was being held—"

"He's alive?" She waits through his awkward silence. "You've known what's been happening!"

"I knew of his intentions," Ahmed admits, "but I did not know he would actually… follow through."

She rolls her anger into a dagger. "What's happened to Tariq?"

"Zora," he says softly. "He was taken to Kober prison. Yesterday they moved him to an unknown location."

Unknown location. Official code for ghost house, the last address of the lost. She loses control, begins to cry.

"Zora, my friend," he soothes. "Please do not grieve. His case has drawn attention outside of Khartoum. That can be his salvation."

She gulps a breath. "Can I trust what you're telling me now?"

"Many of our people have been detained. We know what to do. We've already started to lobby for his release. I will email you the details."

"So, long odds."

He is silent for a moment. "You must come for Turkish coffee. We have much to discuss."

They arrange a time to meet; she hangs up, calming herself before padding down the hall. In her bedroom, every light is on. Abuk sleeps curled in the center of the bed. Beside her are the coloring book pictures of the monkey and the peacock. Zora puts then on the bedside table, covers the sleeping girl with a comforter and kisses her cheek. Her first goodnight kiss is an impulse as natural as her mother's must have been. Switching off all but one light, she sits at her desk. Waiting for her laptop to power up, she rests her eyes on a small photo of Ella in full chanteuse regalia, captured at a moment of singular rapture. The woman who'd raised her had known exactly what she was giving up for a shot at motherhood.

Taking Tariq's paper from her purse, she unfolds it. The script on the flimsy paper will not survive much more handling. She makes three copies, putting one with the original under a tray in the desk drawer and another under the corner edge of the carpet. The last copy she folds and slips into her jean pocket.

Google fills the screen with pop-up news and cutesy icons. She clicks into email. In between a Nigerian scam and a Xanax offer is a message with the subject line: "Concern over arbitrary arrest" forwarded by Ahmed. It's a press release from the Sudanese Organization Against Torture.

The Sudanese National Security Agency has launched a campaign to arrest opposition party members. The names of those arrested include... There in the list: *Tariq Taha.* For a few heartbeats, she can't focus, but the message does not fade. *According to the National Security Forces Act, the security forces can detain people incommunicado for up to nine months without judicial review.*

There's a link to sign a petition for release, a standard tactic of human rights activists. She does not believe the regime can be reasoned with. She covers her face with her hands.

CHAPTER EIGHTEEN

When the doorbell chimes, Zora bolts from bed, confused about where she is. Abuk cries out.

"It's okay, baby," she whispers. "It's okay." Still dressed in her travel clothes, she hurries to the living room.

Bert has let herself in. She's standing in the foyer, removing her gloves. "You're home! You didn't call! My Lord, Zora, you look like a bag of bones."

"Glad to see you, too," she says, reaching for a hug. "What time is it?"

"Almost noon. You're too thin," Bert embraces her fiercely. "Did you find the dinners I left? I'm so relieved you're back. I was worried, especially after I dug up the dirt on that Senoja fellow. He's—"

"A player from Baltimore."

"How'd you know?" She's disappointed that her disturbing tidbit is old news. Zora helps her out of her wool coat. Bert is dressed today in a green polyester dress with lace ruffles at the collar and cuffs. She smooths the sleeves and, with an air of distraction, pulls off her knit cap, frizzing her grey hair into a wild corona.

Abuk appears in the hallway, her plaid dress rumpled and askew.

Bert turns with a start. "Who's this?"

"Abuk Kiir, my niece."

Bert stares at the girl. "Yes. Quite a surprise." Bert musters a crooked smile and takes a step toward Abuk. "Hello, I am Aunt Bert."

Abuk regards her uncertainly.

"Come baby," Zora says, raking her fingers, the way she'd seen Abuk do it.

The girl steps forward, extending her hand to touch Bert's wild hair. Bert draws back.

"Interesting do," Zora allows. 'Static had its way with you."

Bert pats down her hair, dislodging a silver clip that falls to the floor. She and Abuk simultaneously bend to retrieve it, bumping heads. Bert draws back. Abuk picks up the clip, examining its contours with her long fingers as she straightens. Bert extends her hand. Abuk surrenders the clip with a wisp of a smile.

"And how long will you be visiting Washington?" Bert asks.

"Abuk will be living here now. She doesn't know much English yet." Zora ushers them toward the sofa.

"Oh? Oh really?" Bert sits uneasily beside the girl. How can you keep her? I mean, with your career and—"

"Bert, listen. I found her in a bombed-out village. We had a terrifying encounter with riflemen looking for slaves. If I'd left her there, she'd have been snatched. Or she'd be hiking several hundred miles to a refugee camp." She takes a deep breath, steadying herself though another blitz of disbelief over what she's done. "Her grandfather asked me to take care of her."

"Oh my," Bert murmurs, staring at her hands.

"We both knew it was the only choice, short of laying down to die."

Bert's eyes are blinking fast, as though she's flipping through a catalog, searching for a real thing to say. "It makes my head spin to think of bringing a child…is she legal?"

"We had the right documents to get her through customs." Zora watches Bert fiddle with her ruffles. The mood feels raw, as if they are strangers grappling with the aftermath of a violent, tree-downing storm.

Bert rises. "How about I fix some breakfast for you?" She hurries to the kitchen, seeking refuge. Setting a skillet on the burner, Bert opens the refrigerator for a carton of eggs.

Zora moves beside her. "Thanks for stocking the kitchen."

Bert nods. "There's no milk because I know you don't drink it. I didn't know about the girl."

"Not a problem." Zora watches her crack eggs into the pan. "I might as well give you the other big news."

With an apprehensive glance, Bert opens a bag of ground coffee.

"His name is Tariq Taha. He was my translator. I fell in love with him."

Bert drops a scoop of coffee short of the filter. "A Sudanese man?"

"Yes."

"And where is he now?"

"He was kidnapped before we left Kenya."

Bert sweeps up the spilled coffee with her hands, snaps the machine shut and stabs the BREW button. "Good Lord, Zora," she complains, her voice unnaturally high. "I didn't expect you would—"

"I would what?"

"You would bring home a child. Or take up with an African. Someone on the wrong side of the law, no less."

"He was *kidnapped!*" Zora cries, stung by Bert's resistance. The eggs spit. "*I'm* an African, just like them. Why wouldn't I *take up* with them?" She stares at the burning eggs. "Did you expect me to be your token black?"

Bert steps back. The words have wounded as surely as a slap in the face. "I'll go now," she says, hurrying from the kitchen. Zora follows her to the door, searching for words, finding none that fit her disappointment or her alarming need for her aunt's support. Bert stuffs her hair under the cap. "It's such a surprise." She lets herself out.

In the kitchen, Zora splays her hands on the counter, hunching over them. Abuk stands sad faced at the sink. "Aunt Bert...go. Sad?"

Zora shakes her head, relieved that Abuk is learning so quickly to string English words into a reasonable semblance of meaning. "Yes," she admits. She scrambles a new batch of eggs and pushes them onto a plate. Abuk wolfs them silently at the counter while Zora nurses a cup of coffee, angry that she cannot explain to herself, or to Abuk, what has just happened with Bert. When she's finished eating, Abuk wanders down the hall, silent, unknowable.

A knock sounds on the back door. As she pulls the curtain aside, Jackson's stern face appears. She lets him in.

"Girl, you look like hell. Turn on your TV."

"You're my second fun visitor this morning."

"I mean it," he says, brushing past her. "Turn on the TV."

Abuk rushes from the hall to grab the TV remote. Jackson inhales sharply, unsettled at the sight of her.

"She lives here now." Zora points to the "5" button on the remote. Abuk jabs it. The screen blooms with news graphics.

Jackson shakes his head, his face roiling with anxiety. "We got big trouble."

Zora watches the stories flow. "Three GIs and ten Afghans killed in Kandahar—nothing to do with us, right?"

"Zora, just button it." He's more panicky than she's ever seen him. They wait through a story on an outbreak of a new flu in Asia followed by piece chock-a-block with would-be candidates hoping to handshake their way into the White House. "Jackson," she says, "I've got something important to discuss—"

"Shhhh," he waves. "Here it is."

The box headline reads: *Return of Slavery.* "The Government of Sudan," the anchor announces, "has accused the U.S. of sponsoring slave trade in southern Sudan. Interior Minister Musa Ahmed Saef claims the scheme is intended to discredit Sudan's improving human rights record. Zora Monro, spokeswoman for Human Rights Defenders, is seen in this footage with an alleged slave, and Congressman Jackson Sykes, both African Americans, have been implicated in the slavery allegations." The grainy video shows Zora surrendering money to the *jellabiyah* during the raid on Abuk's village, then a shot of her standing on her front porch with Abuk, obviously taken the previous night. Abuk squeals when she recognizes their images on the screen.

"Sonofabitch," Zora hisses. "He was playin' me the whole trip."

Jackson's dour expression hardens. She narrows her eyes at him. "Congressman, what kinda crackheads you got workin' security clearances for you?"

"Woman, don't be crawlin' up my back," he counters. "You're the one brought back *evidence.*"

"She's my niece! You think that report has a speck of truth in it?"

"Doesn't matter if it's true. I gotta deal with public opinion."

"Oh, public opinion, the *massa* of at least one slave here."

Abuk watches them with undisguised discomfort, "Okay?"

"Yeah, baby." Zora sits beside her and watches Jackson pace the room. "They're tryin' to whip up, I don't know, a diversion."

"They?" Jackson challenges.

"You think Senoja's capable of doin' this on his own?"

He flips out his cell phone, hits speed-dial. "Time to track him down." He listens, closes his eyes hard. "Phone's disconnected."

To her surprise, she feels not anger but clawing curiosity. Despite his occasional dazzling ineptitude, Senoja has set and sprung a wicked snare. But who invented this scheme? What could they possibly have to gain? She heads to the kitchen. "Coffee?"

He stalks behind her and grabs her arm. "This is *serious,* and you actin' all down-homey."

"This is made-up shit," she retorts, eyeing his hand on her arm. "And I need some coffee to get me through jet lag."

He releases his grip. "This could hurt my career."

"That all you care about?"

"Both our careers."

She pushes a lungful of disgust through her lips. "Maybe you weren't payin' attention when you toured Sudan, but those people got way more pressing problems. Like surviving attacks by their own government."

Abuk edges though the door looking peevish.

"We neglected introductions," Zora says. "Jackson, meet Abuk, my niece. Abuk, this is Jackson."

He stares at her outstretched hand, shakes it weakly with a strained smile.

"She was driven from her home, mutilated, half-starved and *none* of that's unusual in her neighborhood. *That's* the story. You *know* that's the story."

With a long-suffering expression, Jackson leans against the wall.

"It's a genocide of black folks," she drills. "Where the hell are you and the Congressional Black Caucus on this?"

"Don't play self-righteous," he snaps. "What have you and your human rights buddies accomplished in the last two decades of this mess?"

In silence, she pours two mugs of coffee. She knows talking politics will only drive him away. That will not serve her more pressing need: high-level help with Tariq's release. That's all she wants from him.

"I've got," she says quietly, "an unusual document." She takes the paper from her pocket and unfolds it. "Tariq told me this information could take down the Khartoum regime."

He huffs. "So, now you're dabbling in regime change?"

She's surprised he's chosen to go on the offense. "No, I'll leave that enterprise to you and your policy buddies."

He purses his lips, "What do you want?" He's too good at seeming disinterested.

Unreasoning need rises naked from a memory of Tariq's smile, drowning a warning intuition. "A trade. This information for whatever magic it takes to get Tariq out of Sudan."

He nods, impassive. Taking the paper, he scans it. "You testing my Arabic?"

She shakes her head at his faux modesty. He is that rare creature: a multi-lingual politician. "When you get through translating, I'd like a copy."

As he reads, a subtle smile, like a facial tick, is quickly tamped down. "This your only copy?"

"No."

Folding the document, he slips it into his breast pocket. "I'll look into it." His tone is professionally neutral, and his eyes reveal nothing. With sudden certainty, she knows he has captured a prize, unexpected and undeserved. He will ignore her end of the deal. As he slips down the back stairs, agile as a cat burglar, fear fists in her chest. Giving him the document has been an irredeemable mistake.

"See!" Abuk calls. She is peering out the front window.

"What's going on?"

"Going on truck," Abuk replies, pointing across the street.

A TV satellite truck straddling two driveways is raising its transmission mast. "*Oh, Christ,*" Zora groans. Another truck arrives. "A stakeout." She snaps the blinds shut.

"Stake out?"

"Those people want you and me on TV."

"TV? Okay!"

"No, not okay." She gently pulls Abuk's arm. "Come."

Abuk follows her into the kitchen, her face tense with the battle of finding release for her questions. Zora has seen enough stakeouts to know why they're called "gang bangs," but cannot explain the unpleasantness to Abuk.

"Me…TV," Abuk insists, a fierce pout rising.

Jackson was right on one count: she looks like evidence, never mind the facts. Grandfather Luk insisted that this girl is "the one who knows the way." In her current post-trip fog, she, the adult, does not. Zora wonders if a brush with TV crews might add further credence to the accusation? Did this child's innocent eyes see a vindicating way forward? *Surely, nothing will be gained by hiding. They can't hide forever. And anyway, Abuk needs milk.*

"Okay, you and me," Zora points in turn, "on TV." Abuk grins, victorious.

While they change into fresh clothes, Zora mentally composes message points, crunching the facts into quick sound bites. She might even get a chance to say them. Slipping on their jackets, they step out into the brisk November day. Cameramen and reporters scurry toward the front gate. A young woman, elbowing for position, shoves a microphone toward Zora. "Ms. Monro, is this the slave you bought?"

Zora has seen this reporter, a recruit from a small Midwestern station. Her luscious blondeness almost compensates for her appalling cluelessness.

"This girl is part of my family."

"But the video shows you paying."

"We came under attack. I had the option of getting my head blown off or—"

"So, you *did* buy her?" the reporter insists.

'No. I did not." Zora meets her eyes. "She's a survivor of the genocide."

"Why would you, an African American, buy a slave?"

Annoyed, Zora pushes the microphone aside.

"Ms. Monro," another reporter shouts. "What's your relationship with Congressman Sykes? Was he involved with you in slave trading?"

"We are acquainted professionally. We never have never bought or sold anything together."

A reporter pushes a microphone at Abuk. "Are you able to contact your family?"

"Okay TV!" Abuk answers cheerfully.

It has gone as badly as could be expected. "We're done here," Zora tells them. She slides a protective arm around Abuk and ushers her down the sidewalk.

"Ms. Monro," a reporter calls, rushing behind them. "Who is financing the slave trading business?"

Zora hurries Abuk down the street, wondering how she could have worked for so long with people who endlessly collected diseased branches in a forest of vital information. They duck down a narrow alley that will not accommodate the satellite trucks.

"Good TV," Abuk chimes.

"No, baby." She imagines an editor cobbling together the ridiculous exchange. But the upside is that even a sensational rumor couldn't hold a slot for long in the news cycle.

"Baby'?" Abuk asks.

Zora stops, faces her. "'Baby' means you are special to me." She points at Abuk then folds her hands over her heart.

Allowing a sly grin, Abuk points at her. "You baby."

She nods, accepting the pristine trade of a small endearment. She wants words to reassure, to explain the rush and substance and meaning of this place that, for Abuk, must be alien beyond imagining. She wishes, with nearly equal ferocity, that she could walk away from this child and never think to look back. The impulse surely had shaken both her mothers; only one withstood the assault.

They continue to 19th Street past elderly row houses fronted by narrow gardens that cast the scent of damp earth. Wrought-iron fences bank drifts of fallen leaves, golden in the early winter sun. Abuk huddles against a gust of wind, stuffing her hands under her armpits.

"Cold," Zora says, pulling up Abuk's collar. "You're used to heat. You need a warmer jacket."

"Jacket," Abuk repeats.

Draping her scarf over Abuk's shoulders, she ties it in place. "Let's buy milk."

They come to a building with big windows. Abuk jumps back when the door swings open. Zora gentles her hand on Abuk's shoulder, and they enter together. Abuk blinks hard against the florescent lights. Grabbing a red basket, Zora leads her to the produce section, the only place likely to have any familiarity. Zora tells her the name of each vegetable she touches. She holds up a shiny green apple, watching as Abuk's nose wrinkles and twitches at the scent. Zora shows her how to put some in a bag she can see through.

They walk down the aisles that must look like shiny paths to Abuk. The shelves hold all sorts of cans and boxes with pictures that Abuk pauses several times to inspect. When the come to a section with jars, Abuk is clearly fascinated, grasping and carefully shaking a jar of gherkins. Zora nods for Abuk to put it in her basket.

They've come to buy milk because Abuk is a growing teen. Zora is unaware that it is her favorite food, and they will end up buying a lot of it. She realizes Abuk has never had refrigerated milk. She wonders if it will appeal served cold.

After they pay and are heading to the exit, in walks a woman in a green wrap. She is tall and striking, probably Sudanese. Abuk walks right up to the woman, greets her with the usual touch to her heart and a handshake. She talks quickly as if this chance encounter has unleashed a deluge of thoughts. The woman listens with kind eyes, nodding her head.

The woman turns to Zora and says: "I am Aluot Deng."

"Zora Monro." She shakes the offered hand. "You are Sudanese."

Aluot nods. "I come to this country two years past." Her ebony face is unlined, but her youth seems diminished, as if she has been burdened too early with too much pain.

"I brought Abuk here from Sudan last night," Zora tells her.

"She is from adoption?"

"She is a relative, now in my care."

Aluot smiles. "It is so hard," she says, "for new ones to…adjust."

"Yes. We are struggling just to communicate." Zora wants to say she's desperate for words that Abuk can understand. That she's crazy thrilled to meet a woman who knows both of their languages. Kismet has arrived like a sweet kiss. "Aluot, I wonder if you would join us for our first dinner here, and help with translating for a little while?"

Aluot feigns surprise but she cannot disguise her delight.

"We live nearby," Zora continues, suddenly calm in her need, their need, the luck of the encounter. "I know we just met."

"I like new meetings. Many people here do not speak to foreigners like me." Aluot says this without rancor, as if commenting on the weather. With long delicate fingers, she adjusts the fabric around her face. "My people have custom to be like family. I will come to help you."

'Really?"

"I have no one needing me." Aluot allows, a faint smile playing on her lips. "You save me today from shopping."

"Then today both of us are saved."

As they walk, the conversation shifts between Dinka and English. Aluot's patient translation is a sluice for the flood of Abuk's unspoken questions: Will she see her grandfather again? Will they look for Tariq? Will Senoja come to stay with them? Do other girls live nearby, and where do they gather?

The familial yearnings that occupy this child tumble out, as urgent as they are tender. Zora can offer no sure answers. Abuk appears to accept her uncertainty calmly, without resignation. Through Aluot's translation she tells Zora that she knows they will find a way to gather the ones who are missing.

A sudden wind rustles the oak trees, showering them with bright yellow leaves. Abuk waves her hand to catch one, face lively in the moment. Sniffing the air, she says to Aluot that she would like to sit in the warmth of the fire she smells. Zora says she will get her wish at home.

"Abuk puts me in mind of my daughter," Aluot says. "My sister cares for her until I return to Boston." She tells Zora of her personal campaign to meet Congressmen and advocacy groups to beg them to take action against the demons that govern her country. She tells Zora that she has grown weary of repeating herself. When Zora asks if she has family still in Sudan, sorrow settles like a veil over her face. She nods and goes silent.

The streetlights sputter on, yellowing the dusk as they arrive at Zora's flat. From the foyer, Aluot studies the living room with appreciative eyes and then follows Zora to the kitchen. "We make Sudanese meal," she declares, cheerful again. As Zora empties the grocery bag, Abuk hovers between them, absorbed in Aluot's recitation of her menu plan. Relieved to be excused from cooking, Zora assembles the requested vegetables and spices.

The doorbell calls, and Zora opens the door to find a helmeted bike messenger who offers his delivery log for a signature before handing Zora a large envelope. Shutting the door, she pulls the tab on the cardboard. Inside is a letter from HRD: *You are hereby informed that your employment at Human Rights Defenders has been terminated pursuant to Sections 9 of the Code of Ethics related to illegal activities*. Another paragraph follows but she refuses to read it, flapping the paper against her leg.

Aluot steps from the kitchen. She's removed her outer wrap to reveal her white long-sleeved blouse and loose black slacks. She is thin, almost gaunt. "Bad news comes to you?" Abuk appears beside her. Standing shoulder to shoulder, they wait with expectant faces.

Zora's throat goes dry. "I've been fired from my job," she says quietly.

With studied motions, Aluot dries her hands. "This is how is done in America?"

"One of many ways." She thinks Tom has seized the opportunity to be rid of her, betting that swift distancing from a mortal sinner will be seen as righteous defense of the HRD brand. Conveniently, it does the double duty of pre-empting a charge of sexual harassment, though since their last meeting, she'd made nothing more of the incident. The action seems irrationally punitive.

"You are thinking so hard," Aluot observes. "Let us quiet voices in our bellies; then we talk." She beckons Zora into the kitchen.

"We cook *addas*," she says, lifting a cover from a pot, "soup of lentils. And we cook *mullah,* a stew of chicken, onions and spice. Abuk makes *kisra,* our special bread." Examining Abuk's dough, clucking approval, she appears gratefully in her element and firmly in control.

"I'll set the table," Zora says, earning a puzzled glance from Aluot. "It means I'll put dishes and utensils on the table."

"Set the table, yes." Aluot explains the phrase to Abuk, earning a short snorting laugh. "For *addas* only we need bowls and spoons. We serve all foods on one tray. *Kisra* is for putting food in mouth. Simple. Now watch Abuk make *kisra.* "

They stand beside the stove as Abuk forms thin disks of dough and slips them into a frying pan. She deftly fingers them, testing and turning, absorbed in the motions. Aluot sets a large pot on the other front burner. "Now to make *asida*." She hands Zora a cup of water.

"Aluot, I don't like *asida*."

Her eyes widened. "Where you eat *asida*?"

"In Sudan. The man who made it—"

"A man! Haaah! Men do not know, how you say, technique?"

"It was lumpy paste, just awful."

"You learn right way." Pouring a bit of oil into the boiling water, she measures flour by handfuls into the pot. "Now stir fast."

Zora obeys, rocking her body in a playful rhythm. Abuk giggles, mimicking her motion. As the mixture thickens, Aluot tells her to begin a whipping motion.

"Faster," Aluot exhorts, "or you have paste. Faster."

"Faster," Abuk goads.

"Now put in this *zabady*."

Zora beats yogurt into the thick mush until the texture lightens. Aluot tests it. "Yes, it is good."

They assemble bowls of steaming food on two trays and carry them to the table. The piquant aromas infuse the room, reminding Zora that she's been hungry all day. Abuk hurries back to the kitchen, returning with a dish of pickles arranged in a sunburst, the dash of artistry evidently to soothe any trepidation about the odd new food. Without ceremony, she and Aluot begin eating. They make no pretense at conversation, consuming stew-laden bits of *kisra* with the singular concentration of those well acquainted with hunger. Aluot *is* a much better cook than Adam. Despite Zora's vastly different food fantasies, the first meal at home is a simple, satisfying comfort.

When they finish eating and are wiping their hands with paper towels, Aluot gazes at Zora. "News in letter. How do you answer?"

"It's my right to challenge my removal from the position." She glances at Abuk who is gamely sampling a pickle. "But I don't think I want to go back, not now, with this girl who needs a lot."

Aluot translates for Abuk. Wistfully she adds, "She is beauty. Sweet like ripe plum." Evidently satisfied that priorities are in order, she rises, lifts the serving trays.

"Don't bother with that," Zora says. "Let's sit and relax together."

Aluot shakes her head.

"You need to leave?" Zora follows as she retreats to the kitchen. "Where are you staying?"

"I stay with friends," Aluot says. "In Arlington." Her tone is apologetic, as if admitting a flaw. She rinses the dishes with fervor, as if to rule out conversation. Zora rests a hand on her shoulder and wheedles out the details: she sleeps on a mat in the corner of a small apartment. The place is filled day and night with noisy activity, the comings and goings of anxious people scratching for survival in a place that often bewilders them. She says it is a crazy house. Abuk's arm tugging for translation propels the exchange into confused crosstalk. Then they are all laughing, merry with a new, easy bond.

"You could stay with us," Zora ventures, buoyant with the impulse to ride the luck of their chance meeting. "You can see I need help with this bundle of girl-energy."

"I am here only one more week," Aluot protests, a ritual demurral spoken to the pot she is washing.

"That's enough to get us on track." Zora leans close to her. "Please?"

Aluot explains the offer to Abuk, setting off her riff of celebratory ululation.

"See, Abuk wants you here too. And you can cook all you like."

Aluot grins. "You know *halal* market? I show you."

"As long as I don't have to drive to Virginia. I always get lost there."

Aluot purses her lips. "It *is* in Virginia."

"Well, I think I can handle one trip," Zora allows, drying the pot that Aluot has set on the counter. "What's most important is translating for us."

"Yes. Is most important."

"And one more thing," Zora says. She waves away Aluot's flash of apprehension. "You read Arabic, yes?"

"Yes, it is the language of my education."

"I have a short document in Arabic." Zora folds her hand as if in prayer. "I need to know what it says."

CHAPTER NINETEEN

Effervescent beyond anything Zora had seen or expected, Abuk leads Aluot by the hand to the guest room. Aluot approaches the bed, her demeanor soft with the gratitude of a woman finally granted her rightful comforts. She strokes the puffy comforter, her eyes burdened by tears withheld. "Allah be praised," she whispers. Abuk bounces on the bed, grinning. Her gift for "knowing the way" is, Zora decides, no specious claim. Barely a day off the plane and the child has engineered the first girder of her new life. Zora wants to rest in the calm of the moment. Every coming day will pivot on the presence of this girl in her life.

A loud knock startles them. Dreading another visitor, Zora peers through the front peephole. At first, she does not recognize Mookie. Her dreads are gone, replaced by zigzag plaits. "Got your messages," Mookie says, bursting in, stopping abruptly. "Girl, you look like a damn death camp survivor." She hugs Zora hard. "Nothing like a little scandal to brighten a homecoming." She holds Zora at arm's length. "You freaked 'em at work with that slavery business."

"Mook, that story was bullshit."

"Yeah, I know." She drops her bag and jacket on the floor, follows Zora to the kitchen, sniffs the coffee in the pot, pours a cup, and slides it into the microwave.

Zora waits for a break in her frenetic motion. "You know Tom fired me?"

"Yeah, I know." Mookie meets her eyes. "He gave me your job."

Zora rests her back against the fridge. She should feel angry or betrayed, but neither emotion surfaces. "You'll be good," she says, meaning it.

Mookie says nothing but allows her shoulders to relax. She sips her coffee, eyeing Zora over the rim of the mug. "Girl, what happened to you?"

Abuk appears at the kitchen door, drawing a double take from Mookie.

"Abuk," Zora says. "My friend Mookie."

"Hi my friend Mookie," Abuk greets, offering a hand to shake. For a moment, Mookie is immobile.

"She's my niece," Zora continues, pushing through the weird silence. "And as we see here, even a new arrival can work up a friendly greeting."

"Right," Mookie murmurs, extending her hand. "How ya doin?"

"How ya doin'?" Abuk answers, exactly replicating Mookie's inflection. Her coltish legs look poised for motion.

"She learns English just now," Aluot says, stepping into the kitchen. "I am Aluot, I help her."

Mookie seems to put more effort into concealing her bewilderment. She shakes Aluot's outstretched hand with a perfunctory grin. Zora tells Aluot that Mookie is a colleague from work.

Mookie sets down her mug, ignoring the two interlopers. "You plannin' to appeal Tom's decision?"

"Probably not." As she recounts the short version of the Abuk saga, Mookie listens, distractedly fussing with a loose thread on her jeans, scratching her forehead, glancing at the girl. "It means," Zora concludes, "I'm raising this child."

"*Teenager,*" Mookie corrects. "You best be ready when this filly gets her footing, 'cuz suddenly you gonna be the dumbest woman ever walked the earth." She's had experience with this phenomenon. Her daughter, soon finishing college, had been the product of a rape Mookie survived at age fifteen. Her parenting style, an excruciating blend of tough love and fierce protectiveness, flew in the face of what could have been expected, given that she came up in southeast DC with crack cocaine burning down the 'hood. Her father had been shot dead in a drive-by, possibly a mis-identified target. Her mother, a long-suffering hotel maid, had pushed her cantankerous daughter through Howard University. Mookie's voracious need-to-know, her uncanny instinct for backstory, had blunted most of the workplace resistance to her irreverent, opinionated style.

Her cell phone doodles a complex riff of drumbeats. Flipping it open, she commands, "Talk to me." As she listened, her face twists in disappointment. "On my way." She stabs away the call. "Gotta go." Normally she would follow this sort of disruption with a quip about whatever calamity is demanding her attention, but she simply says, "Nice ta meetcha" to the two strangers. Bewildered by this dismissiveness, Zora walks her to the door. "You haven't heard the part about Tariq."

Mookie arches one eyebrow. "You had time for outta-town dick?"

"Jeezus, Mook."

"Well, not enough sex or too much?"

"Wasn't like that. I…" She looks away, troubled by the rift that seems to be opening between them. "It's…more than I know how to handle."

Mookie slips on her jacket. "You wanna talk, call me."

Zora stands in the door watching Mookie lope to her car, trailing the frayed tether of their pre-trip relationship, realizing how new lives on the family turf could leave her feeling a stranger.

Aluot leans from the kitchen door. "I will translate document now."

Zora nods.

"Your friend did not look happy to meet us," Aluot states, evidently wishing her observation to be a matter of record.

"She's surprised. Give her time."

"Come, bring document. Let us sit together." Aluot moves to the table trailing a floral scent, beckoning Abuk.

Aluot leans from the kitchen door. "I will translate document now."

Zora nods.

"Your friend did not look happy to meet us," Aluot states, evidently wishing her observation to be a matter of record.

"She's…surprised. Give her time."

"Come, bring document. Let us sit together." Aluot moves to the table trailing a floral scent, beckoning Abuk to follow her. Standing behind them, Abuk peers at the paper they've set on the table between them. They point at different lines, talk back and forth, say Tariq's name. Aluot looks at her, tells her in Arabic, "We try to help Tariq."

Abuk smiles, replies, "Auntie and Tariq marry. What bride price?" Aluot translates

"No, Abuk," says Zora. 'Tariq is gone."

Abuk wrinkles her nose as Aluot translates the sentence in Arabic, evidently adding some other words. Zora can only imagine what they are because Abuk's face goes dark and she shakes her head. Her voice is pinched as she responds to Aluot, who translates for Zora. "She wants you to know that no one will marry her because she is not clean, so she will stay with you and she will take care of you when you are old."

This sorrowful bit is too much to contemplate. Zora gives Abuk a wan smile and strokes her hand. Aluot motions for Abuk to be quiet while they continue with the papers.

Zora studies the intricate Arabic script. Snug with her own literacy, she realizes she's not given the gift wide enough definition: she is illiterate in many languages, most disappointingly, this one. She can say five Arabic words but cannot read them to save her life. Without a translator, she's helpless to understand the message that has cost Tariq his freedom.

"Accounts," Aluot declares. "It is list of names and bank accounts. Many big dollars. Many billions." Her tone is indignant as she reads the names and amounts. Zora writes them on a pad.

"I do not know these people," Aluot concludes. The anxious undertone in her voice argues otherwise. She pushes the paper away as if touching it has soiled her; she does not share the thoughts that roil the silence settling between them.

Zora has read reports about three of the men, government officials alleged to have orchestrated mass executions and promoted a practice of brutal torture within the Sudanese security apparatus. A dozen other names are unknown to her. But, if the reputations of the three indicate the character of the larger group, then Tariq has uncovered an exceedingly dangerous network of genocide profiteers. "Many billions" means the stakes are nosebleed high.

Aluot rises, speaks to Abuk, and turns to Zora. "Now we show you how to wear *tobe.*" She walks slowly, like a woman recovering from a blow. Zora decides she is taking refuge in a session of cultural education. Aluot returns with folded emerald fabric, again cheerful, a woman on a mission, and instructs her to stand. She sidles behind Zora, positioning an edge of fabric at her waist. The wrapping and tucking procedure, accompanied by Abuk's furtive giggles, follows an obscure logic that concludes with a decorous drape of the fabric over her head. "We believe," Aluot explains, "grown woman's body should be private in public." She gently adjusts the folds. "But at home, we dress as we like." Smiling, she inspects her work. "Now where is mirror?"

Zora imagines the *tobe* will look like a clownish costume, that her lighter skin will work against the resplendence achieved by her darker sisters. Opening the closet to a full-length mirror, she studies her reflection. The diaphanous wrap announces a mysterious presence, allowing only her face and form to speak. She smiles at the two faces bobbing behind her, bright with pleasure.

"If I wear this," she says, "no one will recognize me."

Aluot chuckles, translating for Abuk. "Sometimes, that is blessing," she advises. "But they remember beautiful vision."

—

After the new residents of the house settle to sleep, Aluot in the guest room, Abuk again claiming her bed, Zora wraps herself in a shawl and steps out back to a bench hunched against a massive oak. Brushing away the tree litter, she lies down on the cold wood. Above her, in the moonlight, the ancient whorled trunk pushes nearly naked branches skyward in a twisting sculpture.

The looks of disbelief from Bert and Mookie felt like repudiations, as if she'd betrayed them by excavating her true identity, by bringing home living proof of her pedigree. How could their allegiance be conditional, their behavior so dismissive?

She breathes in the pungent scent of burning wood, remembering the journey that stripped her soul bare. The long days of living hungry, assaulted by the stench of death, and the nights doused with fear of attack were just bits of the horrors that swarm over her people. This visceral knowing is the fuel Tariq counted on. She wants to believe in the unbearable possibility that millions of lives can turn on this page of information, that she will be fearless in exposing it. She wants to believe she will survive the blowback.

CHAPTER TWENTY

She spends the night on the sofa, laptop perched on a pillow on her belly, trolling the Internet for background on the men on Tariq's List: A CFO of a Chinese telecommunications conglomerate. Two men on the Homeland Security list of suspected terrorists. A lawyer for AmGO with a record of hostile acquisitions in Africa. Of course, Americans would be in the mix. A Russian businessman implicated in illegal weapons transfers in East Africa. A French former mercenary named in an investigation of the Rwandan genocide. A Sudanese government minister with ties to the Islamic Brotherhood, a listed terrorist organization.

Bits of data begin to define their movements in the dark alleys of war profiteering. As covert associates, their range of illicit activity appears limitless, undoubtedly requiring the services of a small army of mercenaries to eliminate interlopers and prying eyes. Merely scratching the surface has induced a kind of loathing fascination that makes her stomach knot.

As frail sunlight seeps through the edges of the blinds, Zora rises stiffly and pads down the hall. She finds Abuk asleep in the center of her bed, face like a chocolate bonbon on the scarlet pillow. Her own momma probably had done her share of "viewing the sleeping child" and no doubt had wondered, as she did now, what dreams whirled in that mysterious mind. It made no difference to her momma that she loved another woman's child. It mattered only that she could love in that singular way. Zora wonders what it will take to live up to that expansive definition of family.

In the bathroom, she splashes cold water on her face. Pausing with towel in mid-wipe, she studies her skin. The color of lightly creamed coffee, it certainly is not "black," her so-called race. That would be Abuk, in primal ebony. She envies a color so unequivocal, the color of her birth mother. She stumbles over the thought, buried in a shallow grave of denied thoughts, that her rapist father must have been pale skinned indeed.

As she pulls on her jeans, someone raps on the back door. Throwing on a sweater, she hurries down the hall muttering: "A United States Congressman and he's still gotta sneak round back." She draws aside the curtain. Outside stands Senoja.

She scowls at him. "You got a death wish, showin' up here?"

"Storya my life," he says through the glass. "You need to hear what I got to tell you."

"I should trust you—ever?"

"Zora, I not messin' with you, for real."

Abuk scurries into the room. "Senoja!" she cries, elbowing Zora aside and flinging open the door. "Hey sugar," he coos. They stand smiling at each other. When he awkwardly extends his hand, she leans into his gruff one-armed embrace. "At least someone's happy to see me."

Zora glares at him. "She didn't lose her job over your lyin' video."

He releases Abuk. "That ain't your biggest problem right now."

Abuk herds them away from the door into the center of the kitchen.

"Well, what *is* my problem?"

"First, I gotta explain that video." He leans against the wall in his extra-large Baltimore Orioles jersey, looking like a man forced to appear in a police lineup.

Zora crosses her arms over her chest. "Yeah?"

He clears his throat. "I was hired to set you up."

"I saw that on TV. Why me?"

"You got media creds. Fit the client's profile."

"What client?"

Senoja peers at the ceiling as if the answer might be dangling there, either to be grasped or to crush him. "Sudanese official," he mumbles. "Wanted to put human rights nags on the defensive."

She squints at him. "You been someone's errand boy."

He shifts his weight, hands massaging the logo on his shirt. "Guy's one scary motha– "

"Do *not*," Zora warns, "use that word in earshot of this child."

Senoja blinks away the reprimand. "Dude had me shot during that raid. A warning to stick with the plan."

"So, they jerked your choke-chain and you delivered my head on a stick. How much you walk away with?"

He studies the floor. "Twenty large."

She huffs her disgust.

"Listen, Zora." He takes a wad of bills from his pocket. "Keep the money you paid me." He offers her the roll.

She pushes away his hand. "You think that's gonna fix everything?"

"Look, I ain't proud of this mess," he admits, "but we got bigger problems."

Abuk inserts herself between them. "Senoja, eat," she orders. His demeanor softens, as if she's invited him to play a game and he cannot resist. He glances at the plates on the counter then frowns at Zora. "Ain't you taught this child how to eat corn flakes? Where the bowls, the milk?"

She opens the fridge, hands him the carton. "Don't get in my face. We just got here." She sets two bowls between them. With a hint of ceremony, Senoja slides the cereal into the bowls and pours milk over each serving. "That's how ya do cereal."

Eyeing her bowl with suspicion, Abuk lifts a bit of the milky mix into her mouth and chews cautiously. Senoja palms the roll of money across the counter. "Zora, take it. You gonna need it to feed this girl."

She watches Abuk finger the wad with vague curiosity.

"I'm right, ain't I?" He mimics Abuk's chewing, causing her to spritz out droplets of milk.

Despite her distrust of him, she is pleased with his big-brother kind of caring. Maybe he's just salving his guilty conscience. Either way, the offering defers a scramble for income. A show of gratitude is, however, out of the question. She slides the roll into the silverware drawer. "Tell me the bigger problem you think I have."

Senoja moves away from Abuk, stands with his arms crossed and meets Zora eyes. "You moved information."

She looks away to pour another glass of tea. "Why you think that?"

"Intel buddy a mine monitors certain sensitive communications. Your list generated lots of chatter last night from AmGO."

She feigns confusion to hide a flash of fear. "The oil company?"

He snorts. "You don't know much about Jackson Sykes, do ya? The Congressman's been feedin' from the AmGO trough. Hands 'em any Sudan intel he happens to trip over."

"What makes you think I gave him information?"

"He told me."

She turns away, furious. Jetlag and desperation made her a fool. First mistake: she trusted a former lover. Worse mistake: she gave highly sensitive information to a *politician.*

"You don't really understand," he jabs, "the *business* goin' down around Sudan." He steps out of the way as Abuk carries her bowl to the sink.

Zora backs against the counter, unwilling to look at him.

He settles on a stool. "Lotsa people making big money. We got weapons dealers, officials on the take, corporations in the oil game."

"The usual suspects." She watches Abuk drift off to the TV. Though the girl makes no demands, she feels the pull of her loneliness.

"And supply contractors and freelance military types. Country's a godamn hot ticket for war-fightin' investment. You know why? Cuz they got all the inside help they need to keep it goin'." His rubs his hand over his mouth as if he wants to stop but can't. "The Sudanese got it in their blood to bicker. The government's just fine with them killin' each other. Gives 'em all the small arms they need. 'Course they save the heavy weapons for themselves to keep stirrin' it up. Serves a whole lotta bottom lines. Business partners stay off the radar, asses covered." He shakes his head. "Girl, you messed with the *cover.*"

She stares at him. A wee part of her mind revels at this confirmation of the list's significance. A stronger instinct insists on immediate, anonymous relocation.

He steps close beside her, props his hand on the cabinet above her, leaning close. "Ain't much billionaires worry about more than being called out for dirty business."

"Like supporting a genocide?"

"Whatever." He moves closer. "You were a *side* project. Just entertainment for a do-nothin' deputy minister. *A side fuckin' project.* Then you spilled to Jackson." He leans toward her ear. "Girl, you in *deep* shit."

She moves away from him, sickened by her naiveté.

"Bitch of it is," he complains, *'My* ass on the line for not knowin' what you had." He pulls on a black watch cap. "I'm livin' on borrowed time here." He moves to leave. "Hard to say what they got in mind for you. Stay inside. Keep doors and windows locked. I'll get back with you when I can." He lets himself out and rumbles down the back stairs.

She bolts the door, stunned. She hasn't even clarified the network's business, much less exposed it, yet the very existence of The List has set off alarms. If Tariq's captors don't already know, they soon will discover he's not only a saboteur but the guy responsible for this breach of invisibility. Jackson's betrayal ensures that they will dispose of him and come looking for her.

She hears Abuk laugh at something on TV, a light melodic sound that survived her life in hell. Like a timer on a bomb, the wall clock loudly ticks away the minutes. Forcing herself to focus, she takes the wad of money from the drawer and stuffs it into a canister below the sink. More channel-flipping in the living room, then MTV's offering of 50 Cent's latest.

Aluot, face puffy from sleep, steps into the kitchen. "Forgive my long sleep. I left you without help." She wears a shapeless blue nightgown, one of Ella's that hadn't made it to Goodwill.

"It's alright. Abuk just finished breakfast."

"I waited for man to leave," Aluot says, setting the kettle on the stove.

Zora wonders if she has heard her conversation with Senoja but decides against inquiring or explaining. Instead, she asks if Aluot would begin the day with an English lesson for Abuk.

"I will." Aluot agrees. She examines the sky from the kitchen window. "Rain will come today."

"If you feel like it, there's wood beside the fireplace. I think Abuk would like to sit by a fire."

Aluot studies her. "You are worried."

She sets out a glass for Aluot's tea. "I have some business to deal with."

Abuk wanders into the kitchen and returns Alout's greeting. Zora realizes the girl does not seem to know when to sleep. Her routine in the village would have been to gather firewood and cook and fetch water every day. Here there isn't anything to do except watch TV. Food comes without harvesting and milk comes without tending cows and water comes by just moving a tap. She can prepare tea but does not understand where the fire comes from. It must all be so strange.

Zora's shoulders are tight with the burden she carries. She retreats to her bedroom. Abuk left the bed smooth, the comforter rolled in the center of the bed with the pillows on top, a fastidious arrangement by a girl who's never known such possessions. It's the only tidy thing in the room. She powers on her laptop.

AmGO's "chatter" must have reverberated along the network's backchannels. A tamp-down response seems to be in motion; there won't be much time to assemble a credible analysis of the network. She's not so naïve to think exposure will end the threat but doing nothing feels like laying down to die.

The links to the Islamic Brotherhood and known mercenaries argue for a search through NSA's database. The vast list of terror-sponsoring organizations offers a few curious hits. Conflicting spellings and DBAs send her down cul-de-sacs until she no longer knows what she is looking for or why. She decides she might be looking too hard for something that's hidden in plain sight. She calls Ahmed, hoping to pick his brain, eager for any news of Tariq. He doesn't pick up.

Unfamiliar female voices rise in the living room. Someone moves pots on the stove and opens the refrigerator. Gathering her research notes into an envelope, she slips it beneath a stack of shoeboxes in the closet, a truly bush-league choice. In a professional break-in search, the stuff would be discovered in about five seconds. She'll get the apartment's security system beefed up, open a safe deposit box. Then again, she may need something less vulnerable to official inspection. On a rising tide of paranoia, she goes to see who's arrived.

Two young Sudanese women greet her with broad smiles, announcing their names in accented voices, shaking her hand. Aluot leans close and whispers, "I invited women from our homeland to celebrate Abuk's arrival." A subtle rebuke lurks behind her smile. She takes Zora's hand. "Come, we prepare meal."

The visitors shed their *tobes*, revealing logoed t-shirts and designer jeans. The lean, long-legged Zahra sets to work chopping meat. Samia, short and stooped, with three prominent scars on her right arm, begins making *kisra*. It's mid-afternoon and Zora has not eaten since the previous night. She's given scant attention to Abuk. They've been cooped up, jet lagged, un-showered, over visited and unfriended. Perhaps Aluot's impromptu dinner party offers a chance to redeem a muted and inauspicious homecoming.

Fully in her element as supervising chef, Aluot directs her to help Abuk chop onions and tomatoes. Knife in hand, Abuk begins peeling a large onion. "*Bas!*" she informs Zora. "Onion" comes the reply. They play this naming game often. With a sly glance and a nod, they launch into a bilingual call-and-response, naming all the vegetables at hand and then moving on to the kitchen implements. When they finally settle into chopping onions, their eyes tear up from the fumes. Amid the sizzle and clatter of the women cooking, Abuk leans gently against Zora, batting the rain of tears that have nothing to do with onions. Zora whispers "Baby" and then more words Abuk doesn't yet know, but "baby" seems good enough.

An hour later, plates of steaming food are brought to the dining table. The room fills with the aromas of roasted chicken and spicy eggplant. As they eat, Aluot jokes about bringing "African time" to America so people will know the pleasure of an unhurried meal. Zahra tells them she has begun nursing classes at NOVA, sharing a comical account of early days in anatomy class. Samia says that she has been lucky to get a job at a café where many Sudanese come for take-out. She has made some friends. One of them is teaching her how to drive but both of them are terrified of attempting the Beltway. The conversation dances between Arabic and English with occasional sidesteps into Dinka. Abuk withdraws into benign listening, her earlier enthusiasm muted in the flood of conversation.

When the serving bowls are nearly empty, when she has mustered the courage, Zora asks to hear what brought them to America, what inspired them to begin again. Aluot shakes her head. "We left terrible memories," she says. "Why do you ask to hear of them?"

Resting her elbows on the table, Zora leans forward as if sharing a confidence. "I don't know if terrible memories ever leave. What I saw and heard in our country will not leave me, and I have not suffered as you must have, or as I know this girl has." She gazes at Abuk, absorbed in gathering a final bite of food. "I want to help her learn how to live here. I think you must know a lot about that struggle." She stops, uncertain. In the following silence, the women exchange glances she cannot decode. "I know it's a lot to ask. Please forgive me if I have overstepped."

"You want to hear now?" Zahra asks quietly.

Zora nods. "While we are together, yes."

Zahra draws herself up, her expression dispassionate, and begins in a low, even voice. "When soldiers came to my village, I was harvesting sorghum in a place near trees. I remember smell of burning before I see smoke from village. I remember thinking I would soon die. But I am taken.

"I am a slave in the soldiers' camp. I pray every day for forty-two days, I pray for death. I cannot speak of the things they did to me." She peers at her hands fisted in her lap, as if waiting for a memory to release her. "God made my life go another way. I remember moon was dark that night. The soldiers drank much. They fell asleep instead of beating me. I escaped into bush." Her dark eyes look beyond them, beyond the room that holds them.

"I walked five nights, hiding when the sun came. It was dry season. I had to dig deep into *wadis* for a little muddy water." She pauses, gazes intently at Zora. "You know thirst that makes whole body hurt?" She shakes her head against a reply. "But I think of my mother and my sister, how I would find them.

"I am in Kakuma camp for ninety-two days. Then miracle comes. I learn I am chosen to go to America."

Aluot murmurs "*Alhamdulila.*"

"When I find my family, we can live again." She presses her lips together, seems to summon a small upturn of her mouth.

"We survive only," Samia says. "You see what they did." She displays her arm, wiping at the three jagged scars as if to erase them. "Cut me. A game!" A tear escapes down her cheek; she rolls and bites her lips. "I am not brave to speak of things that happened. I survive because I find ways to forget."

Aluot rests a hand on Samia's. "Still people suffer and no one sees."

"*I* see," Zora says quietly. "You help me know what I must do."

The doorbell chimes, a merciless intrusion. "Are we expecting other guests?" Zora asks, rising from the table.

"I think no," Aluot answers.

Peering through the peephole, Zora is startled by what she sees: a swarthy, short man in a gray business suit standing on the porch. "Urgent message for you," he calls, evidently sensing her presence at the door. She recognizes the Sudanese accent. "Urgent," he insists, rattling an envelope through the mail slot. It slides to the floor, landing like a white stain on the dark green tiles.

Aluot comes to the foyer. "What is it?"

Wary, Zora picks up the small envelope. It is a fine linen stock, unmarked but somehow laden with warning. The Listers have wasted no time. They know where she lives. She slips her finger under the light seal and pulls out a card. The message is neatly printed in tight block letters: *Meet me 9 AM tomorrow. Westin Embassy Row. Bring document. I will find you.*

CHAPTER TWENTY-ONE

The arrival of the message ends the evening as if a death has been announced, stunning the women into silence that Zora does not understand and cannot breach. "We go now." Samia says. She stands in the door to the kitchen, shrugging on a black coat.

"It's raining. I'll drive you," Zora says. Anxiety knots in her stomach as she watches their nervous preparations to leave.

"We all go," Aluot instructs. "I show the way. Is no good to leave Abuk alone."

Massed under umbrellas, they scurry to the garage behind the building. Zora tugs open the ancient door. Inside, her green Honda gleams in the light of a bare ceiling bulb. The women quickly slide into the seats, Aluot in front, the others in the back.

Zora drives slowly, unsure of her ability, after weeks as a passenger, to navigate in the steady rain. The swish-thump of the wipers offers the only relief from the heavy silence. Aluot repeatedly adjusts the drape of her *tobe*. On the 14th Street Bridge, she clears her throat. "I did not tell you whole truth."

Zora glances at her. "Truth about what?"

The bridge lights flash across her tense face. "I know one name on document. It seems not important. But when big man comes to tell you of danger and then message comes, I am afraid."

In the back seat, Abuk leans forward pointing at the massive flank of the Pentagon. "Oooh!" she cries. Aluot shushes her. "You must know this. Man on list, Haron. He is Butcher of Aweil.

"I know. I have read about his mass executions."

"I *saw* him kill. He is not human." Aluot looks away. "I fear now he will find me and kill me also."

Zora works hard to stay focused on the road. "But you're here in America."

"Hate so hungry can travel far," she insists. "If you show yourself, you will not be safe. Abuk will not be safe." She clutches her hands in front of her mouth. "I will not be safe."

The urgency of her fear claws at Zora. That men like The Butcher could enjoy international reach no longer seems the chaff of conspiracy theorists. If he could brutalize civilians in Sudan with impunity, he and his powerful cronies surely are capable of silencing witnesses wherever they might raise their anxious heads.

When they arrive at the apartment building in Arlington, Abuk watches mournfully as the two women take hasty leave of their company. Aluot remains silent, distant as they drive back to the city.

After a fitful night, Zora awakens in her bed facing Abuk, slack-jawed in peaceful sleep. A wee-hours skirmish with dream demons seemed less violent than the ones in Nairobi. She does not think they will be banished without some sort of professional help. Rain patters on the window. She hides beneath the fluffy barricade of the comforter, allowing the memory of the meeting summons to form up. She considers not going. But will that bring the meeting to her? "Bad outcome" is written all over it.

"Shit," she whispers, rousting herself from bed. After a long shower, she stands in front of her open closet, surveying the clutter of clothes for an ensemble suitable for a rendezvous with a menacing stranger. She unzips her still-unpacked duffel bag and rummages for a pumpkin-hued caftan she purchased in Nairobi. She holds it up to examine the fabulous menagerie embedded in the soft wrinkled cotton. Tiny ibises, like cave drawings, prance along the neckline. Miniature zebras graze at the hem.

A small raven perches on the cuff of the left sleeve. Perhaps her totem would serve as small protection. She finds the hand steamer and works the dress into a wearable state. In the mirror, she watches the fabric slide over her body. Her skin resonates with the vibrant colors, ascending from muted brown to glowing chocolate. She draws red gloss over her lips. Finally, she puts on the family necklace, a talisman to honor the woman who sent her out of harm's way.

The house creaks as the wind buffets it. Pulling out a pair of black leather boots, she considers a new hiding place for her stash of papers. She takes one copy of Tariq's document from the bundle, folds it into a small square and slides it into her bra. "Nobody lookin' in there these days," she mutters. The original and the pages of her research go into a small lock box. In the kitchen, she adds the wad of cash to the box then empties a carton of frozen fried chicken, fits the lock box inside, seals it, and returns it to the freezer behind a collection of ice cube trays and miscellaneous Tupperware.

In the front room, she peeks through the blinds to check on the rain's intensity. Bert scurries into view, wrestling with a balky umbrella against a sudden gust of wind. Surprised, she waits at the open door as her aunt ascends the steps. From under the umbrella, Bert glances up in embarrassed alarm. "Now don't slam the door on me," she petitions, breathing hard as she makes the porch. "Whether you like it or not, we're family and you just can't expect an old Pollock to change her tune in one blinding epiphany. I want what's best for you and—"

"Just shut up and come in," Zora goads.

Bert grins. "Don't you look formidable

"Ya think?"

"What's the occasion?" As she sheds her raincoat, lavender scent sweetens the foyer.

"I've been summoned to an 'urgent' meeting with an unidentified person."

Bert faces her, hands folded in winsome supplication. "You want company?"

Zora hangs her damp coat over the closet door. "I don't want to involve you."

"It's dangerous?" Bert's tone suggests she's intrigued by the possibility. "All the more reason you should have a companion. Maybe we're talking bodyguard?"

"B, you could nail the part thirty years ago on the playground. But this is a different league. Probably armed and twitchy."

"You're serious."

Zora arches her eyebrows. "Would I be making up weird shit like this?"

Bert succumbs to her worried look. Following Zora into the kitchen, she fills the kettle and sets it on the stove. "Let me help you."

"It's not safe."

Bert purses her lips. "You've delivered your disclaimer. I accept the uncertainty. Now just lay out the pieces."

Zora rests against the wall, relieved at Bert's loyal support but reluctant to exploit it. She does not want to be alone with the threat that's reared up. "My translator in Sudan—"

"The man you fell in love with?"

She's been trying to outrun her grief over his unknowable status but the words puncture a reservoir of grief. She covers her face with her hands.

Bert steps toward her. "*Kochanie*, "I'm sorry. I'm sorry I left you alone with all that's happened."

Zora straightens, composes herself. "I promised Tariq I'd find the right channel for information he gave me." She explains the document, what Senoja told her and what the messenger brought.

Rain taps on the kitchen window like children greedy for attention. "You really shouldn't go alone," Bert concludes. "What time do we leave?"

"I already called a taxi." She debates how to leave a message for Abuk, settling on a crayon drawing of the two stick figures holding hands. She sets it on the pillow beside the girl. When the taxi honks, she and Bert dash through the rain. Settling inside, she glances out the back window, mentally reviewing that she'd double locked the doors, closed every curtain. A black Taurus eases from the curb a half block behind them. It follows at a distance as the taxi rumbles through potholes on streets quilted with sodden leaves.

The brick façade of the Westin Embassy Row Hotel looks gloomy in the muted light. The taxi pulls under a red canvas portico where a man in a black cap and heavy overcoat opens the door with a smile. Zora watches the black Taurus pass the hotel and disappear around the corner. Bert follows her into the white marble lobby. At the mahogany concierge desk, several guests cluster, luggage piled behind them, chatting about the miserable weather.

They ascend a short flight of carpeted stairs. A polished white table in the center of an anteroom offers up an extravagant, scentless floral arrangement. Removing their gloves, they wait.

"At least these guys have enough class," Bert observes, "to choose a high-end joint to rendezvous." Her grin does not conceal her anxiety.

A tall man in a dark blue suit approaches them, unhurried. His wiry hair is close-cropped, his skin the color of a chestnut. "Ms. Monro," he says, bowing his head slightly.

"Yes."

"And your companion?"

"Yes, she is. And you are?"

"The one who sent the message." His accent ornaments his words but his dark eyes offer no hint of warmth.

"Mr. Mo, then?" The nickname for "Mohamed" slips out like a racial slur. She is not apologetic.

"As you wish." His grim smile pinches deep lines at the corners of his mouth. "Come, we will sit together."

They follow him down a hall to an empty side lobby, chilly from disuse. Zora sits in one of the plush, plum-colored chairs grouped around a glass coffee table. "Is that your black Taurus following me?"

"Ah, straight to business." He sits across from her. "This is the way of the American woman." His tone says he is returning her insult.

"I'm an African woman," she counters. "What do you want?"

Mr. Mo allows a doubtful glance at Bert sitting in the chair between them. "Ms. Monro, we must talk of sensitive matters. "

"We're listening."

He nods. "You have a document. It is of great value to a few and of no consequence to you."

"You assume a lot," Zora counters. "I've got nothing to say when I don't know who I'm talkin' to."

"It will be safer, for all of us, if you indulge a bit of ignorance." He sits back, resting his right hand on the fat arm of the chair. A small sapphire set in a gold ring glints from his middle finger.

"Listen," she says. "I didn't think much of your summons but I came out on this crappy day. So don't ask me to play stupid too."

With his ringed hand, he strokes his chin. "Mr. Senoja has kept us apprised of your activities. His assistance allowed us to capture Tariq Taha. *Alhamdulilah.* Another terrorist neutralized."

Zora stares past him to a painting on the wall, willing the blandness to absorb her fury. Senoja betrayed Tariq. He's twice played her a fool.

A waiter carrying a tray enters the room. Placing it on the table, he pours tea from a porcelain pot into small gold-rimmed glasses. Mr. Mo waves his hand in offering to the women. He watches the waiter until he leaves the room then turns his steely eyes to Zora. "I require the document Tariq Taha gave you."

Zora meets his eyes. "I don't have a document."

He smiles as if tolerating bad manners. "Such a shame you did not bring it." He caresses the ring on his finger. "We could have concluded our business here."

"I don't know anything about your business."

He appraises her, sipping his tea. "Ms. Monro, if by fate you suddenly become knowledgeable, there will be grave consequences for Mr. Taha."

Bert clears her throat. "I think we're done here." She rises, lifting Zora's elbow.

"Let me further point out," he continues, "that you brought a Sudanese child here illegally. "

Zora's body clenches. She shakes off Bert's grip. Planting her palms on the table, she leans toward him. "You fucking asshole, don't you threaten—"

Bert pulls her from the table and bustles them down the hall to the main lobby. Zora glances over her shoulder to see the man finishing his tea. "*Kochanie*," Bert whispers, "you must never provoke anyone as soulless as that man."

Outside, three taxis idle in a queue, shrouding the brick driveway with noxious exhaust. The rain has eased to a fine drizzle. "That scared me witless," Bert admits, fussing awkwardly with her hat. Gazing at the leaden sky over DuPont Circle, Zora feels all coherence draining from her life. Fear riddles the anger that has been her shield. Suddenly, Senoja appears beside her. "Jes watchin' your back," he says. "Get in the taxi. "

She slaps his face hard. "You goddamn low life. How much did they pay you for Tariq?"

He touches his cheek with a wounded expression. "It wasn't part of any deal. *Get in the cab.*"

"You handed him over all on your own?"

"Can't do this here," he says shoving her into a taxi. The African driver casts wary eyes on them as they clamber into the rear seat. Bert slides in front. The taxi eased onto 21st Street.

"Sucker was no good for you," Senoja mutters.

Her face ices with disbelief. "You betrayed Tariq because you were *jealous?*"

He trains his eyes on the floor, his knee bouncing like a piston. "I was tryin' to protect you."

"You stupid fuck!" she shouts, punctuating each word with a hard punch to his shoulder.

"No violence," the driver commands. "Not in my taxi. I will put you out."

Trembling, Zora heaves herself against the back of the seat. Senoja rubs his shoulder. "You can kill me later if they don't beat ya to it." He pulls an envelope from his pocket and jabbed it toward her. "I connected some of the dots. This is way bigger than you know."

"Driver," she says. "Please pull over." When the taxi lurches to the curb, she turns to him. "Get out."

He shakes his head, dark regret on his face. Dropping the envelope on the seat between them, he swings out of the cab. They leave him shrugged against the cold drizzle amid a stream of umbrellaed pedestrians.

Shaken, Bert turns to Zora. "I've never seen you hit anyone." She wipes a trembling hand across her forehead. "What did he leave on the seat?"

"An information bomb." Zora shoves the envelope into her purse.

When they pull up to the house, Zora touches Bert's shoulder. "I've got to see someone. Will you stay and make sure everything's secure? Abuk cannot go out."

"Now wait! I don't know the girl!"

"Bert, I *need* you to do this. Aluot speaks English and Dinka. Work it out. I'll be back as soon as I can."

Bert slowly pushes out of the taxi and stands at the curb, forlorn. Zora directs the driver to an address in Bethesda. It will be an expensive taxi ride, but she's got no bandwidth for driving. She thinks of Ahmed in his neat suburban split-level, of the party where she'd first heard Tariq's name. Nothing could have prepared her for this fallout. The traffic along Canal Road zips past at maniacal speed. She used to like driving this curvy, tree-lined road by the river. It used to calm her. No chance of that today.

Dim light leaks from the curtained front windows of the house. She rings the bell, waits with mind roiling, for the approach of footsteps inside. She's forgotten her umbrella in the taxi. Fat rain drops splash on her face.

"Zora!" Ahmed cries as he opens the door. "Come in!" He welcomes her with brief hug and helps her out of her coat.

"Where is Tariq?" she demands.

He grimaces. "Our sources have no updates." His eyes telegraph distress as real as hers.

She feels she might cry instead of rage. "Not knowing," she admits, "is the worst kind of helpless." He sighs, hangs her coat and leads her into the kitchen.

"Someone wants a document Tariq gave me," she says.

He glances out the window, smoothing a ripple of surprise from his face. "I did not know he gave you a document."

"You didn't answer my phone message." She drops into a chair. Tenting her elbows on the cluttered table, she grips her hands in front of her mouth. "You could have told me what I was getting into."

He rests his hand on her shoulder. "Let me make Turkish coffee." He busies himself opening a tin, spooning dark grounds into small pot. "I did not know," he says quietly, "if you would make contact with Tariq." He sets two small cups on the table. "A dirty war puts every loyalty to the test. If I had given you background and you had not met him, then how could I know what you would do?" He pours steaming water into the pot. "But you *did* seek him out. It was for you, and him, to decide what would follow."

She spreads her hands on the table, dismayed that her nails look as shabby as her reason for being angry with him. She had, in fact, pursued Tariq with some delight. She let her heart out to play in a war zone. And now it's time to deliver on promises made. As Ahmed reaches into the cupboard for sugar, she slips the document from her bra. When he comes to the table, she hands him the paper and Senoja's envelope.

He unfolds them carefully. As he reads, his face registers growing amazement. "Ahhh, Tariq," he murmurs, glancing at her. "He has a gift for finding jewels in the muck." He moves on to the page Senoja gave her, his lips moving silently. Finally, he looks at her and smiles. "Tariq tells us who the regime's business partners are and how much money they have committed for various "projects." The other document provides useful details about how the network moves money. Together they illuminate the financial investment in the genocide."

Zora stares at him. "People write down that kind of stuff? What…like three million for razing twenty villages, like that?"

He chuckles softly but does not smile. "In Sudan, there is only cash and it passes through many hands. Someone is always minding the transactions. Tariq made a point of knowing those people. He was able to tease out the pieces." His expression darkens. "Who else knows of this?"

She looks away, embarrassed. "Before I knew what I had, I gave a copy to Congressman Jackson Sykes. I was delusional, thinking he'd help get Tariq released."

He huffs, lays the papers on the table. "Surely this information is, how do you say, 'on the street'." He pulls a cherry wood pipe from his sweater pocket and chews the tip of the stem. "The regime will pretend to roll out a new leadership scheme, to toy with international attention." He packs tobacco in the bowl of the pipe and lights it. "If Khartoum cannot use such a change to neutralize this information leak, the business partners will quickly abandon the regime." He draws on his pipe and pungent smoke curls around this face. "You see, they don't mind mass murder as a revenue stream, but to be seen as a financier of genocide is a stain that is hard to erase. It's bad for business." He taps the bowl of his pipe. "Without the partners, the regime will be little more than a gang of rag-tag thugs. We've waited a long time for this unraveling. And it has begun."

Fingering the documents, she tells him of the meeting with Mr. Mo, of his threats to Tariq and Abuk.

His agitation heightens to alarm. "In Sudan, they would drag you from your house. Your body would never be found. Here they cannot be overt, but they have you in their sights. My friend, you are in grave danger."

"So I've been told." She folds the papers and zips them into a pocket of her purse. "But I have to finish this. I have to take the information public."

He gazes over her head, as if considering an idea, then rises and beckons her to follow. In a back bedroom, he removes a padlock from a closet, opening the door to reveal two chest-high stacks of file boxes, each labeled in large Arabic script. "You are holding the big nails to crucify the regime. Here are the smaller ones for their coffin." He pulls a cover off a box. "We have collected military orders, political directives, eyewitness reports of attacks, lists of the murdered and the murderers. The everyday evidence of the regime's brutality. 'Ethnic cleansing' is a cowardly euphemism, don't you think?"

Eyes wide with surprise, she runs her hand over the top box. "You keep evidence of genocide in your *closet*?"

"My dear, what should I have done? We are waiting for a judicial body to take up an investigation of war crimes in Sudan."

Opening the box, she scans the file labels, recognizing a litany of bombing sites. "How'd you get these documents?"

"They were smuggled from sources inside the government and the military. From well-placed people who care about the survival of their country." He selects a file. "Let me read this to you. It's from the executive committee of the Islamic Bloc, urging members to redouble efforts in Al Zarga region."

"'Al Zarga'?"

"An epithet for black Africans." He reads: "'Our task is to create problems for the regional government, to stop production in those areas, assassinate leaders, immobilize public utilities and make the citizens feel the incapability to provide life fundamentals.'" He meets her eyes. "This was in 1987."

She hisses her surprise. "Decades ago!"

"Indeed. The architects of the genocide have patiently followed a detailed long-term plan." He replaces the file and turns to her. "My dear, in the beginning, they held camel races to finance the project. Then oil revenues made them wealthy and business partners scurried for a piece of the action."

"Why didn't you make this information public?"

"The earliest documents were published in obscure newspapers. The rest, we gave copies to government agencies who ought to have found them useful in forming a realistic Sudan policy. But we cannot scatter what, one day, will be evidentiary material." His face seems to drain of energy. "None of this will be worth a dinar unless the leaders of the regime are brough to account."

Rain thrums on the roof, gathering force. Gusting wind rattles the window. The lights brown and recover.

"You have acquired the key," he says quietly.

She leans against the doorjamb, stroking her forehead, wishing, for an ugly desperate moment, to un-know all of it. "Tariq's information is—"

"The breakthrough."

She regards him calmly. "What price will he pay for uncovering it?"

"We will get him out. *Insha'allah.*" The sorrow in his eyes makes a lie of his prayer.

"And now I have endangered you by coming here."

He smiles. "They already know where I live."

CHAPTER TWENTY-TWO

Bert unlocks the door to let Zora in. "Aluot left," she announces, scanning the street before she closes the door and sets the deadbolt. "The poor woman was completely undone when I told her about our meeting with Mr. Mo. My Lord she was scared and oh dear you look dreadful."

Zora brushes rain from her hair. "What exactly did she say?"

"She said just being seen with you is dangerous for her."

"She's right." She peers at Bert. "That applies to you too, don't you see?"

Bert shrugs. "Well, I'm not leaving." She nods toward the living room. "You should check on the girl."

Abuk is crouched in front of the fireplace poking at the burning logs. She wears a bulky sweater, a scarf, thick tights beneath her wrap skirt and furry pink moppet slippers that Bert must have fished out of the back of a closet. "Hi, baby," Zora calls. Abuk turns her head, smiles wanly then continues sparring with the fire.

"She got upset when Aluot left," Bert explains. "I tried reading to her. Some of those old children's books you keep on your shelf, but it's just the wrong vocabulary, so I consulted the Dinka-English dictionary your momma left, but I don't get the pronunciation, and we really have to find a native Dinka speaker." She waits for Zora to finish taking off her boots. "Perhaps you'd like to fill me in?"

Zora settles into the easy chair, grazing Abuk's shoulder with a caress. She tells Bert about her meeting with Ahmed.

"I wonder how," Bert says, "in all this time, Ahmed's managed to keep despair at bay." She rests her hand on Zora's. "He probably is in a state of shock that you have this information."

"Imagine how many people want it to go away."

"Can you hand it off to someone you trust in television?"

"Precious few of those. And they don't control what gets aired. And the genocide has hardly raised official eyebrows at State." She rises, handing Abuk another log to put on the fire. "Maybe a newspaper journalist."

Bert is agitated. "Exposing high level criminals is very dangerous business."

Zora regards her. "I won't sit on this information."

"I'm not suggesting that. We have come up with a plan that keeps us out of danger."

Zora nods, her lips playing with a small smile. "What better use of our days than plotting to bring mass murderers to account?"

—

The early first snowfall blows in during the night. They awake to the spectacle of white-blanketed streets and houses frosted like confections. Abuk's fascination inspires a brief foray onto the front porch to examine the unfamiliar white stuff. Hovering near the door, Zora notices a black Taurus lightly dusted with snow parked three houses down the block. The windshield has been cleared enough for her to glimpse a dark figure at the wheel. Abuk snatches a handful of snow from the porch rail. Shivering, squealing with delight, she dashes back into the house. Bolting the door, Zora knows that Mr. Mo's campaign to break her is in motion. Bert offers Abuk a pan for the snow and, to Abuk's bewilderment, puts it in the freezer. Zora checks that all the blinds and curtains are drawn and the doors bolted, though she ran the same drill the night before. Twice. Paranoia is becoming her new best friend.

She picks at pancakes Bert prepares while Abuk wolfs down a stack. She has research to do that will require sidelining Abuk. A snow day strategy is required. She brings out a box of drawing paper and colored pencils and sets them on the coffee table, expecting Abuk's curiosity to oblige. When she returns from the bedroom with her laptop, Abuk is examining the pencils, running her fingers over them. Zora knows that she's seen people on TV use this kind of thing to make pictures. In her village, they drew in the sand. Zora also knows that this place is too cold for a girl used to 100-degree heat.

"We work together," Zora says. Sitting cross-legged on the floor, she sets her laptop on the coffee table, wondering if the magic of mothering, that generous attentiveness, springs naturally out of one's soul or if each day means learning to love logistics. Ella managed it with treasure hunts and craft fests and baking extravaganzas. The trick seemed to be not minding whatever you think you must give up.

As Abuk unboxes more pencils, Zora checks email. Ahmed's petition to gain Tariq's release seems a long shot. The thought swoops in: her email is under unknown scrutiny. How could she warn friends of possible hacking?

She combs through several databases, hunting for information about newspaper reporters who might take on the Third Reich of Africa. Compared with their Nazi brethren, Sudan's regime has prosecuted a genocide in slow motion. Over twenty-five years, four million dead; the figure would steadily rise if anyone were still counting. The regime masterfully used every tool in the genocidaires kit: unrelenting violence, detentions and torture, press censorship, and expulsions of humanitarian aid organizations. With a shiver of clarity, Zora knows she will not go back to her job. Talk, even the passionate sort, seldom helps people trapped in a killing machine. Policy debate seems a trivial pursuit when bodies are piling up. Her previous angst over lack of eyewitness credentials has propelled her into the dangerous predicament of knowing too much.

"Someone's at the back door," Bert calls.

Zora goes to peek through the curtain.

"I *know* what's happening with Tariq," Senoja says though the glass.

"Son of a bitch," she hisses, unlocking the door, pissed that he used the one thing that would get her attention. "Still working your death wish?"

He snatches off his cap, stamps snow off his boots and steps inside, smiling as if unaware of any discord between them.

Bert arches one eyebrow. "So you are Senoja?" She sizes him up for a moment. "Alias A. Jones. Don't you think reversing the letters of your name is kind of bush league for covert ops?"

He stares at her then coughs one of his phlegmy chuckles. "You're the first to notice."

Abuk dashes in smiling.

"Well, looka my girl," he says, offer a one-arm hug.

She grabs his hand to pull him toward the living room.

"Boots off," Zora orders.

He wrestles out of his boots, sheepishly setting them by the door. As Abuk leads him away, Zora follows, like a wronged spouse in a custody battle, considering how to capitalize on his sudden reappearance.

"We got a artist in the house," he announces, lifting a sketch from the coffee table. "Damn, if this ain't her granddaddy." Abuk grabs the drawing and clutches it against her chest. "Watch TV," she instructs.

Zora stands across from them. "So where is Tariq?"

"Security Police got him," Senoja answers, sitting beside Abuk as she works the TV remote. "At a prison near Khartoum."

"Old news," she jabs. "I wanna know how we get him out."

"We don't." He looks past her. "I came to warn you: walk away from this."

Abuk raises a fisted hand. "Lock and load."

"Damn! The girl watches too much TV," he scolds. "Ain't no way for a child to be fillin' time, listenin' to crap she don't even understand."

Bert steps from the kitchen with a large tray and sets it on the coffee table. "Homemade vegetable soup, toasted cheese sandwiches. Apple pie for dessert." She turns off the TV and sits beside Zora.

Abuk echoes Senoja's sigh of delight. They set to eating as if they've been fasting.

"Senoja," Zora says. "I'm taking Tariq's info public."

He stops in mid-chew. "That'd be paintin' a target on your fine face."

"Not if I give the story to a journalist."

He shakes his head. "They already know it's you." He slurps from the cup of soup. "They gonna get back at you any way they can. And you won't see it comin'. Zora, you gotta leave this alone."

"I can't leave it alone."

Senoja hisses in disgust. "Think your story's gonna change what's been going down for years?"

She watches Abuk eating with canine concentration. "I wanna give the perps reason to worry about payback."

"You still workin' this genocide thing," he accuses.

She can't tell if he's baiting her or simply determined to continue his necessary denial. "Yeah, well I think a few hundred thousand dead civilians is cause for concern. I want your help takin' down the criminals responsible."

"Nah uhh." He wipes his mouth with his sleeve. "Ain't no justice in this world. I stopped lookin' a long time ago." He sniffs, reforming his scowl into a sweet grin. "Miz Bert, I'd love some that fine lookin' pie."

Despite her unfavorable opinion of him, she laps up the flattery and slices the pie. Her expression says she doesn't understand why Zora tolerates him in the house, given his egregious betrayals. But there is something between them, as though they were siblings in a dysfunctional household, poking at each other for ways to cope with their undigested trauma.

Zora paces to the window then turns to face Senoja. "You know from the inside how these guys work. I want you to stand in the shadows and confirm the mechanism. Like Deep Throat during Watergate."

Senoja scowls. "I liked Nixon."

"You would."

"It's a different game now."

"No, it's the same damn game of top dogs gone rogue." She steps closer, looking down on him eating pie in the easy chair. "You just gonna go on playin' errand boy to a bunch of thugs killin' black folks by the thousands? When are you gonna man up with a workin' conscience?"

His face glazes into a hard impassive mask. Thinking he might bolt, she steps closer, blocking his exit route. "You bounce in here whenever you like, eat my food and hang with Abuk, conveniently forgetting you wanted to *leave her in Sudan*." The fire crackles. A snowplow thumps and scrapes down the street. "You almost get me killed and then you sell out Tariq. Dawg, you *owe* me. You wanna see this girl, you wanna be allowed in this house, then you gotta back me up."

He leans forward, hunching over his clasped hands, shaking his head. "I ain't gonna fight you over the girl."

"Good. But are you gonna help me?"

He nods. Bert shoots her a warning glance.

She knows his agreement is provisional. But she still has another card to play at the proper time. "You'll be needin' a better handle than Deep Throat."

CHAPTER TWENTY-THREE

The phone interviews with journalists pose a peculiar dilemma. She has to outline the story. She has to make clear the risk inherent in revealing the information. The latter is, of course, a deal-breaker for most reporters. Exposing a clandestine network, even righteously on so grave a matter, rated comparably with painting "Shoot Me" on one's back, family, home and workplace.

When she does find an interested reporter, his analytical talent comes well-seasoned with dark humor. Big questions with complex answers fascinate him. His name is Mike. He works for a mid-size California newspaper known for its investigative zeal and a display case with four Pulitzers. A UCLA alumnus, his rapid-fire questions and gravelly voice betray him as a caffeine-addicted smoker. He says that during his whole career, he's hoped for a story this big.

Zora convinces Ahmed to provide copies of key documents and even to speak to Mike. He insists on anonymity. Mike's fervor ratchets up. He agrees that an interview with Senoja could provide significant corroboration.

Senoja demands a voice-masking device. Zora enlists RayJ to set up the equipment in the back office of a Northeast club. Despite Senoja's objection to involving an outsider, he hits it off with RayJ. A half-hour before the arranged time for the interview, the two men sit jousting in tech-speak about the latest gear for covert ops. Zora paces the room, half-listening, checking her watch. Senoja seems curiously relaxed. She'll apologize for calling him an errand boy once they're done with this cloak-and-dagger shit. Soon she can watch the fallout from a safe distance, her duty discharged, the burden of silence relieved.

Five minutes before Mike's scheduled call, Zora sends RayJ out. The less he knows, the safer he'll be. Senoja turns to her. "I ain't doin' this." She skewers him with an incredulous look. He turns away. "You a dangerous fool. The dogs gonna know where this info came from. They gonna tie me in. I ain't gonna end up like Tariq, shittin' my pants while they shove a hot wire up my dick." He pushes chairs out of his way and heads to the door.

"You fucking asshole," she calls to his back.

When the phone rings, she tells Mike what's happened, not fully hearing what he says and hangs up dreading he'll need more. She leans against a wall, staring across the room at a scuffed sign reading *This Way Out*. Her eyes burn with tears; she pushes her palms against them, fighting the now egregiously enhanced image of Tariq being tortured.

Three days passed with no pokes from Mike. She frets about how long he'll take to finish the story, or that he'll back out. Bert fusses about their self-imposed house arrest even while encouraging Zora to get out and deal with Abuk's immigration status. She searches for a translator.

Through the flurry of homecoming, Zora had not looked at the video she'd shot in Sudan.. She plays and replays the footage of the raid on the village, the sneering shakedown by the *jellabiya,* the roll of money that had been a stay of execution for a couple dozen innocents. The terror is surreal, ruinous. She sends the files to Mike from a FedEx store. He misses an arranged call.

—

On a dreary afternoon, cranky with cabin fever, Zora takes Abuk to her momma's house. The black Taurus seems not to be on duty, but she takes a circuitous route to test this theory. Christmas decorations have sprouted around the neighborhood. For the first time in her life, she's been oblivious of the holiday's approach.

Reluctant at first to enter the house, Abuk relents when sleet begins falling. They walk quietly into the high-ceilinged parlor that feels like an abandoned movie set. Momma never tolerated matched sets of furniture, instead favoring orphan pieces with "good bones" and "attitude." The fringed purple velvet settee that once seemed fussy has garnered the cachet of family heirloom. Same with the gold brocade Queen Anne chair. Opening the upright piano, she fingers the cherubs carved on the ends of the keyboard and taps a few notes, wishing to hear momma's voice take up a song.

Abuk bounces on the settee, grinning and stroking the soft fabric. Zora imagines she can understand this house belongs to her, more than the house where they live. Many people could live here. But it has to be warmed up. Zora knows Abuk craves to be in the sun with her grandfather.

Long ago, Zora had found safe haven from nightmares here under a hand-made quilt, nestled against momma's warm body, breathing her woman-scent. She wonders if a child's distress infuses a mother with devotion or if fierce protectiveness is a hard-wired impulse. Perhaps it's not possible to understand mother love until it calls you to service. She wants no more ambivalence in this, her new life's work.

She follows Abuk drifting through her old bedroom and back through the rooms of the first floor, gently stroking everything with inquisitive fingers, head cocked, as if hearing distant echoes. This is the home momma paid for with her talent and willed "to my beloved daughter Zora." Selling it would be sacrilege.

As the days lurch by, her need to communicate with Abuk grows urgent. TV watching increases the girl's grasp of colloquial English but also malevolently imprints toxic images. Zora restricts TV viewing time to late afternoon. Bert brings immigration forms that need filling out. There are procedures to follow, and quickly, if they want to head off a surprise visit by ICE.

Domestic rituals thread the days together. Though increasingly listless and sullen, Abuk takes an interest in the household appliances. The refrigerator is a particular favorite with its interior light and in-door ice dispenser. She mercilessly experiments with its operation.

As they sort laundry together, Zora unearths several panties rank with the odor that had afflicted their travel in Sudan. When she holds them up with a questioning look. Abuk frowns and nods. Zora feels a wash of shame over her failure to follow up on the girl's medical condition. The next day she arranges an appointment with the Baltimore specialist recommended by Dr. Kamau. Another abscess has developed. After a brief procedure blessed with anesthetic, Abuk begins a course of antibiotics that quickly restores her energy. Surgical repairs will come soon. Her care requires a messy intimacy that no longer troubles either of them. Bert visits every day, sitting with Abuk near the fireplace to teach her English with magazines and flashcards.

On an overcast day, with no evidence of the black Taurus, Zora makes a grocery run. When she returns, stamping grey slush off her boots, Abuk confronts her. "'In-no-cent'?" she asks. "What means?"

Zora senses a dust-up. "It means—"

"I no this," Abuk complains, displaying a flashcard with a picture of a lamb. She forks her middle and index finger toward her eyes. "I *see* things."

"Yes, you do."

"I *see*." Abuk insists. "I no in-no-cent."

Bert follows them into the kitchen. "This cross-cultural stuff is like navigating a mine field." She begins unpacking a grocery bag.

"I think the mine field is the really terrible stuff she's been through."

'Yes, of course," Bert agrees. "But it doesn't seem to stop her interest in learning."

"Yeah, she's quick. "

"You talk about me?" Abuk demands.

"Yes," Zora answers, "We talk about how smart you are." Abuk frowns, her eyes void of understanding. As she leaves the kitchen, Zora shoots a questioning glance at Bert.

"Rough time for her," Bert explains. "Sadder than usual." She takes a box of cereal from Zora's hand. "Go be with her. I'll finish this and fix a snack."

In the living room, Abuk is huddled in her usual spot by the fireplace. Zora sits beside her.

"*Dit*." Abuk murmurs, "I want *dit*."

"Grandfather Luk." Zora rests her hand on Abuk's shoulder but she shakes it off.

"No *tukul*," Abuk grieves. "No *dit*." She bats away a tear before it can spill from her eye. Creature comforts do not salve the pain of her losses. The only man alive in her family is perhaps trudging toward uncertain safety through a withered, dangerous land.

After thirteen days of uncertainty, Zora logs on to the newspaper website, as she does every day, and discovers The Story: "High Level Genocide Conspiracy Revealed." She reads through the article's naming of names and tracing of partnerships. Mike has made a blistering case. Reaction will be brisk. But who in officialdom will shoulder the burden of responding? She can handle anything but toothless, declawed outrage.

Senoja appears at the back door. When Bert lets him in, he charges past her into the living room. "She okay?" he demands glancing quickly around the room. "Where's my girl?"

"What?" Zora sees fear in his eyes. "In my room."

He hurries down the hall, pushes open the door. Between the bed and the wall, Abuk has built a tent with sheets. The wall beside the tent's opening is plastered with drawings: a girl's face in mid-scream, a *tukul* engulfed in flames, figures running beneath a helicopter. He kneels and parts the sheet over the tent's entrance. Abuk peers at him from the dim space. "How's my girl?" he whispers.

She smiles coyly. "My crib."

He chuckles. "It's kickin', girl." He leans in on one hand. "I was thinkin' you need protection."

"Pro-tek-shun?"

He spreads his arms to block the entry. "You safe," he explains.

She smiles at the bulk of him guarding her. "Okay."

"Yeah, s'all good," he whispers. "Listen, baby. I know you havin' a hard time being here and I know you don't understand what I'm sayin' but I'm…I'm sorry for all the bad shit came down on you."

Abuk's watchful eyes are large and bright.

"You a tough lil shortie. You gonna be fine."

Zora kneels beside him. "What are you doin' here?"

He pulls his head from the tent. "I got a bad feeling soon as I saw the story." He stands up. "There gonna be heavy blowback."

She peeks through the drawn curtain; the black Taurus is nowhere in sight. "The watchers haven't been around for a couple of days," she tells him. A mail carrier mounts the stairs and pushes mail through the front door slot. Noticing her at the window, he points to the porch and continues out the gate. She goes to open the door. In the planter box, stashed like a neighborly gift, is a small white package with no postage, no address.

"Don't touch it," Senoja orders, stepping quickly in front of her. "Get inside." Kneeling beside the planter box, he examines the package from different angles. He sniffs it several times then gently run his finger over the wrapper. With both hands, he lifts it slowly, murmuring under his breath. He removes the twine around the white wrapper. Inside is a pale brown envelope with soft bulges.

"Step back," he directs as Abuk comes up behind Zora. Opening a pocketknife, he slits the envelope along its seam and carefully examines the contents. Satisfied, he withdraws a folded piece of faded orange cloth. Dropping the envelope on the porch, checking the street, he brings the cloth inside and locks the door. In the foyer, he lifts the fold, revealing a rust-colored stain. Beneath it are two lines of Arabic script penned coarsely on the fabric. "It's a piece a prison shirt." He lifts a second fold. A slip of brown paper flutters like a dying moth to the floor.

"Read it," she says, her voice brittle.

He rubs his hand nervously across his forehead, picks up the note. "It says: *'Death was the only mercy for the terrorist Tariq.'*"

The words hit Zora like a punch to the stomach. "No! NOOOOO!"

He balls up the cloth with angry hands. "They got wind of the story too late to stop it. They want you to know how pissed they are."

Zora slides against the wall to sit on the floor, hugging her knees to her chest. Silently, Abuk curls beside her.

"Good Lord!" Bert exclaims, coming from the kitchen. "*What* is going on?"

Senoja brushes past her on his way out the back. "I can't protect none of you now. You best get gone."

Zora wants to howl but her lungs resist efforts to breathe. Her body trembles violently. She rises unsteadily, wrestles on a coat, and flees the house. Stumbling along the root-buckled sidewalk, she gulps harsh-cold air with an open mouth. A sharp wind lashes her. Horn blaring, a taxi swerves to avoid her. She backs to the curb, shivering in the cold. Her eyes, glazed with wind-whipped tears, refuse to focus.

She grasps at shards of memory. His dazzling green eyes, luminous with desire. Then, dark with grief among the ruins of their people. Then wicked with challenge. He'd calculated she would honor blood ties. That she would carry forward his work, knowing the cost to them both. She had not believed that the price would be his life. His murderers deserve to die in agony like rabid dogs.

Suffocating dread settles upon her. All her life, she'd invented tricks to parry fear. Long jumping into her child's bed had thwarted the grasping phantom beneath. Glib retorts had neutralized high school taunts. Forthrightness had disarmed detractors of her work. But Tariq's murder is neither imaginary nor provisional. No sleights-of-mind will change the fact. Chilly raindrops spatter on her face. She remembers that Mr. Mo had two targets in mind. In the eerie umber light, she realizes she's abandoned Abuk. Crazy with fear, she sprints home. At the door, Abuk flies into her arms, crying pitifully against her chest. Curling on the sofa with her, Zora strokes her back, whispering reassurances.

Late in the evening, after Bert has held them both, letting them weep, after she's made hot chocolate and set logs on the fire, she tells them she will stay over. After midnight, Zora shuts the lights. The house seems to shudder in a keening wind. The windows rattle with crackling sleet. She lays beside Abuk, wakeful, like a wounded warrior awaiting the next battle.

CHAPTER TWENTY-FOUR

Before dawn, Zora sits numbly at her desk. There will be no retrieving Tariq's body for proper burial. Whatever had been left of the man she knew would have been destroyed, the fact of his existence erased. His execution had been both punishment and warning. There would be no memorial service among those who knew him in Sudan. There would be only private grief amid an ocean of anonymous sorrow over lost brothers, fathers, husbands. In their homeland, lives got erased without consequence.

From the memory card of the camera, she pulls up images she had deliberately avoided: Tariq, trudging along proud and stubborn as shit, towel on his head. Tariq burying a dead boy. Tariq and Abuk sleeping in the Land Rover, sick and worn. Tariq talking passionately with Luk. Abuk would want that one. She printed a copy and put it on the pillow beside Abuk's face.

Grasping for the comfort of routine, she checks email, finding one from ThelmaJ. After "Remember me? The Customs lady at Dulles?" Thelma asks if Zora would come talk to her church group about the troubles in Sudan. Behind her in bed, Abuk moans and begins thrashing her arms. Zora does what she'd learned to do when the phantoms invade: hold and comfort her until they are banished.

As the sun elbows through morning clouds, Zora pads to the kitchen and makes coffee. Bert comes in yawning, her hair comically mussed. "*Kochanie,* will you eat some breakfast?"

"Not hungry." Zora pulls her gaze from the kitchen window, the only one un-curtained these days. "I want to get Abuk enrolled in school. She needs something normal and regular outside this house."

"I suppose so." Bert begins preparing coffee. "With her fuzzy immigration status, it won't be simple."

"I filed the papers."

"And she'll need vaccinations because they don't want epidemics started by new students from exotic places. And she needs new clothes. And we don't know if she'll be safe, thanks to Mr. Mo. And she's not even literate though she should be in middle school. But you're right, of course. She should start school."

"Just the sort of pep talk I needed."

Abuk wanders in her pink flannel robe. "Morning good," she grins, holding up the photo Zora had left. "I see *dit.*"

"*Nam, ana saeed.*" Zora says. "I am happy." She kisses her cheek. "Do you want to go to school?"

Abuk furrows her brow.

"*Madrassa,*" Zora says. "*Dire temche…al madrassa?*"

Abuk smiles. "Okay!"

"Learning Arabic in your spare time?" Bert asks.

"A phrase here and there. It's easier to pronounce than Dinka."

Zora sees Abuk relax when she uses familiar works. Seeing her grandfather's photo seems to energize her.

The sun finally burns off the clouds. Zora wants to be anywhere but inside the too-familiar walls. If she thinks too long about Tariq, she'll be reduced to a weepy mess. If she worries obsessively about Abuk, she'll turn pathologically isolationist. "Abuk, let's go out," she says, glancing through the front curtains. The black Taurus is absent. Perhaps Mr. Mo believes Tariq's murder has punished her. Is she a moron to imagine that will be the end of it?

The day is unseasonably mild, an unexpected reprieve. The warming sun in the winter blue sky melts the icy residue of the night's storm. Abuk lopes down the street to commune with a wandering cat that darts under a parked car. She waits for Zora to catch up, smiling into the sun.

As they walk together toward Dupont Circle, a black SUV pulls beside them. Three men in uniforms jump out of the vehicle. The largest, a broad-shouldered guy with a military buzz cut, accosts them. "Zora Monro?"

"Who's asking?"

"Immigrations and Customs Enforcement." He touches the ICE badge on his shoulder. "You're harboring an unaccompanied minor who entered the U.S. illegally. We are authorized to take her into custody."

Zora puts her arm around Abuk. "She's not unaccompanied. She entered the country with me through Customs at Dulles."

"I have a court order to detain her." He reaches for Abuk.

Zora blocks him. "Let me see that court order."

The other two men, dark-eyed and stony faced, flank him. He holds up a document with a DHS logo and a scrawled signature. "How 'bout we do this nice and easy." The two flankers grab Abuk's arms and pull her toward the vehicle. She screams, twisting to escape. Zora reaches for her. The big guy wrenches her arm behind her back. She cries out for help. The door slams shut with Abuk inside, screeching wildly. The big guy lets go of Zora. She reaches for the handle, yanking frantically on the locked door. She pounds on the window. The vehicle speeds away. She chases it for a half-block, memorizing the tag number. Wheeling around, she sprints back to the house.

Crashing open the front door, she calls out: "Bert, ICE has taken Abuk!" She runs out back and flings open the garage door. The car will not start. Cursing, she keeps turning the key until the balky engine sputters to life. Jamming the car in reverse, she backs out, grazing the doorframe and speeds off in the direction the SUV has taken. She drives up Q Street, slowing to look for the SUV at each intersecting street. The traffic signal at Connecticut turns yellow; the car ahead stops, evidently driven by the only person in Washington who does not speed up to beat a light. It dawns on her that she has no clue where ICE takes detainees. She heads back home to find out.

Bert meets her at the door waving a piece of paper. "ICE Detention and Removal field office for DC is in Fairfax, Virginia."

Zora dials the number.

"They couldn't possibly be there yet," Bert counsels.

She hangs up and dials Mookie who answers with "Hey, I'm sorry I haven't called"

"Mook, can you find me the name of the judge that handles ICE detention orders for minors in DC?"

Mookie is silent for a moment. "They took your girl?"

"Snatched her right outta my hands."

"I'll get back a-sap."

Bert wrestles on her coat. "I'm going with you."

In rush hour traffic, they crawl toward the 14th Street Bridge. Bert sighs. "Well, the Feds actually have a bit of a case since you are not yet her guardian and she has no official immigration status and you had that unwarranted but very public allegation of slave trading, so it was only a matter of time until ICE came knocking."

"You're blaming me?"

"No, but I did encourage you to get her registered."

"Mr. Mo arranged that scene," Zora says.

Bert looks surprised. "You think he has that kind of leverage with a US government agency? Or would he use a favor like that just to punish you?'

"A small favor to protect big money?"

Bert runs her hand over her mouth. "Oh. Oh no."

They drive along Arlington Boulevard. Bert fiddles with the radio, finally settling on NPR. The reporter describes the uproar about a Swedish minister's complicity in Sudanese bombing of civilians. And, in the wake of recent disclosures by a California newspaper, a congressional hearing had been set to inquire into US corporations' involvement in Sudan.

"And so it begins," Zora observes. "The Committee will question and badger right on through the entire dog-eared agenda of moral and legal outrage. Then everything will just go on as it has."

Bert peers at her. "Cynicism doesn't suit you. Especially not on this. You helped stir the pot."

"It's a black hole suckin' the life outta anyone that gets involved." She speeds up as a knot of traffic dissolves. "I just want Abuk back."

They find the ICE facility in a nondescript office park off Route 66. A uniformed man behind a Plexiglas–enclosed counter does an obvious double take on Zora. His badge identifies him as J. Polter; he seems flirty enough to be helpful. She explains the circumstances of Abuk's arrest and asks to see her.

"No young girls on today's schedule," Agent Polter replies. He pecks at his computer. "Nobody in the system named Abuk, or like you describe. Anyway, we don't snatch little girls off the street. They come through the court."

"But the guys wore uniforms like yours with ICE badges. One of 'em waved a court order at me."

Bert shakes her head. "Who'd wanna impersonate ICE agents?"

Agent Polter frowns. "You see the plates on the vehicle?"

"Yeah." Zora gives him what she'd scribbled on a slip of paper.

He taps them into the system. "Vehicle reported stolen two days ago." The creases in his forehead deepen; he meets her eyes. "That makes probable kidnapping by men impersonating Federal officers in a stolen vehicle."

"We know who it is," Bert chirps. "Well, not his name."

"A hunch really." Zora demurs. "Nothing specific that would help."

Agent Polter throws her a quizzical glance then resumes tapping on his keyboard. "Puttin' a BOLO out on the vehicle. You got a photo of the girl?"

Zora makes a show of searching her purse, ashamed that she does not carry Abuk's photo, mortified that she has no photos of Abuk except the one in the passport "No, not with me."

"Can you fax it when you get home?"

"Yeah, sure.

"Here's the number. Give me yours."

In the parking lot, Bert scurries to keep up with Zora's march to the car. "You played it too close to the vest in there. "

Zora turns on her. "Abuk is *not* their concern. They wanna nail criminals masquerading as Feds. I don't trust them to handle it without a bunch of commando-types bustin' down a door and getting my girl killed." She slides into the driver's seat trembling. "Abuk must be scared shitless. I didn't protect her. I *promised* she'd be safe."

For the first time in their long, complicated life together, Bert sits speechless.

As they pull from the parking lot, Mookie phones. "Gotcha the judge's name."

"ICE didn't snatch her. SUV was stolen."

Mookie curses. "A kidnap?"

"Looks that way. ICE is on it, but you know where that goes. I'm not sure what to do."

"I'll come by in a half hour or so. We'll talk it through."

Zora hesitates. "Lemme call you later, Mook." She stabs END, uncertain if she wants to involve Mookie, both to protect her and because she has not understood her strange unavailability.

At the house, Bert prepares a salad and soup. Zora refuses to eat and retreats to her room. Sitting on the corner of her bed, she surveys the scatter of Abuk's clothes and drawings. The girl has slipped into careless housekeeping habits, contrary though they are to her natural orderliness. Among Abuk's sketches, she finds one of herself, a portrait without eyes. Over her left shoulder Abuk had drawn a small self-portrait, rendered like an angel whispering counsel.

Rather than "save" Abuk, she's managed to make her feel unseen. She didn't rally to protect the new center of her life, snatched like plunder in a secret war. She could even be dead. The thought makes her gasp for air. In a rush of fury, she grabs a lamp from the desk and hurls it across the room, shattering a framed Miro print. Shouting curses, she throws a jewelry box and, with gathering force, a makeup kit, a glass cherub, and a shoe. As she grabs a vase of flowers, Bert catches her arm. "Lord Jesus, Zora, get a grip." Seizing the vase, she embraces it protectively. "Child, I gave you this as a *gift*." She inspects the welter of shattered objects, shaking her head. "Abuk can't come home to a mess like this." She leaves the room.

Lightheaded, Zora stands breathing hard. She hears Bert rummaging in the kitchen closet, then padding back through the hall. She comes through the door armed with a broom and dustpan. "Cleaning helps you think," she declares, handing them to Zora. "This will take you a while. Fortunately for both of us." Her expression shifts from agitation to resolve. "I'm going to think by the fire."

Bert usually handles her distress with restraint, an endearing trait that now rankles Zora. Alone in the room, she swipes the broom over a shelf to clear shards of glass. The print has suffered a gash across one of the artful faces. She'd stopped liking that print ages ago. Sweeping the detritus off the rug, she cannot remember ever throwing objects in rage. Rage feels safer than fear. The possibility of losing Abuk terrifies her.

Her phone signals an incoming text message. She flips it open to read: *10 lee st ne 9pm come alone.* The sending phone number registers as "unavailable." She knows this is about Abuk. Pulling a map from her desk drawer, she locates the street in Anacostia. About a half-hour drive. It's 7 o'clock. Waiting here would be pure torture. Grabbing her coat, she heads to the door, tells Bert she'll be back, then circles to the kitchen for a box of crackers, a carton of juice. Abuk will be hungry. She's always hungry. She snatches a blanket from the bed, Abuk's heavy coat from the closet, the digital camera.

A light sleet is falling. She drives slowly, intent on the route she's planned, crossing the river on the Southeast Freeway Bridge into an unfamiliar neighborhood, bleak in the raw winter night. After cruising a dozen blocks, she finds Lee St., turns onto it and begins checking the numbers. Number 10 is a boarded up three-story house. She circles the block, returns to a spot down the street from the house and parks behind a beat-up Toyota. Switching off the engine and headlights, she slouches down to wait. A lone streetlamp at the corner flickers garish orange light. The house looks like a squat old woman who've given up any pretense of self-maintenance. An abandoned refrigerator lies like a beached dolphin among a wash of plastic bags and household trash. The naked frame of a bike, stripped of wheels, seat, handlebars and chain, hangs from a U-lock on rusted a chain link fence.

A few houses away, multicolored Christmas lights leak feebly from a second-floor window plastered with posters. A town car turns onto the street, stops in front of a boarded-up storefront. A man in a baseball cap steps quickly from the shadowed entrance to the car. The front window slides down to accommodate a quick exchange. She slouches further down; the car passes. A siren wails a few blocks away. Her phone rings. She quickly silences it. Bert, of course. She taps out WAIT and sends the message.

Damp cold settles in the car. She checks the time. Still a half-hour to wait. Turning on the engine for heat would betray her presence, probably with bad results. She pulls the blanket around her and tries to remember if Abuk was wearing enough to keep her warm.

Two men in black coats emerge from the alley beside the house. Purposeful shadows, they stalk down the other side of the street. She presses further down into her seat, watching them in the side view mirror until they reach the corner. A dark Taurus pulls up, they get in, the car drives off. No wasted motion.

She rummages in her purse for the camera. After she gets her girl back, she will shoot photos until Abuk begs her to stop. She thinks of the moment when they'd first met, how Abuk's dark eyes had riveted her. She hadn't known then what those eyes had seen, nor imagined how much she'd come to care about improving what they saw.

A figure staggers down a stoop nearby and vomits on the sidewalk. The sight makes her retch. The malaise of this neighborhood feels like early-stage Sudan. Gut the soul of a people and they *will* find ways, however sad, perverse, or humiliating, to inhabit the carcass of life. How could a revolution ever be a surprise?

At nine o'clock, she slides out of the car. Quietly closing and locking the door, she steps gingerly across the sleet-slicked street. As she passes the alley toward the house, she hears "Z" like an exhaled breath. A dark shape motions to her. She knows the silhouette. "Senoja!" she whispers.

He grasps her arm, puts a finger over his mouth, draws her into the shadows, and gestures with his head to follow him. They step around piles of trash to a battered door. A jimmied padlock hangs open from the bent hasp. Inside, he leads her by the hand through a lightless passage to another door. He pushes it open. A flashlight on the floor beams meager light on a cot. A human shape lies covered in black tarp, trussed with ropes. Senoja quickly stifles Zora's cry with his hand. Abuk emerges wide-eyed from a dark corner. She allows herself to be embraced; her body heaves with soundless sobs.

Senoja retrieves the flashlight, switches it off, and pulls them toward the door. With sure steps he guides them back through the passageway and outside. Replacing the broken padlock with an identical new one, he straightens the hasp and snaps the lock shut. Scanning each entrance to the alley, he takes Abuk's hand and leads them to a recessed garage with no door. He motions them into the back seat of a black sedan. From the driver's seat, Senoja turns to Zora. "I wanted ya to see how they was gonna leave her tied up like that to die. You gotta take this serious."

"Jesus, I been goin' crazy! *Of course* I take it serious."

Regret flickers over his face; he turns away. "When boss man sends his soldiers back here and they see I messed with the plan, I'll be joinin' y'all as a mark. Hard to say what their next move'll be. I ain't stayin' to find out. Got me another gig as far away as I could get. It's on you to keep this girl safe." He starts the engine. "Gonna take you to your car."

Zora holds Abuk tightly as he maneuvers out of the alley and around the block. The street is empty. "Revenge gets outta hand," he says softly, as if he is talking to himself. "These dudes never think what it means to mess with children."

"Senoja, I–"

"No way I'd let shortie go out like that." He stops beside her car. "I can't be protectin' you two no more. Just get outta here. Now."

Zora touches his shoulder, whispers "Thank you." As she gets out of the car, Abuk leans forward, encircles Senoja's head with her skinny arms and kisses his cheek. She hops quickly into Zora's car, clambering over the center console into the passenger seat. Zora scoots in and locks the doors. Senoja drives away. They watch the taillights until his car disappears around the corner.

Abuk touches the tears that spill from Zora' eyes. Zora imagines she wants to tell her about being tied up, how hard it was to breathe, how cold it was, how they made the dummy body from papers to trick the evil men who left her there. Zora strokes her hand, knowing she will hold her tears for a little while. They watch the messy sleet falling from the sky and breathe the heated air.

CHAPTER TWENTY-FIVE

"Oh sweet Jesus!" Bert wails. She locks Abuk in her arms. Abuk goes rigid against her for a moment then surrenders. Bert grabs her by the shoulders laughing, touching her face as if to confirm that her flesh is still warm.

"Senoja saved her," Zora reports.

Bert doesn't seem to hear as she ushers Abuk to the bathroom. "Let's get you out of those clothes and into a hot shower."

Zora thinks that Bert is like a nervous mother, fussing about. Probably Abuk's aunties looked after her, but not in the way of someone who mistakes you for their own child. Maybe it is something you can pretend until you believe it. Maybe she can believe she is part of a new family. Perhaps she does not mind there are no men because men usually bring trouble. Except her grandfather.

The hot water makes Abuk stop shivering. She holds her face beneath the flow and lets her tears join the stream down her body. Being tied up like an animal in a cold dark place is just like being a slave. She thinks she would rather die than have it happen again. If wicked people could come and take her, and even Auntie couldn't stop them, then maybe she will never go outside again.

She sits down in the shower of water, holding her knees to her chest. She think that someday it might not be cold in this place and she will *need* to go out. That was how her life had been, out in the sun with her work and her friends. It would be better if she knew people to visit. Auntie talked about school. Girls must be allowed there. That could be a safe place.

The hot water feels so good. Auntie is not knocking on the door as usual. She doesn't like anyone to use a lot of water. This makes no sense. The water flowed without having to be carried. Like magic. She did not know enough about this magic. She shuts off the water and slowly dries herself, then studies her reflection in the glass. She sees bruises where the man held her arms. She knows he was Sudanese by the way he talked. He told her she was going to die. She spit on him and he spit back. He forced her against the wall like he would have sex with her. That's when she kneed him between his legs. The other man stopped him. His talk was different. The wrapping they'd put around her smelled like a dead animal.

She puts on her warm robe and goes into the room where they keep the fire. Zora and Bert make a place for her between them on the long soft thing they call a sofa. When she sits down, Zora wraps a blanket around her. All the sadness feels like thorns in her heart. She tries to stop her tears but they come falling down. The tears that were hiding when Senoja told her he would go far away. Tears for her friends buried in the ground of their village. And for grandfather. She misses him like her heart will die.

After a long while in the warmth of the fire, Zora feels Abuk's body relax, hears the soft breathing of sleep. Bert whispers that rescuing Abuk was unexpectedly heroic of Senoja and wouldn't he be pleased to know they thought him brave. Cocooning in comforters, they sleep as falling snow hushes the world.

—

Zora stands at the kitchen window watching fat snowflakes splat against the window. TV's "Storm Center," rife with bundled-up reporters, trumpets a foot of snow on the ground and more on the way, changing to freezing rain. The city is paralyzed. A probable white Christmas is two days away. Finding the kind of safety they need will be nearly impossible until the weather clears

Feet stamp outside the back door. Bert pops in, cheeks florid. "The neighborhood's a wonderland!"

"Didn't know you'd gone out."

"Let's go get a tree!" Bert says, pushing the door closed against a sudden gust. "It's never too late for a merry Christmas." She dusts snow from her hat. "We could all use a bit of fun."

Zora puts water on for tea. "I don't want Abuk out yet."

Bert's expression suggests she thinks otherwise. "At least take the child out in the yard to enjoy the snow. I'll go and enjoy buying a Christmas tree."

Zora adjusts the scarf around Bert's neck. "You're a member of our 'marked women' group."

"Of course," she says. "'Stay aware and carry on' is my new mantra." She winks, pulls on her gloves and leaves.

Swirling snow mounds on the fence and frosts the shrubs in the backyard. The dreamy landscape beckons like a school-snow-day fantasy, offering respite from cloistering in the house. Zora coaxes Abuk out of her tent and takes her by the hand to the closet. Abuk stoically cooperates with putting on the heavy leggings, the boots, the sweater and coat but, by the time Zora pulls a cap over her head, her fragile calm dissolves. Her arms and legs whip into an awkward dance to shed the layers. Zora backs off. "Yeah, stay inside," she soothes. "It's okay baby, I'm not leavin'." She kisses her cheek. "Have some tea."

Pulling the door shut against a gust of snow, Zora ventures down the stairs, feeling for sure footing. The quickly massing Sudan scandal has weakened the holiday season's usual sappy hold on the media. Reporters of all stripes are weighing in on the iniquities du jour. Before leaving on break, two key Congressmen ream the CIA Director for the agency's cozy alliance with the Sudanese Security and Intelligence Agency, a major purveyor of terror in their own country. Eager to firewall the administration, the White House press secretary hastily affirms that a full array of sanctions on Sudan remains in place. It is a skirmish with no consequence.

The International Court issues an indictment of the Sudanese President for crimes against humanity, forcing an ugly dilemma on purported allies: preserve a relationship with the regime or honor the obligation to extradite an accused war criminal should he arrive for a visit. His travel options depend on who is willing to thumb their nose at current or future distain.

A Swedish minister quickly is drummed out after a human rights group produces several years of flight records from his former company's airstrip in a Sudanese oil field. Seems the company has been generously accommodating the Sudanese Air Force as it bombed rural villages into ruin.

Amid renewed rumors of a coup, Sudanese ministers pack off their families on private late-night flights to European capitals. Under tight curfew, the capital morphs into a heavily policed ghost town. The situation is riveting but an unraveling regime, even an Islamic one, can hold headlines for only so long. A redemptive outcome assumes the media's ability to "sit and stay" with the ugly facts. She does not believe they are capable of this.

She sees Abuk framed in the window, watching her, mournful in the way of the old woman in Sudan who wished for a painless death. She beckons her with a gloved hand. Abuk shakes her head and turns away.

Bert returns with a three-foot spruce, excited. "So I'm waltzing down the rows of mixed evergreens and I run into—literally— a girl with a scarf over her face, and the scarf falls away and I can see she's disfigured and I blurt out "what happened to you?" and a woman comes over, and she isn't upset like the girl and I didn't mean to upset her but it was so startling and she tells me that the girl is her niece and she was burned with acid and she brought her to the US for asylum and I told her about Abuk and what's happened to her and she told me about this organization in Arlington that works with survivors of torture. She gave me a number to call for counseling services."

"You never cease to amaze."

"Well, Abuk is struggling and I really have no idea what to do for her and isn't it funny how people show up with help just when you need it?"

Zora nods. "You have a gift for reeling 'em in." They carry the tree inside and shed their coats and boots in a scatter. "Mini Spruce" gets staged near the front window. As Zora makes a phone call, Bert brings boxes of Christmas decorations from the bedroom closet. Under Abuk's impassive gaze, she begins removing the shiny ornaments from their boxes.

"A miracle has occurred," Zora says, stepping from the kitchen. "I found an Arabic-speaking social worker who will make a house call. Tomorrow!"

"We're lucky some people don't celebrate Christmas." Bert hands her a box of lights. After she wrestles the green wiring out of the package, she hands one end to Abuk. "Baby, come and hold this," she prompts. With vague curiosity, Abuk takes hold of the plug and sits watching her circuit the tree, arranging the tiny lights over the green branches. With a tray of assorted ornaments in her hand, Bert moves in to begin decorating.

Fingering a shiny silver ball, Abuk hangs one on a branch just the way Bert has done. She thinks it makes no sense to put pretty things on a prickly bush, but she likes the way they look. It helps her not think.

When they have hung every bauble from their years-old collection, Bert unboxes a black angel with gossamer wings. Clinging to Zora's hand, she docks the angel to the top of the tree. Then she gazes at Abuk with mischievous delight, plugs in the lights and steps back, smiling beatifically.

Abuk cocks her head, frowning as if she's been asked to comment politely against her will. "Bogus," she declares.

Bert sighs. "That would be one of your new words."

"Well, for the uninitiated, it's gotta seem a bizarre use of a baby tree." With her foot, Zora nudges the empty boxes into the corner. "I been thinking about something you said: that momma kept the secret so long because she was afraid of losing me."

"That's a theory."

"I think she wanted to protect me."

Bert adjusts an ornament. "Go on."

"She wanted to spare me from knowing my very personal connection with suffering that just goes on and on. No matter what anyone does."

Bert drapes a hand gently over Abuk's arm. "I think Ella would want you to focus on knowing what you *can* do." She nods Abuk toward the kitchen. *Fotoor.* Let's eat."

As they clatter in the kitchen, Zora packs away the empty boxes. "I've been thinking about something else," she calls. "Movin' to momma's house." She goes to the kitchen door. "My income's disappeared. Her place is paid for. That eliminates having to pay rent. I've got the money from Senoja to pay the other bills until I figure out how to make a living again."

Bert slices and begins chopping an onion.

"Might be a safer for Abuk–"

"Living in Southeast? How's that safer?" Bert argues. "And don't kid yourself that we're out of the woods with Mr. Mo. If they want to find you or Abuk, moving isn't going to throw them off."

"I can't live worryin' constantly about what some crazy bastards might do. She can't live cooped up like a house cat. We'll put in a security system, get Abuk some sort of—"

"Bodyguard?" Bert pushes a pile of onions to the side of the board. As she reaches for a tomato, Zora snatches it away. Abuk chuckles softly when Bert tries to grab it back, pretending to be annoyed.

"Look B," Zora says. "I don't have all the answers. But you're gonna see me stressin' if I've gotta keep payin' rent with no job. I'm lookin' at the right-in-front-of-us way to keep it all together."

Bert nods.

Zora grabs two more tomatoes and begins juggling them, provoking another small chuckle from Abuk. "You wanna learn how to do this?"

Abuk shakes her head. "I want eat."

"Okay." She hands her a tomato and gives the other two to Bert. "There's a new charter school near momma's house."

'Uh huh." Bert lights a burner and sets the skillet on it.

"Abuk can start school. And I hear there's a PTA."

"Good." Bert quickly chops the tomatoes.

"We could do a little renovation on momma's kitchen. Repaint the bedrooms." She sidles over to Bert's right side. Taking the cue, Abuk positions herself on the left. "You wanna move there with us?"

Bert glances at Abuk then at Zora. "So, you're looking for a financial partner and live-in child protection?" She pushes the chopped vegetables into the pan; they hiss in the hot oil.

"That's a touch raw," Zora pouts. "Are you so in love with your little condo?"

Abuk takes the wooden spoon from Bert's hand and stirs the vegetables.

Bert offers a sly grin. "Let's cut to the chase." She steps back from the stove and perches a hand on her hip. "It has to be a *cook's* kitchen. And I get the front bedroom."

CHAPTER TWENTY-SIX

The media hoopla over genocide profiteers quickly tanks, as if gentlemen's accommodations have been discretely arranged. The Sudanese government escalates its campaigns against tribal groups though its military has lost its sugar daddies. Senior officials rail against Western interference while sending massive amounts currency out of the country. Rumors of infighting among the cabinet swirl behind international criminal indictments. Exponentially rising inflation sparks violent public demonstrations in the capital.

Zora reads these signs with ambivalence. She would happily watch the sons of bitches in power mercilessly subjected to their own brand of brutality, but that would not portend well for governance after they are eliminated. She prays that, on the other side of the maelstrom, the threat of reprisal that circumscribes her life will evaporate. But she still can hear Senoja's warning *never* to underestimate the memory or methods of powerful men professional at revenge.

The transfer of residence consumes nearly a month. During all the back and forth, they see no overt signs of watchful eyes. They paint the bedrooms of the old house in brilliant hues, eating take-out Chinese as they sit in paint-spattered clothes on paint-spattered drop cloths. Every weekend they move some furniture to the house. To stanch the anxiety that has dogged her since Abuk's kidnapping, Zora hangs blackout shades on the front windows and installs a sophisticated security system. Abuk builds a bamboo-framed canvas hut in Zora's childhood room. Her sessions with the social worker seem uneven. Sullen grief ambushes her without warning and drives her into seclusion in her hideout.

On a self-serving hunch, Zora makes a long overdue call to Thelma Johnson, the Customs lady. After Zora's speech about the Sudan situation to her church group, they gather for lunch in the church basement, showering her with questions. Thelma prompts for news about Abuk. The story of her kidnapping incites both outrage and a surprising offer: three retired army buddies want to put together a "protection detail." Like doting uncles, they begin dropping by the house on a rotating schedule "to make sure the ladies are secure." Bert is over the moon with the appreciative new cookie tasters and lunch cadgers.

Abuk stoically submits to a pre-enrollment medical checkup and a battery of immunizations. Zora skirmishes briefly with a school counselor over a recommended special-needs placement for Abuk, finally convincing him that an illiterate thirteen-year-old growing up in a war zone is traumatized and *under*educated, not mentally handicapped. One of the "uncles" walks her to school every day, relaxing into his own brand of doting behavior. Ted, a paunchy, balding man with laughter in his eyes and a VFW pin fastened to his shirt pocket, brings stories of his childhood in rural Alabama. Sports enthusiast Howard, a lean man with arthritic knees, teaches her how to dribble a basketball during the six-block walk. Bookish, bespectacled Robert walks with a cane and brings stickers for her notebooks or artsy patches to sew on her bookbag. Anticipation of their company dissolves her resistance to rising early for school. At the end of the day, she waits for their arrival, proud that she has been singled out for their attention, oblivious of snide jokes from boys about the "geezers."

With ESOL classes and a patient tutor, she quickly develops a startling command of English. She reads aloud everything: food labels, street signs, flyers, menus, newspapers, magazines and books, and *Jeopardy* clues. At home she begins hogging the computer, eager to web surf for pictures and stories about Sudan. She has posted her drawing of her grandfather among other family photos on the fridge.

Zora devotes her days to slogging through the labyrinth of U.S. Immigrations, determined to gain legal status for Abuk. There are more lengthy forms to complete. Perfunctory civil servants and a voluble attorney seem to parcel out information in tiny packets, as if the full extent of requirements would be alarmingly Kafkaesque. And in fact, the stories she hears from fellow petitioners cooling their heels at the INS office fuel her fear that the process will chew up her money and her sanity. She arms herself with late night research into immigration law and resettlement procedures. She practices patience as documents are drafted and amended and reviewed and stamped and filed.

On a bright February Saturday afternoon, a packet of mail plops through the slot. As the new self-appointed mail manager, Abuk swoops in to fetch it. She says likes the surprises that come every day and she gets to keep the ones Auntie calls "junk mail." This day, there's a large envelope covered with bright blue letters; it ought to become hers. The other envelope is small and brown with pink birds on the stamp. From "Nyy-roow-bee," she says, experimentally hanging on each syllable. She delivers the envelope to Zora at her desk.

Glancing at the postmark, Zora asks: "Who do we know in Nairobi?" The message inside is handwritten in graceful script on lined notebook paper. She reads aloud:

I am writing on behalf of Luk Jok Kiir.

"*Dit*!" Abuk cries, leaning energetically on her shoulder.

"*He came to Kakuma refugee camp in Kenya on 10 December.*

He was very ill but is recovering. He requests news of his granddaughter, Abuk.'"

Squealing with delight, Abuk dances around the room while Zora gapes at the letter, dumbfounded that Luk kept her card and managed to get a message through.

"I want to write back!" Abuk crows. Grabbing a pad of paper, she sprawls on the floor and with lip-biting concentration prints a message with a red marker. Singing softly, she draws elegant little faces in the corners of the paper. When Bert arrives home from her new part-time job as a tutor, Abuk meets her at the door and pours out the news.

"We'll have a party!" Bert proclaims. "A celebration."

Abuk calls to Zora: "You good with that Auntie?"

"Auntie?" Zora steps into the hall.

Abuk flashes an unreadable expression, her mouth pinched in a taut line. "I always think you are my Auntie."

Zora gazes at her. "Well, I'm thinking you are my daughter."

Abuk offers a smile. "I like that."

"Good. As long as we're together, we get to work out what it means."

"I'm the Auntie," Bert insists. "And the party will also be a housewarming. We haven't done that yet."

"Housewarming?" Abuk asks.

"A party for friends to bring joy to our home." Bert winks and dances a little jig.

"B, you weird. Can Mattie come?" Mattie is Abuk's first friend at school.

"Yes, Mattie and her mom and dad."

"Mattie no has dad. Like me."

"I'm sorry. I never heard what happened to your dad."

"Not me either." Abuk shakes her head. "He was killed." She watches dismay grow in Bert's eyes. "I have *dit."*

"Yes," Bert says softly. "Yes, you do."

The party is set for the following Saturday night. The three women spend all day preparing. Bert plans a menu in honor of her sisterly years with Ella and their Soulish cuisine: a big pot of goulash, kielbasa, three fried chickens, two pans of cornbread, greens and mashed potatoes. Working deftly around her, Abuk prepares a chicken *mulla* and *kisra.*

Late in the afternoon, they begin decorating. Abuk tapes her drawings on the walls of the parlor, draping each with yellow crepe paper. Zora strings star-shaped lights around the doors. At dusk, when the aroma of baked pies wafts through the house, she steps outside to put candles in holders near the front door. Across the street, a black Taurus idles, a silhouetted man behind the wheel. She drops back inside the door, fear rising like a lit match. Holding her breath, she stares at the nightmare car, expecting a threat to uncoil. A woman hurries from a neighboring house with a small boy in tow. She opens the back door of the Taurus, lifts the boy and fastens him in a child seat. She gets in the front seat and kisses the driver. The car moves away. Zora backs inside the house and closes the door. Leaning against the wall, she slowly breathes her way out of a pointless panic attack.

Mookie and her daughter Dessie arrive with a bottle of champagne. Zora hadn't seen Dessie for a long time. The girl has made her way well into a woman's body. She wears short dreadlocks, a white silky blouse that teasingly reveals her ample cleavage, a cherry red skirt that barely covers her ass, gold, strappy spiked heels and big hoop earrings. Her raucous laugh conspires perfectly with her office vamp ensemble to announce a formidable female in the house. Though Mookie had been laying low for weeks, she was relieved when Zora called to invite her, admitting that she missed her, especially with all the juicy scandals cropping up around Tom. She pops the cork of the champagne bottle. "Let's get this party rollin'!"

Ahmed arrives with his wife, Pamela, an Irish woman with green eyes and short red hair that's gracefully ceding to grey. Their first granddaughter was born two weeks ago. They brought photos. Ahmed is buoyant, allowing himself to imagine the end of war in his country. "After all," he proclaims, "A new member of the family deserves new hope."

When her two friends arrive, Bert hurries out of the kitchen in her pink apron. She introduces Sadie, a Rubenesque woman in a flowing burnt orange dress. Sadie decided to resume churchgoing as a hedge against years of agnosticism; that's where she met Bert. She's been hoping to find a respectable man, but a good woman friend, one who shares her passion for cooking, has been just as lovely an outcome. She's recently taken up belly dancing. There could be a demo tonight, she says, offering a twitch of her hips.

With her is George. Tall with thick grey hair, he's a retired Air Force pilot who's devoting his "golden years" to teaching immigrant children to read. He met Bert at the tutoring office just after she'd begun working there. His eyes twinkle as he watches her regale the other guests with a story of Zora's first visit to the Polish side of the family. He tells Bert he's interested in discovering out just how fabulous a cook she is. With fetching delight, she leads him by the hand through the dining room to taste-test her culinary treats.

Abuk's personal bodyguards come with their wives, Ruby and Helen, dressed to the nines in polyester and pearls. Howard, a widower, brings a lady friend named Jasmine. As usual, they have small treats for Abuk, who thanks each with a firm handshake.

RayJ breezes in with a friend named Landy who's brought a saxophone. "Two other dudes comin'," he tells Zora "Piano man and drummer." He winks and kisses her cheek. "We be jammin' tonight."

When Mattie and her mom, Flora, present themselves at the door, Abuk lopes from the kitchen with a whoop. She and Maddie perform a ritual of rapid hand signals before dashing off to Abuk's room. Flora, a wide-bodied Ugandan woman in a dazzling red kaftan, says that the two girls have something special between them. She wants Abuk to come soon for "that American custom," a sleepover.

Before Zora can answer, she sees him ascending the steps. RayJ's piano man has rich brown skin, green eyes, and a knockout dimpled smile. RayJ chuckles, circling his arm around her waist. "Zora, this my man Jua. You two deserve to know each other."

The drummer, a short dark-haired man, maneuvers around them with his conga to claim a spot on the old Queen Anne chair. "Petey's not much for talk," RayJ whispers, "but he lays down a sweet beat." As if on cue, Petey begins stroking out a soft slow rhythm. Jua steps to the piano and fingers a little burst of notes. Zora catches his eye. He offers back a welcome-to-my-world smile. Landy readies his sax. Their rendition of *I've Got You Under My Skin* brings the old couples dancing into the room. When they switch gears into R&B, the women blend their voices as backup for Jua's full-bodied *Maybelline.*

Before the next song can begin, Bert announces: "Come and eat!" To applause, she and George bring platters of food to the dining table. The girls race down the stairs to be front and center at the buffet. Talk and laughter fill the room as everyone lines up to fills their plate.

Watching them, Zora knows her tribe finally has gathered. A hard search delivered some of them. Others arrived on the wings of serendipity. Like that fine Jua, showin' up like a gift. The house is full of the old family vibe; she can rest her back against this collective strength.

The party churns into the wee hours until a cop raps on the door and asks them to quiet down. "Neighbors complained," he says apologetically. Bert hands him a plate of cherry pie with ice cream.

Early the next morning, when the windows are still patinaed with frost, Zora hears Bert leave for church. She burrows under the comforter. Simply venturing out of bed on such a cold, overcast morning would require courage she does not want to muster. At 8:52 am, the doorbell awakens her. She shambles downstairs in her robe, unable to imagine who would presume to make an early call on Sunday. A uniformed policeman tips his hat, asks if this is the residence of Bertha Monrowski. The question confuses her; no one ever calls Bert by her given or maiden name. He asks if she is a relative. Nodding, Zora snaps alert.

"And what is your name?

"Zora Monro."

"I'm Officer Trent. Ms. Monro, I'm sorry to inform you—"

"Oh god no," she breathes.

"Ms. Monrowski's car was broadsided on Connecticut Avenue. She was killed in the collision." Silence.

"I'm very sorry for your loss." Silence.

"The driver of the other car was a young woman. Minor injuries but she was hysterical. She said the light turned green for her before she reached the intersection. Ms. Monrowski's car came speeding out of nowhere. Didn't slow down." Long silence.

"Will you come to the morgue to identify the body?"

She nods. She remembers that Bert had been fussing about her car needing new tires, asked if she could borrow Zora's if the roads were icy. Throwing on a coat, she struggles into boots and remembers to leave a note for Abuk. She allows the officer to hold her elbow, guide her to the car.

The morgue is a blur of antiseptic green and stainless steel. Bert's body, covered with a sheet, lies inert on the metal table. Zora wants to pick her up and carry her home, rest her in bed. A man in green scrubs asks her if this is Bertha Monrowski and she wants to say "No, not this ruined lifeless body. The real Bert went to Mass and will pick up some donuts on her way home, maybe a Sunday paper. They would be going grocery shopping later." She would not let Abuk see Bert this way.

She signs a form. Someone puts her in a taxi. She does not notice who is driving or the route they take but she knows the sky never looked bleaker.

Abuk is standing in the kitchen, the note in her hand, a look of fearful need on her face. "Where you go?"

"Abuk, baby, a bad thing happened." She says the words of the story, what she knows, the simple facts, calmly, until Abuk starts to cry and she holds her and cries too.

On a cold, rainy day, they bury Bert beside Ella. Everyone that feasted on her housewarming cuisine shows up at the gravesite. Sadie cooks for the wake. As she sets out a tray of fresh rolls, she says to Zora how strange it was. Such an annoyingly cautious driver as Bert would never run a yellow light, much less barrel through a red one. Was there a problem with the car?

Zora remembers someone saying that the massive damage would make it hard to confirm a malfunction. But the question nags, as if a part of her mind knows the answer but is shouted down by the matron on duty.

Bert's absence scours away any pretense of household routine. Zora warms up whatever food people have brought, and they graze distractedly, without much appetite. Abuk spends the days in her hut and the nights beside Zora, fitful, sometimes weeping. The uncles stop by and sit outside her lair, quietly telling stories or just keeping her company. A counselor will be coming by to help her get back into school.

Since Abuk suspended herself from the task, Zora retrieves the mail from the foyer floor. At her desk for the first time in a week, she pushes aside a pile of papers to sort the stack of mail. She puts the junk circulars in Abuk's box. The bills—fuck the bills! She opens a condolence card, reads the short note from Thelma. The dear woman comes by every day to "check in, see how ya doin'" and leaves without needing to be asked. At the bottom of the stack, she finds a card neatly printed by a foreigner, if the style of the numbers tells the truth. Inside is a white note card:

We are deciding how many more dead bodies you deserve.

She throws the card like a hot coal across the desk, circles her arms across her face. Bert died because she borrowed *her* car. Senoja warned she wouldn't see it coming, the "get-back," Mr. Mo settling the score. It felt like the twist of a knife plunged deep.

Abuk pads in, rubbing sleep from her eyes. Zora reaches for her, holds her close. She wants no more fear or sorrow for this child. Enough has been heaped upon her. But an unknowable threat is hard to evade. *How long before it ends?*

Zora realizes her grief is but a tendril of the vast suffering that snakes among all who have been trapped in the hopeless place where she first drew breath. She gazes out the window at a shrub leafing out too early in the winter-burned yard. "The one who knows the way" slides from her embrace to study a map of their homeland taped to the wall. "When can we go home?" she asks, innocent, fierce, touching the red dot that marks the crucible of their lives.

Zora wants to stroke her cheek. "For now, baby, we *are* home."

Abuk pulls away, then turns back toward her, searching her eyes as if she has made a confounding statement. Their homeland clings to them, and they to it, with equally compulsive love and fear. When all the girls stopped singing of warrior victories and cattle wealth, the vast hot soul of their people had been sold to the highest, cruelest bidder. They did not know what price, what song of resistance, would be required to buy it back.

Acknowledgements

My happy fortune has been to be assisted by numerous knowledgeable individuals who may not have always been aware of their important contributions to my work. My heartfelt thanks to ElTom and Alice Umbarak, Ken Isaacs, Ted Dagne, John Ashworth, Steve Wondu, Ami Henson, Jemera Rone, Guot Juac, Francis Bok, Dr. Victoria Wells, Dave Sampe, Dr. David Bradt, Wanjiru Kamau, Dr. Warren Cooper, Moses Luba, Maina Muthee, the entire staff at Samaritan's Purse hospital at Lui, Sudan, Thomas Abel, Kamau Gachigi, Suliman Giddo, Omer Ismail, and Omer Ihsas.

My gratitude also to Peter Porosky, an early mentor and critic; to Leslie Keenan for patiently coaching me though a year's worth of rewrites, and to Richard Peabody for the morale-boosting that came with publishing my stories.

Big thanks to Dianne Pearce, my editor and publisher, and to David Yurkovich, designer of the cover and book interior.

I'm especially grateful to my husband Dave and my daughter Nikole for gracefully accepting my detachment whenever I was writing. Fortunately, both are far better and more motivated cooks than I.

The central character of this novel is named in honor of Zora Neal Hurston, the first published black woman in the U.S. and one of my heroes in women's struggle for necessary transformative influence on the course of human affairs.

Susan Burgess-Lent

Susan Burgess-Lent is a veteran international aid worker, Emmy Award–winning documentary editor, and author dedicated to amplifying voices often ignored.

She founded Women's Centers International, a nonprofit that establishes community resource hubs for women displaced by conflict and poverty.

Her published works include *Trouble Ahead: Dangerous Mission with Desperate People*, a nonfiction book (Amazon 2019); *In the Borderlands* (Xlibris, 2000); short stories in anthologies including *Gargoyle Magazine* and *SFWC's 2022 Anthology*; and scores of essays on social justice and women's rights on her blog SusanBurgessLent.com and on Substack.

Susan lives and works in Oakland, California with her family.

www.ingramcontent.com/pod-product-compliance
Lightning Source LLC
Chambersburg PA
CBHW030905060726
47591CB00005B/1428